THE DEVIL'S ADVOCATE

ASHLEY JADE

First published in USA, March 2019
Copyright © Ashley Jade

This is a work of fiction. Names, characters, businesses, places, events and incidents are either the products of the author's imagination or used in a fictional manner. Any resemblance to actual persons, living or deceased, or events is purely coincidence.

The Devil's Advocate

Cover Photographer: Wander Aguiar

Cover Design: Lori Jackson at Lori Jackson Design

Editor: Ellie McLove

KA Stalter

The Devil's Advocate

"These violent delights have violent ends
And in their triumph die, like fire and powder.
Which, as they kiss, consume."

—William Shakespeare, Romeo and Juliet

Prologue

DAMIEN

"Most people don't get to take control of their own destiny." I motion to the file I placed on his desk. "Don't think of this as a death sentence...think of it as an opportunity to go out the way you want to."

Hands in his pockets, he walks over to the large window in his office and sighs. It's a beautiful view. It's a shame he won't be enjoying it much longer.

"I didn't know I was terminal until last month. I thought the treatment was working."

"Why didn't you drop out of the race when you received your diagnosis?"

His jaw tics. "Cain Carter will run this town into the ground with his self-serving stance on things, if not his arrogance alone... and then, like the cancer in my lungs, he'll spread his disease to the White House. I'd rather win the race for mayor and die in office. This way he'll be one step behind instead of one step closer to being in a position of power."

Satisfied with his response, I light a cigarette and offer him one. He looks at it longingly before declining, like he stands a chance at beating his illness.

He doesn't. Otherwise, I wouldn't be here.

Neither would he.

"As I suspected, our interests are aligned." When he gives me a questioning look, I say, "I don't want him to be mayor either."

"You never struck me as someone interested in politics. Your father wasn't."

"A lot can change in eleven years." I take a long drag. "And unlike your opponent, I don't want to follow in my father's footsteps."

He snorts. "Didn't you take over your father's hedge fund investments after he died four years ago?"

"He left everything to me...big difference." I shrug. "In turn, I chose to focus on the investments I wanted to keep and let go of the ones I saw no potential in."

Turning, he assesses me. "That's putting it mildly. Rumor has it withdrawing your father's investments led to the demise of five companies and put eight-thousand people across the U.S out of a job."

"That's the pesky thing about rumors—they aren't always based on truth." I stub my cigarette out in a nearby ashtray. "It was six companies, and just shy of ten-thousand employees were laid off."

He tuts. "You're horrible. No wonder people call you the Devil."

"I never claimed to be a hero. It's not my job to rescue a sinking ship."

"And yet here you are trying to offer me some kind of deal. Why?"

"My reasons for wanting Cain Carter to lose the election are personal."

"Then I'm afraid I can't help you." He juts his chin toward the door. "You can exit the same way you came, Mr. King."

I don't budge. "You only have fifty-thousand in your savings account." He starts to protest, but I pull out my phone and look down at the screen. "I already checked to see if you or your wife have any hidden accounts, but you don't. Your son has a few bonds from his christening ten years ago, but they're not worth much." I whistle. "You used quite a bit of your personal money to fund your campaign. Of course, your medical expenses aren't helping your financial situation, given you recently made a check out for ten grand to your insurance company."

His nostrils flare. "How did——"

"Same way I accessed your medical records." I tuck my phone inside my pocket. "But me hacking your files isn't what's important here, Mr. Covey…what I can offer you is."

"You're not half as smart as your father was." He walks over to his desk and swipes the file. Papers scatter on the floor. "In case you missed the memo, you marched into my office with—I'm a dying man. There is literally nothing you can offer me. Nothing that matters anymore."

I rub the stubble on my chin. "You're right, I don't imagine there's much I can offer you." My gaze flickers to a framed picture of his wife and son. "But what about them?"

For the first time since I walked into his office, he looks open to me being here.

I take the opportunity to drive the nail into his coffin.

"Funerals are expensive. Not to mention property taxes, monthly utilities, food, the medical debt you've accrued, and of course, college for your son. That fifty grand will go quickly. I predict it will last your stay-at-home wife a year at most, and that's being generous…after that, your family will be on their own."

I can see the pain in his eyes. The pain of a man who will die long before he ever planned to. The pain of a man who knows when all is said and done—he will have left his family with nothing but a collection of medical bills, a house they can't afford to live in, and a pile of ashes.

"Memories of loved ones are nice, but they aren't security. Your death will hurt worse, and your family will resent you more for it if you leave them with a financial burden."

"What exactly are you offering me?" he questions, his voice barely above a whisper.

"A chance to provide for them. If you agree to work with me,

3

you'll leave them with enough money that neither your wife or son will long for anything ever again."

"What do you want in return?"

"To take your place in the election."

He looks at me like I've sprouted another head. "*You* want to become mayor?" He chuckles to himself. "You can't be serious. Not only are you unqualified, you don't know the first thing about the position."

"The town bylaws state that a mayoral candidate must be over the age of eighteen and have a high school diploma. I assure you, I meet both requirements...and then some."

"Fine, you're qualified to run, but this is the first time you've stepped foot inside this town in eleven years. Things may have changed, but reputation and perception are forever. Those who knew your father are happy he's dead, and those who believe the countless rumors about you think you're a ruthless monster. No one in their right mind would ever vote for you."

It's not so much the votes I'm interested in—it's the look on Cain's face when he sees I'm his new opponent.

I swirl the amber liquid in my tumbler. "People will vote for the person who gives them the better incentive. Cain's weakness has always been that he's too selfish. He doesn't care about the little people. He's too busy kissing the asses of those who are already in power. He's failed to realize that the real power lies within the very people he's underestimated."

He pours himself a fresh glass of whiskey. "I think you're forget-ting what kind of town Black Hallows is. There are no *little people.* Every boy has a Rolex by the time he's thirteen, and every girl has a thousand-dollar purse by the time she can pronounce a designer's name. Just like their mommies and daddies."

"Then I'll need to give these people something they can't resist."

"What? More antique shops and yacht clubs?"

"A scandal. More specifically—a reason to doubt their golden boy."

"Good luck with that. Cain's track record is as clean as they come."

Quite the contrary. Cain's a very dirty boy.

My soon-to-be co-conspirator waves a hand. "But none of that matters. You still can't take my place. The primary elections are over. The candidates are locked in."

"What if one of the candidates dies?"

His face turns ashen. "I'd still be on the ballot. If anything, my death would encourage people who would have voted for me, to vote for Cain, given he's the one with a pulse." He blows out a breath. "And hypothetically speaking, with over a month left, there's still enough time for the committee to nominate a new candidate or hold another primary election. And given your history, there's no way the people of Black Hallows would vote for *you* to take my place."

I finish my drink and place the glass on his desk. "Let's not give them the option to vote."

He pinches the bridge of his nose. "This isn't an ice cream shop your daddy can bulldoze to the ground and turn into a gym, Damien. This is—"

"Article fifteen of the Black Hallows town handbook specifically states that if a mayoral candidate dies ten days or less before polling day, officials will authorize the political party to nominate a new candidate—and as long as the new nominee receives the majority vote from the *political party*, voters are not required to vote in."

"How am I supposed to get my party committee to give *you* the majority vote if I die?"

"Easy. You do what politicians have been doing since the beginning of time."

"What's that?"

"Paying people off and offering favors under the table in exchange for their *support*."

His distressed expression tells me he's mulling it over. "Okay, look—even if I could get you the majority vote, there's no way I can

5

guarantee you the win. Hell, I can't even guarantee *my own* win at this point. Cain's been ahead in the polls since day one."

"Let me worry about the election. The only thing I need you to do is move some pawns out of my way."

"I wasn't aware we were playing chess."

"Life is nothing but one big chess game." I grin. "Some people are pawns...others are kings."

He fidgets with his wedding band. "How can I trust you'll keep your word?"

"I'll transfer the money to a private bank account a few hours before you...pass on."

He rubs the back of his neck. "Do I look like a fortune teller? How am I supposed to predict what day I'll die? The doctor said it could be weeks, maybe even months."

I fix my cufflinks. People tend to feed off my energy and if I remain calm and relaxed, so will he. After all, what I'm offering him is nothing more than a business deal.

"Remember what I said earlier about taking control of your own destiny?"

The look of horror on his face tells me the realization of what I'm asking has finally dawned on him. "You want me to kill myself."

I fish my cigarettes out of my pocket. This time when I offer him one, he accepts. "Think of it more like—ending your pain and making sure your family is taken care of. Some might call it a heroic act."

He takes a long pull from his cigarette. "You're a sick bastard, King. This is...I don't want to die."

"None of us do. However, death is inescapable for everyone and something we have little control over."

"I'd like to see my family one last time."

"You will. The election is still thirty-nine days away."

He blows out a heavy breath. "Do you have a specific date in mind?"

"Why don't we make it a month? During that time, you can tie up your personal loose ends and tell me how much you'll need from me to garner the support of the committee."

He looks down at the calendar on his desk. "The annual masquerade ball is in thirty days."

"I know. I recently purchased the Vanderbilt castle."

He looks at the picture on his desk. "My wife loves the masquerade ball."

"Then give her one last memory with you she'll never forget."

He rubs his temples. "I'm going to have to tell the committee about my health and that you're—"

"No. I don't want anyone knowing I'm back in town until I'm ready. I need the majority vote, not all votes, so I highly suggest you only tell the members you trust about me. If someone leaks the information regarding your health or my whereabouts, I'll withdraw my financial offer of support for them and *you* so fast both your heads will spin. Understood?"

He nods. "I'm close with a few members, I'll ensure they keep their mouths shut about everything until it's time."

"Don't screw this up, Covey. Your family is counting on you."

"I know." He clears his throat. "I can do this." He shifts some papers on his desk. "If you don't mind, I have some things to take care of."

"Of course." I start to leave but pause when I reach the door. "I'm so happy we're working together *SpankMeMommy74*."

Behind me, glass shatters and he mutters a curse. "I have no idea what you're talking about."

"It's your username on an app called *Temptation*."

"You're mistaken, I've never heard of any app called *Temptation* and I certainly wouldn't subscribe to it, I'm a married man."

Digging my phone out of my pocket, I spin around. "You're logged in right now."

Proving my point, I send him a message and sure enough, the cell phone on his desk vibrates.

"Son of a bitch. I knew nothing about the app until I received an e-mail addressed to my wife. They offered me a free membership

7

due to the mix-up. I was told it was anonymous and nothing could be traced back to me."

"Nothing can. Unless you're the developer."

He shifts his feet. "I signed up the day after my diagnosis. I wanted to see what my wife was hiding from me. I've never——"

"Relax. Your secrets are safe with me." Reaching behind me, I turn the doorknob. The look on his face when a woman wearing leather and holding a paddle walks in is half embarrassed and half intrigued. "Consider Mistress Veronica a gift from me to you. Life's too short not to seize an opportunity when it's right in front of you."

Chapter 1

EDEN

*I*t's not Cain. It can't be.

Cain wouldn't bring me here just so he could hurt me like this.

He loves me.

I wipe away the tear making its way down my cheek.

Despite my brain's insistence that the man leaving in a haste isn't Cain...another tear falls.

His lips.

Everything else about the man, his hair, his tux, even the way he kissed the woman on the dance floor...I could chalk up to coincidence. But I know those lips.

They're the same lips I've dreamed about kissing since I was fourteen.

But my heart isn't convinced. It needs proof. I refuse to believe Cain would betray me like this.

I take a step forward, preparing to follow him out of the ballroom, but the ground beneath me tilts and I stumble instead.

I'm trying to gather my bearings when the lights above me change colors, illuminating the room in a red glow.

"Take it easy, sweetheart." The man next to me nods at the now

9

packed dance floor. "Cocktail hour just ended, and you're already hammered."

I blink in confusion. *I'm not drunk.* Anxiety shoots through me like a rocket and I clutch my chest. It's becoming an actual struggle to draw in air.

Oh, God. I'm having a panic attack. Right here in front of all these people.

"Why don't we go somewhere more private for a little while?" the man shouts in my ear so loud I wince. "This way I can look after you."

The man tugs on my hand, but I yank it back.

Nausea churns my insides. I need to get out of here, but my feet won't move, no matter how much I plead with them to.

Cain. I need him. He's the only one who can help me through this.

Instinctively, I peruse the room for him while I pull out my phone, ignoring the little voice inside mocking my efforts.

Angelbaby123: I feel like I'm going to pass out. I'm on the dance floor.

I think I spot him, but strobe lights start flickering and the music changes—filling my ears with uneven beats, dark harmonies, and intense tempos.

My senses kick into overdrive, making it impossible to concentrate, but I scan the room in a last-ditch attempt anyway and send a text directly to his phone instead of the app.

Eden: Please, Cain. I need you.

"Fine, be that way," the man next to me snaps. "I was only trying to help, you drunk bitch."

"What?" I can't understand a word he's saying. I want to ask him to repeat himself, but the lights flash...and then it's nothing but darkness.

A few people scream, but it's drowned out by a spooky, evil laugh that crackles through the speakers.

A moment later, the lights turn back on, sheathing the room in a blood red hue again.

My legs finally get the signal and I put one foot in front of the other. I'm halfway to the exit when the lights go out for a second time. It's so dark I can't even make out shapes, let alone walk.

Terror spirals through me when a muscular arm wraps around my waist.

I open my mouth to yell at the asshole who won't take no for an answer, but I'm slammed against a wall.

"Wh—" My eyes adjust, enabling me to see the tall figure wearing a black mask in front of me. My heart takes flight when I inhale the scent of Cain's aftershave.

"Cain." I smile, feeling both relieved he came to my rescue and stupid for ever thinking he would bring me here to hurt me. "You found—" My voice catches when he presses his palm over my heart. The part of me he owns and controls. The part of me that will forever be tethered to him.

I look down when his hand compresses, painfully constricting the organ. "What are you doing?"

I try to maneuver out of his hold, but he's too strong. Whenever I inhale, he pushes down harder. Fear pumps through my veins and I grip the collar of his jacket, urging him to stop.

White spots form in front of my eyes and the hand gripping his collar falls limp at my side. It physically hurts to breathe. I'm going to pass out if he doesn't let up in the next few seconds.

I flatten my back against the wall, hoping to catch a shallow breath, but the crushing weight becomes so unbearable, I give up.

My knees buckle and I start to fall—but suddenly the force is gone.

I suck in air so fast I cough, and try to push him away, but he leans in, his mouth hovering over my ear. "Remember that feeling, Eden." His voice is deep and raspy...different. "Because it's only going to get worse."

11

My blood runs cold. *It's not Cain.*

"Who are you?"

I feel his lips curve against the shell of my ear. "A friend."

My cheeks heat when he nuzzles my neck and plants a kiss where my pulse is beating erratically. "My friends don't hurt me."

I know I should be running away and finding Cain, but I need to know who this man is and how he knows my name.

And why my body responds to him the way it does...even though it's obvious he wants to harm me.

"You're right." His teeth scrape my flesh as his hand slips through the slit in my dress. "I'm definitely *not* your friend." The vehemence in his tone is chilling, yet his touch is soft like velvet. "Consider me a messenger." He gives me an evil grin that makes my stomach drop. "Cain's waiting for you upstairs."

I blink in confusion. "Cain sent you to get me?"

That doesn't seem right, although it's not entirely out of the question. Cain has people to do his bidding for him. But it's weird he would send one of his employees to fetch me.

The tip of his finger slithers up my thigh and I glare at him. "I suggest you keep your hands to yourself, *sir*. Because if Cain ever finds out you touched me, I guarantee you'll be out of a job." I crinkle my nose. "And probably a few teeth."

He smirks. "It's a shame we didn't meet under different circumstances." He captures my hand with his free one and kisses my finger. The one I cut on broken glass. "Last bedroom on the second floor." He plucks the string of pearls against my hip bone. "The one next to the closet."

With that, he releases me.

Chapter 2

DAMIEN

I look at my watch. Eden should be arriving in approximately one minute. Two if she second guesses her decision on the way up.

Three if she starts wondering why her little pearls are damp after our encounter.

I light my cigarette and take a long drag before I chuck it over the balcony. I have just enough time to grab a good spot and watch the show unfold.

The small suite Cain's currently in shares a bathroom with another suite—enabling me to slip inside undetected.

Turning the knob, I enter the adjoining bathroom. Given I can't hear them on the other side of the door, my guess is they never made it to the bedroom and they're screwing in the foyer.

My lips quirk. This is working out better than I hoped. With Cain in the foyer, he won't have enough time to dislodge himself from his new fiancée before being caught.

Eden's going to have a front row seat to Cain's betrayal.

And my, oh, my…what a show it is.

Creeping behind the open bedroom door directly across from

where they are, I watch as the woman drops to her knees and takes him into her mouth.

Cain grips the small table behind him. I assume it's to stop himself from winding her hair in his fist and shoving his cock down her throat.

Amused, I observe her lick around his pink mushroom head daintily, as though she were a queen enjoying a snack in the public eye.

Cain's jaw works as he caresses her head, offering some encouragement. It's almost comical. He's trying to be a gentleman when he doesn't even look like he's enjoying himself all that much.

Can't say I blame him though. His soon-to-be wife doesn't seem to have a kinky bone in her body. As if proving my point—her movements stop altogether when he grips her hair and tries to push his dick farther inside her mouth.

"Don't treat me like a whore, Cain. It's rude."

I bite my lip. Cain might be able to convince himself marrying this woman is for the best, but I bet his cock is seriously regretting his arrangement with the governor now.

If there's one thing I know about Cain...it's that he craves all the things he shouldn't. *He's tempted by the forbidden.*

His fiancée will never be able to satisfy him...because society says she's exactly what he's supposed to have.

That alone should be enough for me to feel vindicated, but it's not. Not by a long shot.

I want Cain so drunk off lust he can't see or think straight.

I want to take everything from him and then bring him to his knees...both figuratively and literally.

And then, when he's at my mercy—I want to destroy everything he ever cared about. Everything I took from him.

His hopes. His dreams. His precious stepdaughter.

After I expose who he really is. *All his secrets and sins.*

"Sorry," Cain mutters through clenched teeth before his voice takes on a softer tone. "It felt so good, I couldn't help myself."

The woman beams, lighting up like a Christmas tree. Despite

her father being governor, it's clear she doesn't recognize a bold-faced lie drenched in sweet talk coming from a politician when she hears one.

Then again, Cain can be awfully convincing when he wants to be.

And his latest stepping stone isn't immune to his charms, because when she starts up again, she's a little more eager to please. She even manages to get half of it in her mouth and draw a low moan from him.

Just in time for the door to open.

A grin pulls at my cheeks and my cock jolts to life.

Eden has no idea she's my bait. *The pretty fish for my hungry piranha.*

The look on her face is a mixture of outrage and anguish. My fallen angel is so shocked, so overwhelmed at the sight, she can't even move. She just stands there, her glassy eyes darting from Cain to the woman—completely devastated. Looking every bit the gorgeous tragedy she is.

The one I created.

Margaret stands up, fixing the top of her dress. "Excuse you. Can't you see this room is occupied? Get out."

Ignoring her, Eden's eyes flick to Cain, taking in his tousled hair, undone bow tie...and the dwindling erection he's stuffing into his pants.

She's like a crime scene investigator who needs to process every piece of evidence before accepting what's right in front of her.

She doesn't want him to fall from the pedestal she's placed him on any more than he does.

Because deep down she knows...the fall won't kill Cain.

It will only kill *her.*

"Cain," Eden chokes out, her broken voice barely above a whisper.

Cain's brows draw together, it hasn't quite dawned on him yet due to the mask she's wearing, but it's clear something about her holds his interest given the way he's studying her.

15

The spell is broken when the governor's daughter crosses her arms over her chest. "Do you know this woman?"

Cain clears his throat, his expression quickly changing from enthralled to impassive. "I have no idea who she is."

Margaret, not one to be played for a fool, squints her eyes at Eden. "How do you know my fiancé?"

Eden rocks back as though she's been sucker punched. "Fiancé?" Her slim, curvy frame shakes so badly I can practically feel the ground tremble from my spot behind the door. "You're—" Her hand clutches her chest. "You're getting *married*?"

And there it is. Betrayal and heartbreak in its rawest form.

The look on Cain's face is priceless as recognition dawns on him and he realizes his world is about to come crashing down like a sledgehammer.

And this is only the beginning.

"E—" He catches himself. "Our engagement hasn't been announced yet."

"How could you—" A sob breaks free, but she shakes her head and balls her fists, fighting through the sting. "When were you planning on telling me?" A bitter laugh erupts, and she looks up at the ceiling. "God, who am I kidding? You weren't—"

"Who the hell is this woman, Cain?" Margaret shrieks.

"Yeah, Cain," Eden taunts, sauntering toward him. Her infuriation is now as palpable as her heartbreak. "Who am I?" Cain looks like he's going to have a coronary when her fingertips graze her mask. "On second thought, I should probably stop being rude and introduce myself." She licks her red lips. "Welcome her to the fa—"

"That's *enough*." Cain snatches Eden's wrist a second before she pulls her mask off. "I think everyone needs to calm down and remember we are at a public event." Cain looks at Margaret. "I need a few minutes to deal with her. I'll meet you downstairs shortly."

Eden's eyes become tiny slits. "Deal with me? Wow, Da—"

Cain's other hand slams over her mouth. "I said *enough*," he seethes, the timbre of his voice taking on a dark tone. "Disrespect me again and you'll regret it."

Eden's eyes go wide. It's clear she's never seen this side of him before.

There's so much she doesn't know about the man she loves.

With a huff, Margaret walks toward the door. "Deal with her quickly. And make sure this is the first and last time I see or hear about one of your little whores." She gives Cain a look that could freeze a tropical island. "I would hate to have to tell Daddy that this little problem of yours prevented us from getting married. Or worse…led to you losing the upcoming election."

With that, she walks out, slamming the door behind her.

Cain turns his attention back to Eden who's attempting to get out of his grip.

With one hand still covering her mouth, he pushes her until her back meets the wall. "I never wanted you to find out this way." He sighs heavily. "I wanted to tell you, but—" His face twists and he removes his hand. "Fuck."

I smirk when I notice the impression of her teeth on his palm. *Good girl.*

"But you're an opportunist who wanted to have his cake and eat it too," Eden finishes for him, tears welling in her blue eyes again. "You didn't want to tell me the truth. What you wanted was to string me along for however long you could before you pulled the rug out from under me."

Cain snickers. "String you along?" He leans in, crowding what little space he was permitting her to have. "Maybe I should talk to that shrink of yours about these delusions, because last time I checked—*you* spread your legs and stuck your fingers in your cunt in hopes of getting my attention that night, not me."

It's clear Cain's statement struck a chord, however, Eden recovers from the blow and raises her chin, meeting his stern gaze head-on. "Yeah, well…it worked, didn't it?"

His lids lower, his stare settling on her ample breasts that trigger him with every intentional deep breath she takes.

I squeeze my growing erection. *Triggers us both.*

Eden might have the face of an angel...but her body was built for sin.

Perfect for enticing corrupt men like her stepfather. And depraved men like me, who have a score to settle.

It's a shame the little lamb won't realize she's in the middle of a dangerous game until it's too late.

Obsession can be deadly.

And the man she loves led her straight to the slaughterhouse.

His throat bobs on a swallow. "It did." The tip of his finger dips between her cleavage. "But I'm not the first, nor will I be the last man to succumb to easy pussy, sweetheart."

Hurt splashes across her face and she shoves him away. "I'll be gone by the time you get home."

She's halfway to the door when he speaks. "Goddammit." She freezes and I watch cautiously as he creeps up behind her, his hands twitching. "I told you to stop pursuing this thing between us."

Eden looks down at her shoes, unaware of the evil rearing its ugly head behind her. "But—"

"Eden." The tiny hairs on the back of my neck stand on end when he takes a step closer and raises his arms, his brown eyes darkening with malice. "I *warned* you."

Chapter 3

EDEN

*E*very word Cain utters is the equivalent of a dagger piercing my skin. I close my eyes as the last one slices through my flesh and bone—making a beeline for the shattered organ that still beats for him.

Despite his betrayal. Despite the pain pumping through my veins.

Despite the little voice in my head chastising me for loving a man who cares about politics and his image more than he'll ever care about me.

The heart wants what it wants. *Even when it's broken.*

"You can't help who you fall in love with," I whisper, tears prickling my throat. "Because trust me, if I could, I'd pick someone —*anyone*—else to give my heart to right now."

Someone who deserves it.

I reach for the doorknob with shaky hands. If I spend one more moment in this room with him—he'll sever the rest of me. The little shred of sanity I'm barely hanging on to.

My breath leaves me in a rush when Cain spins me around, then presses me against the door.

"Eden." He says my name like a small prayer as he frames my

face in his hands. "I know it hurts, but please try to understand where I'm coming from."

I shake my head. I can't. I won't. Not anymore.

I'm tired of seeing things through Cain's eyes and making excuses for the way he treats me when he's never once bothered to see things through mine.

Because if he did? He'd see how much pain I'm in. And if he truly loved me the way I love him…it would kill him.

But he doesn't. And now the stone-cold realization is staring me right in the face.

Loving someone isn't dangerous.

Falling in love with the wrong someone is.

Cain Carter's been the air I've longed to breathe from the moment I laid eyes on him…but right now? *He's suffocating me.*

And I need to find a way to let go of the anchor dragging me down before it's too late.

"Why should I, when you never once thought about what it feels like from my side? Then again, why would you? Why think about my side when your side is so much better, right? It must feel great knowing you're loved by someone who would do *anything* in the world for you. Someone who lets you use them because one second of your attention is better than a lifetime without it."

His jaw works. "You need to find a way to accept we can't be together…just like I have." I start to protest, but his fingers skim my throat, causing my heart to kickstart back to life. "I don't want to hurt you."

No, I won't give in. I won't let him shut me up like he always does. "You're *already* hurting me, Cain. Because I'll never know what a love like mine feels like in return. Even though you're the key to my happiness…according to you, I'm the key to your destruction. Our two sides will never meet in the middle. I'm the girl you want to stay away from…and you're the man I cling to."

Something ugly and painful twists my insides, puncturing the dam of anguish I've tried so hard to hold back. "You're not capable of loving me the way I love you. You're not capable of choosing *me*…you never will be. Even though I choose you with every single breath I take."

His thumb grazes my cheekbone and for a moment, I see the tiniest flicker of genuine emotion in his eyes. The kind that makes me believe he feels the same way for me.

"If you weren't my stepdaughter. If you weren't so young—if things were *different*—I'd choose you. In any other lifetime but this one, I'd choose you and never look back."

And therein lies the problem. "No matter the obstacles—I still choose you. In this lifetime…in *any* lifetime, I'll always choose you." He tightens his hold and I reach for his wrists, caught between wanting to keep him close and wanting to push him away, because his touch feels like salt in the wound he created. "Please, don't marry that woman. We both know it's only for show and you don't really care about her." I lean into his touch. "Choose me, Cain. Love me back and I'll love you harder than anyone else ever has or ever will. I'll—"

"Eden." He presses his lips to my forehead. "I can't." His mouth brushes the tears running down my cheek. "I can't." Tension coils low in my belly when his expression changes from pained to hunger and his lips find my neck. "I *can't*." I suck in a breath when he ventures lower, his stubble scraping the sensitive skin between my breasts. "I shouldn't."

With a groan, he takes my hand and places it on his bulging erection. "You see what you do to me?" I squeeze his length through his pants, and he props his arms on either side of my head. "How fucking crazy you make me?"

His muscles tense as I rub him harder. The friction is so intense between us I'm surprised we don't burst into flames.

In one swift motion, he unzips his pants and rocks into my hand. "Why don't you get on your knees and finish what Margaret started like a good little girl?"

And just like that, a tiny piece of my heart plummets…falling from the pedestal it was clinging to with everything it had.

He said her name.

The woman he's going to marry. The one he never told me about.

The one he's choosing over me.

Cain realizes his mistake the moment I remove my hand. "I'm—"

"Don't." He's not sorry. *He never is.*

Closing my eyes, I wait for the sharp, shooting pain radiating through the center of my chest to lessen enough that I can walk out of this room.

As if he can sense my impending departure, Cain's body sinks against mine, his lips softly tracing the shell of my ear, keeping me enslaved. Funny how the same feature—my favorite feature of Cain's—causes me both pleasure and pain.

Often in the same breath.

"I love you, Eden."

Then why did you trick me into coming here so you could break my heart?

Reaching behind me, I turn the knob. "Then why does it hurt so much?"

My feet barely touch the hallway floor when he closes the door. No doubt afraid someone might be watching.

My heart pangs as I touch the rustic mahogany. *Eleven years between us but a lifetime apart.*

He's going to marry Margaret. He's going to become mayor. He's going to get everything he ever wanted...and live happily ever after.

While I'll be left with nothing.

Too bad the man who tried to kill me on the dance floor didn't finish the job.

Chapter 4

CAIN

_T_he last thing I need is a scandal ten days before the election. And by my count, I have not one, but three on my hands. The reporter, Margaret, and my stepdaughter.

Muttering a curse, I look up at the ceiling. _I have less than twenty-four hours to put these fires out before word starts to spread._

The reporter mess will work itself out soon enough—but if it doesn't, I know exactly how to pacify Katrina.

Smiling to myself, I give my dick a languid stroke.

Margaret is going to be a trickier situation, but as long as she doesn't figure out the woman in the mask was Eden—I can fix things with her before the night is over.

Sadly, it will involve surrendering myself to another boring blowjob. My fist tightens around my erection. Let's hope her snatch can take a dick better than her mouth does—otherwise the next four years will be hell on earth for me.

A deep groan fills the room and I pick up my pace, my thoughts drifting to Eden. The solution is simple—send her off to college. Keep her far away from all of this. Let her fall in love with a boy her own age—not a man who happens to be her stepfather—and live happily ever after.

Let her forget about me and move on.

Let her go because I love her.

Unfortunately, both the organ beating inside my chest and the one my hand is wrapped around have serious issues with that.

Not only do I want her so much it physically hurts, but somewhere along the way, Eden became so much more than my stepdaughter. More than the desire I can't indulge in.

She's my trusted companion. My loyal pet who waits at the door for me day in and day out. And despite how many times I've hurt her—that gorgeous face always lights up like the sun whenever I come home.

She's my secret superpower. My beautiful angel and my darkest craving.

She's a saint a man like me doesn't deserve.

But she's also become…my greatest liability. *It's dangerous to want someone so much they can destroy you.*

My head lolls back and I close my eyes, thrusting into my palm as images of taking her innocence flash through my head. I've tried to do right by her—tried to keep her away from the worst of me, but I'm hanging on a ledge…barely holding on. And if she's…

A door creaking followed by the sound of footsteps has me scrambling to tuck my dick inside my pants.

The corners of Margaret's eyes crinkle when she sees me. "Didn't mean to interrupt you."

I bristle. I don't like that she came back up here snooping, but it's better she caught me with my hand on my dick instead of Eden's. "Can't blame me for trying to finish what you started."

Margaret blushes like a school girl before her expression turns grim. "I'm surprised the blonde you asked me to leave you alone with didn't help you out."

Fixing things with her will be easier than I thought. "I'm not in the habit of disrespecting the woman I'm going to marry. You wanted her gone. She's gone."

I can tell she wants to cave, but she eyes me suspiciously. "For how long?"

I give her a small smile. I just have to charm her enough to let her believe my intentions are earnest. "How long do you plan on staying married to me?"

She opens her mouth, but whatever words she intended to say are lost when she clamps it shut.

I tip her chin. "If this is going to work between us, I think it's best we don't keep any secrets from one another. So, what is it you have to say to me?"

She wrings her hands. "What's her name?"

Despite the slight roll of my stomach, I keep my expression impassive. "Would you hate me if I told you I don't know?"

She tries to speak, but I cut her off. "I'm not trying to butter you up. Truth is, we hooked up in a bathroom at a benefit party over six months ago. She never gave me a name and I didn't ask her for one. Shortly after our encounter, I ran into one of David Covey's campaign managers and he introduced her as his new girlfriend." I shrug. "Needless to say, if I was interested in her before, I certainly wasn't after that exchange."

Margaret fixes my bow tie. "She was awfully irate for a woman you claim to have only slept with once."

I place my hand on top of hers, halting her movements. "You're not stupid, Margaret. If you take your personal feelings out of the equation and think logically, I'm sure you'll realize Covey obviously hired her to get dirt on me. As tragic as Karen's passing was, it gave Covey's team an advantage because up until our arrangement, I was a twenty-nine-year-old widower. And to be frank, a whore bending over a bathroom sink was ideal for a man who wasn't interested in anything more back then, and they knew it." My nostrils flare. "I have no doubt her outburst earlier was designed to make you suspicious and cause a rift between us before the election." I drop my hand. "It obviously worked."

I walk past her, but she reaches for my arm. "I had no idea."

"That's exactly my point. You had no idea, and yet you chose to believe the worst in me before I could explain. I'm not sure I can be with someone who doubts me and questions the truth. My wife should be my biggest supporter—not my biggest adversary."

"I'm sorry for doubting you." She goes back to fixing my bow tie. "You're right. The people in this town will chew you up and spit you out at the first sign of weakness. We need to be a united front at all times."

"Are you sure you can handle that?"

She zips up my fly. "I'm not the one who needs to worry, Cain. I've never been the subject of gossip and scandals."

"Wh—"

"Word of advice? You've already been married once—lucky for you it ended in death, not divorce. However, if you have plans to be more than just the mayor of Black Hallows, I'm the wife you want beside you. But I won't be made to look like a fool. Therefore, I suggest you learn to like my hand...or get used to your own for the duration of our marriage."

Despite wanting to throttle the woman, I reach for hers. "I'm becoming rather fond of yours."

"Good." She smiles. "We should head back downstairs. Daddy has some important associates he wants to introduce you to."

I steer her toward the door. "Let's not keep them waiting any longer."

I go to turn the knob, but she stops me. "Is there anything I should know about? Any ghosts from your past that might come back to haunt us?"

I meet her gaze head-on. "No." With a wink, I lead her out of the room. "And for what it's worth, I don't believe in ghosts."

Because all of mine are buried.

Chapter 5

EDEN

*T*hey say your life flashes before your eyes moments before you die. Your fondest memories, greatest achievements, the people you love—it all zips through your mind like a slideshow.

Heartbreak is a lot like death.

Only for me...there aren't people. There's just Cain.

Every single one of my flashes revolves around him. And every positive flash is immediately followed by one that hurts so much I wish I was actually dead so I wouldn't have to suffer through the pain any longer.

I close my eyes as another one spikes through me like the jagged teeth of a hungry animal ripping through its next meal.

I watched from the sidelines as his tuxedo-clad body pressed against some woman wearing a sophisticated purple dress and they swayed to the music. I couldn't tell if they were friends or lovers... not until his dance partner closed the distance between them.

I smiled. Thinking how sweet it was to see a couple in love show affection.

That is until his hand lifted—the glint of gold from the diver's watch I got him last Christmas was nearly blinding as he cupped her flushed cheek before his lips—those perfect lips of his—moved against hers tenderly in a soft kiss.

A kiss that lingered long enough people took notice.

A kiss so beautiful it made the people on the dance floor clap.

A kiss so powerful it broke my heart.

Cain kissed her like she was his everything…and I was his nothing.

The organ in my chest recoils as I touch my tear-stained lips. "He never kissed me."

"Who?"

I nearly jump out of my skin at the sound of a deep voice. I was so wrapped up in my sadness, I didn't hear anyone approach.

I shift on the granite bench I'm sitting on so I can see him. Unfortunately, he's standing in front of the balcony doors on the terrace and the distance combined with the black mask he's wearing keeps his identity a mystery. The only thing I can make out from his shadow is that he's tall and his frame is muscular.

It's odd he would be here given you can't access this balcony without entering the bedroom first.

I probably should have gone back downstairs, but there was no way I could face all those people. Not in the state I'm in. I figured the best option was to find another bedroom so I could gather my bearings and figure out what to do next.

Only, I haven't a clue what to do next. I have twenty dollars in cash and an account Cain oversees and puts money into whenever I tell him I need some. I have no car. No place to go. No family or friends to call for help.

I'm all alone. Dependent on a man who brought me here so he could shatter me for sport.

The one and only thing I know for certain is that I don't want to see him…with her. And given Cain's marrying the woman, it makes going back home a very bleak thought. One I can't bear.

So I won't.

I'll hide out in this abandoned castle until someone with authority kicks me out…or my organs cease, and the flesh falls off my bones.

I'll stay here until it doesn't hurt anymore.

Lifting my mask slightly, I wipe my cheeks with the back of my hand. "Didn't anyone ever tell you it's rude to be nosy?"

I'm not in the mood to talk. I just want to be left alone.

"Didn't anyone ever tell you it's rude to answer a question with another question?"

The timbre of his voice sends a shiver down my spine. Goosebumps graze my arms when I realize. *He's not just anyone.*

"You're the man who hurt me earlier."

That gets a chuckle out of him. "I'm not the man who hurt you."

I swallow hard when he takes a step forward. The light from the moon illuminates him enough to reveal his black mask and beautifully severe features. For a moment, I'm utterly hypnotized. Those blue eyes are so vibrant even the purest ocean in the Caribbean wouldn't come close to capturing the pigment.

"That would be your stepfather."

Trepidation coils my insides like a noose around a person's neck before an execution. Not only is he the man who attacked me on the dance floor, he's also the man who helped me when I crashed into the waiter and knocked over his tray.

The man who sucked the blood from my finger and then left without a trace.

My response is automatic. Right out of the Cain Carter politician handbook. *Deny, deny, deny.* "I have no idea what you're talking about."

Head whirling, I reach for my phone. I've never seen him before tonight, and yet, he not only knows who I am—he keeps showing up like a ghost out of thin air to either help, harm, or intimidate me.

It doesn't make any sense.

As much as I don't want to talk to Cain, I'm not stupid or stubborn enough to be alone with a nosy jerk who knows more than he should.

With shaky fingers, I type out a text.

Eden: I'm out on the terrace in one of the bedrooms upstairs. Some guy has been following me around tonight and he just showed up again. He knows things about me he shouldn't. I'm nervous.

I hover over the send button for the better part of a minute before I clear the message and place the phone down beside me on the bench. I don't want to need Cain. I don't want him to swoop in and be my savior when he's the asshole who broke my heart.

So, I won't give him the option. I can handle this myself.

Given I'm still wearing my mask, I can be anyone.

"Listen, I don't know what your deal is, but you have me confused with someone else." I straighten my shoulders. "I'm not who you think I am. I'm also not in the mood for company. Please go."

Any decent human being would leave at this point, but not him. He takes it as an invitation to sit down next to me.

"Fine, buddy. It's your funeral. I came here with my husband tonight and he's gonna kick your ass if he catches you out here with me."

I once read an article that said if you're a single woman being approached by a man you're not interested in, you should pretend to be waiting on your spouse.

I see the faintest hint of a dimple peek out on his right cheek as he looks down at my finger. "You're not married."

"Just because I don't wear a wedding band doesn't mean I'm not taken."

He fetches a pack of cigarettes out of his pocket. "You not wearing a wedding band has nothing to do with my observation."

I fidget. It's on the tip of my tongue to ask him what led to that conclusion, but I don't have to because he says, "No man in their right mind would let you out of their sight."

I roll my eyes. "Wow, smooth—"

"Not because you're attractive or irresistible. But because a man in love doesn't leave the object of his affection alone at a party. He also doesn't keep her locked away like a dirty secret while he fucks other women and marries them."

His statement is like a lethal kick to the heart. "I can get security to throw you out."

Smirking, he fishes his lighter out of his pocket and lights his cigarette. "But then you'd have to go down there with all those people."

I inwardly wince. *He has me there.* People are my weakness. Especially the people in this town.

Crossing my arms over my chest, I glare at him out of the corner of my eye. "If you don't leave, I'll call the police to escort you off my property."

There. I'd like to see him talk his way out of that one.

I'm not sure what to make of the expression on his face. "You live here?"

The smile I give him is as arrogant as he is. "Would you like to see the paperwork?"

Cain once told me people will believe anything you feed them if you sound convincing enough. *Looking back, that should have been a red flag.*

He rubs the dark stubble on his chin. "Yeah, actually, I would." My stomach knots when his gaze darkens. "Given *I'm* the owner."

My smug expression falls. It's not so much his words—although that's enough to make me want to piss myself, it's the absolute possession behind them. Like he's prepared to dismember and obliterate anyone who threatens to take what belongs to him.

I clutch the granite so hard my knuckles turn white. If I thought I was nervous before, it's nothing compared to now.

I bite my lip until I taste blood. I'm too afraid to speak for fear I'll say something to make it worse.

If agoraphobia is a chink in the armor I pretend to have—anxiety is my Achilles' heel. The living, breathing succubus I live with day in and day out, and no matter how strong I try to be, or how many medications I try to numb myself with—it will always be my weakness. The root of nearly every issue I grapple with daily.

Unlike my mother, who was a force to be reckoned with, a weapon in and out of the courtroom, I'm like a defective gun. Because even though I act like I can hold my own and rise to any challenge when it's time to battle—my bullets are the equivalent of cotton candy. Sweet sugar that dissolves into nothing.

Or as Cain would say, I'm all bark and no bite.

Cain—who's downstairs with his fiancée.

Cain—who wanted me to finish him off after *her* mouth was on him.

Cain—who tricked me into coming here by getting my hopes up, just so he could hurt me.

Cain—who only told me he loved me when he realized I reached my breaking point.

Because you can only be tethered to someone for so long before the cord begins to strangle you.

They say there's a thin line between love and hate. But mine's so thick I can taste it.

And it tastes like nicotine and sin.

It happens so fast I don't give him time to react…or myself time to think about the repercussions.

I maneuver myself on his lap and crush my mouth against his.

If the man is surprised by my assault, he doesn't let on. If anything, he's complacent—almost like he was expecting it.

As if he knows I need this.

Digging my nails into his shoulder, I lick the seam of his lips, urging him to part them for me. A rough sound escapes him, and a flash of heat settles between my legs when he opens his mouth and the tip of his tongue flicks mine…before he pulls away.

No doubt wondering why the girl he found on his balcony—the one who claimed to live in *his* home and then threatened to call the cops on him a moment ago—kissed him.

Oh, God. He must think I'm psychotic.

Embarrassed, I wipe my mouth. "I'm sorry. I don't know why I did that." I start to get off him, but his hand finds the small of my back, keeping me there.

"Yes, you do."

I shake my head, but he holds my gaze, imploring me to tell him the truth.

I did it to get back at Cain.

"I had too much to drink."

He drags his thumb down my spine, lowering the zipper of my dress. "Eden."

"I'm not Eden."

The fingers skimming my vertebra spasm. "Then take off your mask."

"No."

"Shame you're so stubborn." He traces a line from my neck to the swell of my breast with his free hand. "Good girls get rewarded."

I'd laugh if he didn't have that scary look in his eyes that makes it clear he'll tear someone limb from limb if they cross him.

Hell, maybe I should let him. Cain already destroyed my heart...he can finish the job.

"Good girls, huh?" I smile coyly. "You clearly don't know a thing about me."

Because good girls don't get labeled the town whore.

Good girls don't fall in love with their stepfathers and then seduce them once their mothers are out of the picture.

And good girls most definitely don't start writhing on a stranger's lap to avoid answering his questions.

"You're right, I don't." He stares at me for a long moment, his lips curling into a sly grin. "Well, I do know some things."

I don't want to give in to him, but curiosity is winning the battle. "Like what?"

Face impassive, he slips a digit inside the top of my dress. "I know today is your eighteenth birthday."

"I told you—"

"I know your mother Carol Williams died in a car accident last year."

"Congrats, you can Google."

His fingers drum over my skin. "I know you think her death was a blessing."

My retort stalls in my throat. I can't deny or defend that statement because it's the truth.

My mother didn't treat me like normal mothers treat their children. I was a burden, and she made sure I knew it every single day.

She hated me because I was nothing like her. I didn't look like her. I didn't act like her. And I certainly wasn't smart like she was. We were night and day. Complete opposites.

Given she never talked about him, she must have hated whoever my father was with the fire of a thousand suns.

It's what made her hate me with the fire of a thousand and one. Because no matter how much I tried to earn her love...it never came.

Especially after the scandal with my teacher, Mr. Delany.

She loathed me for embarrassing her and almost ruining her reputation and career. Whatever glimmer of hope I had of ever winning her love vanished after that.

In turn, I ended up falling in love with her husband.

Cain's the only one who ever cared about me. The only one who didn't treat me like a walking fuck-up.

He gets me in ways no one else ever will.

The mystery man's stubble scrapes my collarbone as he nips the edge of my jaw. "I know she kept you away from people. Locked you up in that house like some kind of animal."

"You don't know what you're talking about," I whisper, looking up at the stars to keep my emotions at bay. "Please stop."

But he doesn't. "I know you're obsessed with a man who will never love you back." He plants a soft kiss on my throat. "So tragic."

"Go to hell."

He catches my wrist a second before my hand connects with his cheek. "I vacation there, little lamb."

"Maybe you should stay there permanently next time."

His hands find my ass and I gasp when I feel how hard he is.

"Maybe you should learn to tell the truth." His lips quirk. "But we both know you won't...because fighting with me turns you on."

"No, it doesn't," I lie.

My thighs clench as his tongue slithers along my clavicle. He's right. Provoking him stirs something in me. *Something dark and provocative.*

"You're like a goddamn bomb waiting to explode. Looking for the right reason to detonate." I open my mouth to argue, but sparks of pleasure race over my skin when he raises his hips, creating delicious friction against my pearls. I whimper, needing more, but he laughs darkly. "You're ruining my pants, little liar."

The damp spot beneath me makes me blush, but my pride forces me to give him a big smile. "Consider it payback for ruining my night." I scramble to my feet. "Enjoy the rest of your evening, asshole."

"Shame we're not on the couch in your living room." His lips twist into an evil smirk. "Perhaps you would have given me the same show you gave him."

My blood runs cold. Up until now, every word out of his mouth was a rumor.

But there are only two people who know about that night. And he's not one of them.

"Who are you?"

His expression is downright menacing as he stands up. "Do you believe in ghosts?"

I shake my head, not understanding. "You're not a ghost."

Anxiety swells in my chest as he walks forward, pinning me against the railing. "You're right. Ghosts have souls." Panic works its way up my throat as he fastens his hands on my hips and lifts me off the ground. "I don't."

My stomach churns with fear. What could I have possibly done that would warrant a man I don't know to terrorize me like this?

"What—why are you doing this?"

Silence is my only response.

I eye the balcony doors. They're less than twenty feet away. Not far at all.

I could kick him in the balls and make a run for it.

The second I move my leg, he tsks. "I wouldn't do that if I were you."

"Help," I scream, praying someone below can hear me. "Hel—"

Horror surges up my spine when he slams a hand over my mouth, causing half my body to slip over the railing.

One wrong move and I'll fall. *He's got me right where he wants me.*

Something he's taking pleasure in judging by the look on his face.

God, he's like a cat teasing a mouse. Drawing out the inevitable.

Nausea barrels into me when I make the mistake of turning my head to the side and looking down. The flowers in the garden are tiny specks and the pool is merely a puddle. There's no way I'd survive.

He's going to kill me on my birthday. The thought sends a ripple of anger through me. I've barely led what would constitute a life and he's going to take it.

Hot tears roll down the sides of my face. *Cain.*

My life is flashing before my eyes and he's all I can think about. Everything that ever mattered to me has revolved around him, and the very last memory I have of us…is him breaking my heart.

"Eden—"

"I hate you."

My anger rises, and I claw at his face until his mask falls off. If I'm going to die unjustly, I deserve to know who's responsible for it.

How can someone so beautiful be so vicious?

I barely have time to process the thought because I'm hoisted into his arms.

"No, you don't." In the blink of an eye, he dangles me face first over the iron barrier separating me from my death. "You hate *him*."

Head whirling, I try to kick my legs, but it only makes my shoes slide off my feet.

"Cain." It sounds like a plea. "Cain."

"He can't rescue you," the man rasps, his hold on my legs growing slack. "He's too busy with his fiancée."

White hot pain slams into the center of my chest and I choke on a fresh batch of tears.

"I bet he's pulling down her panties...burying his face between her legs."

"Stop," I plead because the truth hurts too much.

"Or maybe he's got her bent over a desk and he's fucking her brains out."

"Why are you doing this?" I choke out as my mask slides off my face and into the darkness.

"Maybe he's dancing with her in a room full of people, showing off his soon-to-be bride to the world. Something he'll never do with you."

I close my eyes as agony slashes through me, chipping away at the remainder of my heart.

He's right. It's a sobering realization. Like a child finding out Santa doesn't exist or a believer finding out there is no God.

"Please." My voice comes out frail, the last thread unraveling. "Kill me."

Chapter 6

DAMIEN

"*K*ill me," she repeats. Her voice is weak. *Desperate.* Like a wounded animal suffering and begging to be put out of its misery.

Hell, maybe I should. It's what I came here to do. *What I'm supposed to do.*

Lord knows a mercy killing would be less painful than the truth.

But murder's always been Cain's easy way out.

She squirms, attempting to wiggle out of my grip. "Please."

My cock twitches. My fallen angel isn't the type to give up without a fight. She can be quite feisty and stubborn when she wants something.

Unfortunately, what she really wants is something Cain will never give her.

He's not capable of it.

Because people like me and Cain are flawed. There's a crack in our code. A vacancy in our chest that we fill with wrath for those who have hurt us.

Just as darkness is the absence of light...we too are missing something. Something that prevents us from being righteous.

Because that's all evil really is. It's not the boogeyman or the monster under the bed. It's not demons or hellfire.

Evil is merely the absence of good.

People can condemn the wicked all they want. But deep down, we're all evil.

Some are just better at hiding it.

And others…offer deals for our services.

"I won't kill you." I loosen my grip. "If you agree to my proposition."

"Not interest—" she screams, slipping from my grasp.

Leaning over the railing, I latch onto her ankle. "Care to reconsider?" My muscles contract and I wrap my other hand around her calf. "Decide quickly, little lamb. As much as I enjoy your company, I'm not sure we can *hang* out much longer."

When she doesn't respond, I try a different approach. "Statistics prove most people who commit suicide regret their decision seconds before they die."

"I didn't push myself over this railing, psycho. *You* did."

I smile down at her through clenched teeth. "And now I'm offering to help you."

"If you really wanted to help me, you'd let me go."

Obstinate girl. "We both know you don't want to die, Eden."

"You don't know what I want."

"You're wrong." Before she can protest, I haul her back over the edge. When she struggles, I slam her wrists against the railing and press my body against hers. "He'll only keep using and hurting you until there's nothing left. He'll keep destroying you until his high from the pedestal you keep him on wears off and you're completely useless to him."

Running my nose along the side of her neck, I inhale her sweet apple scent. "But you already know that…it's why you asked me to kill you." My cock thickens against her pert ass. Her smell is addictive. Like virtue and sin. As if heaven and hell had one dirty, corrupt night together and she's the tantalizing vestige. "Cain's little lamb finally realized death is the only way out of the hell he's keeping her in."

She trembles, and I know my words ring true. "But it doesn't have to be. There's another way. One that will make him pay for all the pain he's caused."

Her voice is broken glass when she finally speaks. "I love him."

Eden's loyalty to Cain is impressive.

Unfortunately, it means she'll have to learn the hard way.

You can't always save a person from drowning.

Sometimes it's best to throw them a life preserver so they can learn how to save themselves.

I trace a finger up her arm. Her skin is warm, despite the cool October air. "Will you still love him after he marries Margaret?" Not waiting for a response, I nip the delicate flesh of her shoulder. "How about after he gets her pregnant with his child?"

I don't have to see her face to know there are tears in her eyes. But tears aren't enough.

I need her to break.

"Will you still love him when he gets everything he ever wanted...while you're left with nothing but a broken heart?"

When all his lies come out and his sins are revealed?

She lets out a shaky breath when I press the blade of my knife against her spine. "I don't have all night, little lamb. Are you in or out?"

Her body tenses. "I don't even know who you are."

"Right now, I'm your worst nightmare." I slice through the fabric of her dress, revealing her pearl G-string and supple bare ass. "But I don't have to be." When she flinches, I flick her earlobe. "Nice pearls."

The pulse in her neck jolts. "What exactly is it that you want from me?"

"Your cooperation."

"And if I don't?"

I dig the point of my knife into her back, just enough to pierce her skin. "You'll wish you begged me harder to kill you."

If she's under the impression I'm going to grant her mercy, she's dead wrong.

Despite how he uses her, there are strings connected to the black thing in Cain's chest, and Eden's the only one who can control them.

Which officially makes her the best weapon in my arsenal.

I need her.

"Time's up."

"Wait," she shouts. "You can't seriously expect me to go along with whatever it is you want when I don't even know your name."

I put my knife away. "You're right."

She relaxes, drawing in a deep breath. "Thank—"

My hand finds her throat. "You no longer have a choice."

Eden belongs to me…whether she likes it or not.

Chapter 7

EDEN

"*I* kissed you because I'm mad at Cain," I admit, attempting to reason with him.

"What?"

"You wanted the truth, right?" I swallow thickly against his palm. "Well, the truth is—you're right about everything. My name is Eden and I'm Cain's stepdaughter. And as you already know, I'm in love with him." Turning my head, I study him out of the corner of my eye. "You don't have to tell me who you are. I figured it out. It all makes sense now."

Not only does this man know too much about my relationship with Cain, he obviously wants to harm me.

And there's only one person I can think of who would want me gone.

Margaret.

"You know who I am?"

I nod. "Margaret is the governor's daughter. It's why Cain's marrying her...and how you know so much about me." I close my eyes as I recall the lipstick mark on Cain's collar the night we hooked up in the living room.

It was only three weeks ago. Cain had to have been seeing Margaret by then. He might have even proposed to her.

Which explains why he avoided me like the plague after. *Guilt.*

"He must have felt guilty for cheating on her, so he came clean about what happened. In turn, Margaret became jealous and hired you to take care of the problem...*me.*" Indignation hits me square in the chest. "I know you have orders to follow and all, but I'd really appreciate it if you could give her a message."

"What's that?"

I straighten my shoulders. "Tell her I said—suck my dick." I give him a menacing smile. "On second thought—tell her to learn how to suck one first. Maybe then her fiancé wouldn't have to ask me to finish him off."

His blue eyes sparkle with amusement. "You're smarter than you look."

The confirmation nearly knocks me off my feet. Part of me was hoping I was wrong.

"I can't believe she hired you to get rid of me." Clutching the railing, I blow out a breath. "That bitch thought she was so cute pretending not to know who I was earlier." I laugh. She's not so smart after all. "Cain's going to have her head when he finds out." I glare at him. "Yours too."

The man runs his nose along my hairline. "Your stepfather deposited the money into my account this morning."

I freeze. "What?"

"I told you he was—"

"No," I interject because he's clearly lying. "You're wrong. Cain would never kill me."

I don't care what Margaret told this guy to say. There's no way I'll ever believe Cain would hire someone to kill me. He may not feel for me the way I feel for him, but I know he loves me.

He's my family.

That's what he told me the night my mom died.

"You said it yourself, Eden. Cain's marrying Margaret because she's the governor's daughter. And if his new fiancée was upset after

44

finding out how *close* you two are… he'd do anything to get in her good graces again." He licks the tear running down my cheek. "Or rather, he'd do anything to win the election…including sending his favorite little lamb to the slaughterhouse."

I shake my head. His brainwashing won't work on me. "No. He loves—"

I'm so fucking close to getting everything I ever wanted…and I won't let you or anyone else ruin it.

I can feel the color drain from my face as I recall Cain's words that night.

The realization that this man may actually be right slices through me like a hot knife through butter.

Nothing is more important to Cain than this election.

Not even me.

My blood turns cold as my mind puts all the pieces together. "Cain wanted me to come here. He bought me a dress." Nausea barrels into me and I wrench the torn dress off my body. I don't want anything of his anywhere near me.

"How could he do this?" I choke out. "How did it come to this?"

Easy. *Because he knows how much I love him.*

He knows my obsession with him knows no bounds…and death was the only way to keep me away for good.

The man cornering me grazes his teeth down my neck. "I know it hurts." He walks his fingers down my abdomen, stopping above my pubic bone. "But I can make it better."

"No, you can't," I whisper.

The only one who can fix this is Cain.

My breathing hitches as his hand ventures lower. "I'll protect you, Eden." He skims my pearls with his thumb and I arch toward him instinctively, as if my body knows he's my lifeline.

I just don't understand why. Why would a man who was hired to kill me…offer to save me?

"What's in it for you?"

My pulse accelerates when his finger slides along my slit. "Apart from this?" He tugs on the string of pearls, sending them scattering. "Revenge."

The hairs on the back of my neck stand up. "Against—"

I don't get to finish that sentence because he shoves two fingers inside me. "Your stepfather."

I start to speak, but he works me faster, driving into me with meticulous, swift movements that have me spasming against his palm. "And you're going to help me. Understand?"

Against my better judgment, I nod, head whirling. I'm so close to coming I can't see straight. However, he removes his touch before I can.

"Good." He secures one of my wrists to the railing. Upon closer inspection, I notice it's his bow tie. "Because if you screw me over... I'll kill you both."

My heart thunders in my chest with his threat and then stops beating entirely when I look down at my wrist.

Cain tied me up in the closet earlier.

But what if it wasn't Cain?

I don't have time to ponder the thought though, because he guides my free hand to his zipper. "Take it out."

My hand trembles as I wrap it around his length. He's thick and long. A mixture of power and terror covered in silk. He makes a noise deep in his throat as I run my fingers over the veins and ridges, stroking him from root to tip.

"Bend over and grip the railing," he growls. "I want to see your pussy."

Nerves bunch in my stomach as I proceed to do what he asks. The position leaves me fully exposed.

Something he enjoys given the hum of approval he makes. Slowly, he pushes two fingers inside me and spreads them, stretching me. "Beautiful."

My cheeks heat. Something tells me he isn't the type of man to dish out compliments.

I gasp when he removes his fingers and the smooth head of his cock glides along my lips. "Look up at the stars and hold your breath."

"Why?"

"Because this is going to hurt."

"What's—"

"Taking what's his," he groans against my ear as white-hot pain surges through my body.

Tears sting my eyes when his hand curls around my hip possessively and I exhale sharply when he thrusts again, as if staking his claim.

My legs turn to jelly. I don't know why he hates Cain so much, but whatever the reason, it's clearly a personal one.

It still doesn't give him the right to take something from me without asking. "I don't recall giving you permission."

"I don't recall asking for it." Pain gives way to pleasure briefly as his hand drifts between my legs and he whispers, "Tell me to stop."

My pulse skitters when he finds the spot that lights all my nerve endings on fire. However, my pleasure is short-lived as images of Cain and Margaret together discharge one by one through my mind like bullets hitting a target.

Did they laugh as they planned my demise?

Did Cain feel anything—shame or sorrow—when he paid this man to end my life?

"No." I clutch the railing, my anger and hate are wrapping around me, coiling so tight I can't breathe.

Reminding me that Cain will always be inside me.

Because even though I hate him now…I loved him, first.

And deep down, I know I'll continue loving him…with all the broken pieces he left me in.

It's the cruelest punishment there is. To continue loving someone who's given you every reason to hate them.

"Don't stop," I say, the organ in my chest turning to steel. "Keep going."

I want Cain to burn like I do.

I want him to know I didn't go peacefully when he ordered someone to kill me.

That he didn't get this part of me.

Someone else did.

I whimper in both pleasure and pain as the man takes me in harsh, primitive thrusts.

He fucks the same way he threatens...with no mercy.

"What's your name?" I question, my breath choppy. "You're inside me and I don't even know your name."

Wrapping my hair around his fist, he tugs my head back, angling his mouth over my ear. "Damien King."

With that, he picks up his pace, fucking me so hard I cry out as I lose my balance.

"Come on, little lamb," he taunts, gripping both my hips to steady me. "Take my cock like a good girl."

I start to speak, but he pinches my clit and my knees go weak.

"No—I can't. I can't come," I utter, my body at odds with itself. "It hurts too much."

"Trust me," he snarls as his hand leaves me. "If I want you to come, you will."

His dick pulses and he shudders, finishing inside me with a violent growl.

And then there's nothing but the sound of the bitter October wind howling in the distance.

"That was my first time," I whisper as he slips out of me.

I regret the words the moment they leave my mouth.

"I know." His laugh is callous. "You bled all over my dick."

As if on cue, liquid begins trickling down my thighs. I start to turn around, intending to ask him if I can clean up, but he halts me.

"We're not done yet."

His rough palms skate down my body as he drops to his knees.

My pulse quickens. "What are you doing?"

He spreads me open with his thumbs. "You want your reward, don't you?"

I moan when his mouth finds my pussy and he peppers kisses along my slit. "Yes."

I want him to ease the pain.

My eyes flutter closed when he flattens his tongue against my clit, licking me in long, brisk strokes.

His tongue slides in deeper and he groans. "You taste like my cum."

His dirty words make my thighs clench. "Oh, God."

"God isn't the one eating this little cunt until it creams all over his face," he growls low and deep. "I am."

Blood whooshes in my ears when his mouth latches onto my clit and he begins sucking me in a staccato rhythm that has me rocking against his jaw.

"Damien, I'm—" I tremble and squeeze his tongue, coming so hard and fast I'm grateful he tied one of my wrists to the railing.

I expect him to stop, but to my surprise, he doesn't let up. He laps at my orgasm like a man starved.

"That feels—" The sound of someone banging on the glass door cuts me off. "What—"

Something sharp pricks my skin...and then there's nothing but darkness.

Chapter 8

CAIN

Cain: I'm having my driver pick you up shortly. I'll let you know when he's here.

*G*rit my teeth when another two minutes go by and she doesn't respond. Eden doesn't ignore me. No matter how angry she claims she is.

Then again, I've never hurt her this much before.

"Shit."

"Cain," Margaret hisses under her breath.

Governor Bexley clears his throat, no doubt annoyed with the lack of attention I'm paying to his friend.

I need to get my head back in the game.

"Everything all right?" Senator Dodson questions, not bothering to hide the trace of annoyance in his tone.

Tucking my phone into my pocket, I give my head a shake. "Sorry, my assistant forwarded me an urgent email." I glance at Bexley who frowns. "Everything is fine. There's been a change of schedule for my meetings tomorrow is all. Evidently my assistant considers that an emergency."

Margaret pats my arm. "That's because she knows how much it

irritates you when your affairs aren't in order." She tilts her head back and laughs. "Cain can be a tyrant when it comes to organization and planning."

Dodson chuckles. "My father always said being precise was a trait of a great leader."

Margaret beams at me. "Indeed, it is. No one works harder than my Cain does. I miss him terribly while he's gone all hours of the day and night, but I know it's only because he wants the best for the people in this town."

Her father raises his glass. "He's going to make a great mayor, and one hell of a governor some day."

They all raise their glasses at the same time my phone vibrates. "Excuse me, gentlemen." I motion to my phone. "I have to take this."

I can feel everyone's eyes on me as I head to the restroom, but I have to handle the Eden situation and get her home before she does something stupid.

Like find Margaret and tell her the truth.

I curse when I check my phone and realize it is in fact an email from Claudia updating my schedule for tomorrow, and not a text from Eden.

Bringing my cell to my ear, I take a sharp left—dodging the bathrooms—and head up the staircase.

I curse for a second time when it goes straight to voicemail. "Goddammit, Eden, I have neither the time nor the patience for one of your teenage tantrums right now. The driver will be here in fifteen minutes to take you home."

Since there's no telling when this little stunt of hers will end, I continue up the stairs. I have about five minutes to get her the fuck out of here before Margaret or Bexley come looking for me.

A pit forms in my stomach when I glance at my watch and recall today's date. No wonder she's so upset. *It's her birthday.*

Cain: I'm sorry.

Even to my own eyes, my half-hearted apology appears trite.

Cain: You're the last person in the world I want to hurt.

No matter how often I continue to do it.
After finding the suite I was in earlier empty, I try the one at the end of the hall.

I'm barely a few steps inside when my phone pings.

Eden: I'm already home.

I go to respond, but another text comes through.

Eden: Now stop texting me. I'd like to salvage my last two hours of the birthday you ruined.

I hover over the reply button before deciding it's best to respect her wishes. Maybe when she's calmer, she'll give me a chance to explain that Margaret or no Margaret…we can never be together. Not the way she wants.

Although I can't seem to find the will to let her go like I should.
Scrubbing a hand down my face, I pace around the room, scanning my brain for the right words to pacify her.

I come up empty.

With a shake of my head, I laugh. A stupid eighteen-year-old girl shouldn't have me tied up in knots like this.

I'm a grown man. I'm the one in control of this situation…*not her.*

Eden's young, impressionable, and according to her therapist—a bit mentally unstable due to her anxiety and the lack of motherly affection she received from Karen growing up.

Therefore, she'll do whatever the hell I tell her to.

Because she loves me.

Because she wants me.

Because I'm the only one she has.

And when I see her later…I'll make sure she doesn't forget it.

I squeeze my growing erection through my pants. *I'm going to take what's mine.*

Mind racing, I unzip my fly and fist myself. *Every untouched perfect inch of her.*

Licking my lips, I spit in my hand and drag my palm over my shaft.

The moment I get home, I'm going to rip apart those long legs and mar that sweet, innocent cunt of hers with my cock. *I'm gonna show her exactly who it belongs to.*

And if she protests or tries to put up a fight, I'll give it to her *harder.*

I quicken my pace, jacking myself off so fast the room spins.

So fucking hard she cries and pleads for me to stop.

But I won't.

Because she's mine.

I halt my movements when I hear a woman mewling in the distance.

Whether it's due to pain or pleasure, I'm not sure.

She does it again, and like a moth to a flame, I chase the sound into the bedroom of the suite—only to find it empty.

I look around, desperate to find out where it's coming from. My skin prickles when a deep grunt, punctuated by skin slapping together, assaults my ears next.

Like a bloodhound hunting down a scent, I track the noise to the French double doors across the room.

Dick firmly back in my hand, I wander over and peer through the glass.

I nearly come on the spot.

Both of their backs are turned to me, but there's no mistaking what's transpiring out on the balcony. Some man in a suit is fucking a woman senseless.

Tension in my dick skyrockets and I have to force myself to suck in air as he continues pounding her into the railing as though she were nothing more than a ragdoll. His harsh thrusts must be too much for her to take though because she starts to lose her balance.

Just when she's about to topple over, he grips her hips and bites out, "Take my cock like a good girl."

His voice punches through me and heat sears my thighs when she whimpers. An eerie feeling crawls up my spine, but I disregard it and thrust into my palm at the same time he rams into her.

My balls tingle thanks to the show they're giving me, and I know I'm liable to come any minute—but then he growls and his body convulses.

"No. Don't you fucking stop," I grumble under my breath, my needy cock protesting the injustice. "I'm not finished yet."

Just when I'm debating going out there to have a crack at her, the man drops to his knees, granting me a perfect view of her naked back and plump, bare ass.

Jesus fucking Christ. The moon illuminates her smooth skin, messy blonde hair, and soft curves. She looks like a sexy angel.

My dick pulses and I jerk myself faster when he slides his thumb along the seam of her pussy and separates her lips, exposing her.

I shift my stance, trying to get a better look, but his head inches closer, blocking my view.

Asshole.

Closing my eyes, I press my forehead against the window and sigh. There's no mistaking that the moans coming from her now are ones of pure ecstasy.

She enjoys having her cunt eaten like a dirty little whore.

I squeeze my aching shaft, imagining every illicit thing his mouth is doing to her.

My breath comes out in short, jagged bursts against the glass as I watch the back of his head move up and down and she starts writhing against his face.

I'm so close. So fucking close…

"Damien, I'm—"

Instantly the hairs on the back of my neck stand on end. That *name*…her *voice.*

No. *It can't be.* I'm hallucinating.

I shake my head, convinced the stress of the election is responsible for my current state.

However, my blood turns cold when the man turns his head and a pair of creepy blue eyes meet mine.

His lips curve into a vicious smirk, drawing my attention to the blood on his jaw before he spears her with his tongue again.

My teeth clench as I process what's happening.

Eden. Damien. *Eden.* Damien.

It's the equivalent of stepping on a landmine.

I go to turn the knob, but I can't. When I push harder, I realize both balcony doors are fastened shut from the outside, preventing me from opening them.

Rage twists my insides as I bring my fist to the glass and pound on it. "Eden!"

She doesn't know who Damien King is. She doesn't realize he's dangerous. She doesn't know…

She doesn't know the truth.

"Eden—" My stomach sinks when she goes limp. One of her wrists is tied to the railing, causing her body to sway ever so slightly —my very own pendulum of doom.

Damien stands up and walks toward me with an amused expression on his face. "You look like you've seen a ghost." He gestures to Eden, his eyes becoming tiny slits. "Guess that makes two of us."

Dread claws at my chest. *He's like a piranha teasing his meal.*

He's got me right where he wants me.

It's all I can do not to find a sledgehammer and break through the glass door separating us so I can rip his jugular out with my teeth.

I open my mouth to speak, but my phone vibrates.

He blows a line of smoke in my direction. "You might want to answer that."

My jaw tics as I bring my phone to my ear. According to the screen, it's Andrew Jones—the head of the committee for my political party.

It's odd he would be calling me when I saw him downstairs earlier.

"Hello—"

"We have a problem," he says, cutting me off. "David Covey is dead."

I want to remind him that it's not so much a problem as it is a blessing, considering he was my opponent, but I'm too shocked at the news. "That's...when? He was here tonight—"

"I know. I'm not sure of the details yet, but I have a friend who works at the medical examiner's office and she said she'll let me know what happened when she does. In the meantime, I called an emergency meeting with the committee so we can come up with a game plan. Governor Bexley was kind enough to offer us his home to set up camp for however long we need it, since townhall is closed until the morning. I'll see you there in say, fifteen minutes?"

"Yeah, I just have to..." I clear my throat. "I'll be there."

"Everything okay?" Damien questions after I hang up. There's no mistaking the taunting bite in his voice.

"Fu—" My sentence stalls when I hear the front door of the suite open.

"Cain?" Margaret calls out. "Are you in here? Cain?" she repeats and panic lodges in my throat. The click-clack of her heels tells me she's heading for the bedroom.

I look past Damien to Eden and my chest tightens.

Damien, appearing to enjoy the dilemma he's created, rubs his chin. "Quite the predicament you're in."

"I'll be downstairs in a minute, Margaret," I bellow over my shoulder. "Just finishing up in the bathroom."

Every muscle in my body contracts in aggravation when I turn my attention back to Damien.

I should have known he wouldn't stay away forever.

"This isn't over," I snarl, stabbing the door with my finger.

Damien's lips twitch in amusement. "Not by a long shot." He licks his blood tinged thumb. "But don't worry. I'll take good care of her."

Chapter 9

EDEN

a beam of sunlight breaks through a crevice in the dark curtains, rousing me from sleep. The streak of light is harsh when I open my eyes, and I turn my head away.

Grogginess has me combating the urge to fall back asleep, and the pulsating in my temples makes it hard to formulate a cohesive thought, but I know one thing is certain.

This isn't my bedroom.

My mouth is bone dry and my throat is thick when I swallow. However, it's nothing compared to the dull ache between my thighs and the throbbing pain in my left wrist.

I try to examine the cause of it, but I can't...both of my wrists are tied to the bedpost.

I suck in a rush of air when I peer down at my naked body. Confusion, followed by a wave of anxiety, shoots through me like a cannon as I recall the events of last night.

I had sex...with someone named Damien King.

The man who was hired by my stepfather and his new fiancée to kill me.

Tears prickle my eyes. On second thought—sleep seems explicitly better than reality.

No. I can cry over his betrayal later. Right now, I need to figure out who this Damien King dude is and what else he wants from me in exchange for his *help.*

Given he drugged me and has me bound to his bed—my virginity obviously wasn't enough for him.

I fight back a shiver. *What the hell have I gotten myself into?*

As if answering my question, the bedroom door opens and it's not long before his tall, muscular frame is parked at the end of the bed, studying me as if I were bacteria under a microscope.

I'm disgusted that my first thought is how attractive he is, instead of preserving my dignity.

He crosses his arms over his chest, his gaze unwavering. The longer he stares at me, the more humiliated I feel.

Which is exactly what he wants.

My mother once told me vultures' prey on the weak and broken…and she wasn't talking about the birds.

Stuffing down my embarrassment, I look him straight in the eye. I refuse to let him reduce me to nothing.

He's the one who should feel ashamed about tying a naked girl to his bed…not me.

"You drugged me." I don't pretend to disguise it as a question or an accusation, we both know what he did. "You realize you could have killed me, right?"

"It was a sedative." The corners of his lips curl up. "And you didn't seem to care about dying last night."

I don't know what irritates me more—his apparent amusement over my suicidal thoughts…or that he's right.

Since I don't have a retort, I scan his tattoos which are on full display due to him not wearing a shirt. They're intimidating, but beautiful. I rake over the words, 'Trust No One' in bold, black ink before focusing on the tattoo that draws my attention the most. Smack dab in the center of his neck is a large skull with intricate orange and yellow flames expanding across his throat. Every time he swallows, I watch them move—almost like they're flickering.

"Did it hurt?"

His response is short and gruff. "No."

It's on the tip of my tongue to ask him if he ever feels anything period, but I have more important things to worry about. "Are you planning to untie me in the near future?"

He narrows his eyes, but I don't mistake the hint of a smirk on his face. "That depends."

"On?"

"You." He walks over to the side of the bed. "The police department will be making a statement regarding David Covey's death later today."

I blink, not understanding. "What does that have to do with me?"

His hand sweeps down the underside of my arm. "The committee has been authorized to nominate someone to fill in the vacancy."

"Spectacular. But again, I'm not sur—"

He places a finger over my lips. "The committee will be nominating me." His eyes darken as his finger journeys south, lingering between my breasts. "After the funeral, they'll officially announce me as the new candidate."

My mouth drops open in shock. "Wait, *you're* running against Cain."

I don't bother hiding the disbelief in my tone. The man is crazier than I thought if he seriously thinks he stands a chance against Cain.

His jaw hardens. "Is that a problem for you?"

"Not for me, but definitely for you. There's no way in the world you'll win."

And why would he want to run for mayor of Black Hallows in the first place?

I'm not sure what to make of the expression on his face. "Your support for Cain is compelling. However, you'll need to take it down a few notches tomorrow."

"What's tomorrow?" I question as he releases one of my wrists.

I attempt to undo the other one, but he shakes his head in warning.

"Tomorrow is the funeral. You'll be attending with me."

Anxiety flickers in my belly. "No. Margaret and Cain are trying to kill me, remember?"

"No one will touch you," he bites out, his face contorting into something dark and menacing. A contrast to the soft kiss he places on my raw and tender inner wrist. "I'll make sure of it."

I yank my hand away. "No." Turning onto my side, I fiddle with the fabric still keeping me hostage. "I'm not going, and you can't make me."

I refuse to intentionally make myself a target so the people in town can make fun of me. Last night was bad enough...even with my identity hidden behind a mask.

My belly dips. *I swear some of them knew exactly who I was, and they were just waiting for the right moment.*

Relief fills me when the knot loosens and I'm able to free myself. Unfortunately, my victory is short-lived because Damien rolls me onto my stomach and pins me to the mattress with the weight of his body. "If you insist on acting like a child, I'm going to treat you like one."

I want to tell him I'm not acting like a child—I'm battling with an issue he knows nothing about—but he doesn't deserve to know those personal details about me.

"Treat me however you want. I'm still not going, asshole—"

My breath leaves me in one big whoosh when he jerks both my arms behind my back and fastens them. Before I can process what's happening, he maneuvers me into a position that forces my head down and my ass high into the air.

I start to argue, but the sharp sting of his hand against my flesh cuts me off.

My vision goes blurry when he does it again. He's spanking me as though I'm a child in need of discipline. *It's utterly humiliating.*

"Is that all you got?" I hiss, refusing to surrender.

The next one is harder than the first two, but I bite my lip and concentrate on maintaining control.

The man can beat me until I'm black and blue if he wants... I'm still not going to that funeral.

"Guess all your muscles are for show...because you hit like a girl."

I don't know why, but provoking him stirs something inside me. *Something wicked and provocative.*

It's as if he's unknowingly providing me an outlet for everything I've been keeping inside.

I steel myself, preparing for him to issue the next one, but he doesn't.

I'm even more confused when he flips me and hovers above me, caging me in with his forearms.

His dark eyebrows knit together as he peers down at me. "Does he hit you?"

For the first time since we met, I detect a genuine note of concern in his tone. However, I don't understand who he's referring to or why he's asking me this.

"Who?"

"Cain."

I'd laugh if he wasn't so serious. "Cain would never hit me."

He'd only pay someone to kill me.

"Karen?"

I shake my head. "No."

That would have required her to acknowledge my existence.

He surveys me for what feels like forever before he speaks. The intensity behind his sharp blue eyes nearly steals my breath. "Why are you so fucked up, Eden?"

I've seen dozens of therapists over the years, and not one of them has ever *asked* me that question.

They always told me.

"I—" I don't know him well enough to open up about my mother...or my insecurities and fears, so I do the only thing I can.

I turn the tables around on him.

"Why are you?"

He doesn't answer, but something is simmering beneath the surface. My entire body vibrates when he edges forward. We're so close we're practically melded together.

My skin prickles and the space between us tightens. There's an inimitable energy between us. A current flowing from him into me —connecting me to a man I don't know.

A man who's given me every reason to fear him.

It's the strangest thing I've ever felt.

I part my thighs without thinking and he settles between them effortlessly, like a puzzle piece clicking into place. A breath shudders out of me when he moves his hips and I feel how hard he is. I wish he wasn't wearing pants so there wasn't a barrier between us.

I close my eyes and inhale his scent. I have no idea why I'm so drawn to him, but I don't have the strength to fight or deny it. Whatever spell he's put me under is working.

I gasp when his hand finds my breast and he gives it a squeeze before venturing lower, cupping me where I'm damp and needy. I spread my thighs wider and nearly choke at the feel of his skin against my slickness. He's barely even touching me, and every single nerve I have is on fire.

Raising my hips, I move against his hand, slithering like a snake. Pleasure sizzles up my spine when my clit makes contact and my temperature skyrockets when I look up. His eyes are stormy with lust, and his jaw is clenched. There's something incredibly arousing about the intent way he's watching me get myself off.

A rough noise escapes him when I repeat the movement and my wetness seeps into his palm. I'm so turned on I can't see straight.

"Please," I whimper, needing more.

"Only good girls get rewarded."

I hiss when he presses his hand to my clit before removing it.

"You gonna be a good girl for me?"

I nod. I'll do anything he wants right now. My body is completely at his mercy.

My cheeks heat as I watch him lick the length of his palm, his eyes burning into me like hot coals. It's sweet torture the way he proceeds to tease me with his fingers, slowly dipping one in before pulling away.

"Please," I beg, growing frustrated. "Ple——"

The second his fingers are inside me, my body goes into overdrive. He pumps them vigorously and I arch my hips, meeting him halfway. The soreness from earlier fades to a dull ache as he works me faster.

"That's it. Ride my fingers."

Wet sounds fill the room and my head lolls back as the first stirrings of my orgasm hit me. The tip of his thumb swirls against my clit, keeping a steady rhythm as he kisses the column of my throat.

My toes curl, and I begin panting. It feels so good, I can't speak. I moan against his lips and he flicks my tongue, teasing me. I open my mouth wider, demanding more, and his tongue plunges inside, greedy and urgent as he swallows the cries of my climax, his heart beating like a jackhammer against mine.

I'm still wrapping my head around what transpired between us and why it feels so *intense*—when he pulls away abruptly.

His expression is stone when he stands up. I'm not sure what I did wrong, but I feel the cold front he's giving me down to my bones.

He points to a door across the room. "That is your bathroom. One of my servants will bring you something to eat in a little while." He strides toward the exit. "There are clothes for you in the closet, including a dress for the funeral tomorrow."

I sit up in bed and glare at him. "I already told you, I'm not g——"

"Yes, you are. I'll drag you in there kicking and screaming if I have to, but either way, you're going."

"Why?" I demand as he turns the doorknob. "Why is it so important for me to attend the funeral of a man I've never met before?"

"Because we have a deal." He gives me a menacing smile as he turns around. "And you better get used to it, little lamb, because you'll be attending a lot more functions with me in the future."

I swallow hard as bile works up my esophagus. "No. I'm sorry, but I can't."

His eyes flash in challenge. "You can...and you will."

I feel the color drain from my face. The only thing I can do is tell him the truth. "You don't understand, Damien. I have—I *can't* do this. Please—"

"The only reason you think you can't is because you've convinced yourself you can't. Last night—"

"Last night was different," I interject. "Last night—"

"Was for him," he seethes. "But you're not Cain's anymore. You're *mine*."

The possession in his tone is absolute.

"You didn't untie my hands," I yell when he opens the door.

"Not my problem."

Chapter 10

DAMIEN

"*D*id he leave a note?" one of the many reporters crammed into the room calls out.

Newly appointed police chief, Raymond Trejo, hesitates briefly before responding. "Yes, he did. However, out of respect for the family, it won't be released to the public." He points to another reporter. "You."

"What about the election? Is Cain Carter our mayor now?"

The cameras flash, and I look across the room to the man in question. He stands stoic in a dark pressed suit, the corners of his lips turned down in a frown. One might mistake his grim expression for sadness due to his opponent's tragic death...but they don't know the real Cain.

The only thing Cain's upset about is officials granting Covey's committee authorization to nominate someone else.

According to the handbook, had David Covey only waited a few more days to off himself, Cain would have won by default.

Such a pity.

Chief Trejo clutches the sides of the podium. "Uh, well, that isn't my particular area of expertise, but as I understand it, another person will be stepping in to...fill the vacancy."

"Do you know who?"

"Your guess is as good as mine." He gestures to William Anderson—the head of David Covey's political party—and the man who will ensure I have the majority vote from the committee when they meet in secret later tonight. "Let me hand it over to the one who can answer your questions."

Cain eyes the podium like a hawk as Trejo and Anderson trade places, no doubt chomping at the bit to know who his new opponent is.

He won't find out now, though. I specifically instructed Anderson not to tell the public about me until it was a done deal.

I don't want to give Cain—or his precious governor Bexley—the chance to persuade someone on my committee to change their vote.

"Evening, everyone," Anderson starts. "I know you're all anxious about the upcoming election. However, out of respect for the family, we won't be revealing who the new candidate is until after David Covey's funeral."

Instantly, reporters' hands fly up and they start pummeling him with questions.

"Isn't the public supposed to nominate the candidate?"

"The election is just over a week away, is that enough time for the town to make an informed decision by polling day?"

"Given Covey was terminal, did he ever disclose who he'd like to take his place?"

I can practically see the hairs on Cain's neck stand on end as he whispers something to the man next to him.

"Please, everyone," Anderson stresses. "I know you're all concerned about the upcoming election, however, right now is about David Covey. We'll be holding another conference the day after the funeral to discuss the events going forward. Now, excuse me while I spend the rest of my evening mourning the loss of a great man."

～

"What the fuck are you doing here?"

I glance up at his reflection as I finish washing my hands. "Last I checked, this was a restroom. Do you really need me to go into specifics?"

"You know what I mean. I distinctly remember telling you never to set foot in this town again."

"The conference was open to the public." I fish my cigarettes out of my pocket and light one. "And technically the Vanderbilt Castle—my new home—isn't part of Black Hallows. It's just outside of it." Turning, I blow a line of smoke in his face. "Might want to do some research on your town before the election, Mayor."

Despite his impassive expression, a vein in his forehead begins to bulge. "I'm gonna cut to the chase, Damien. This little stunt of yours is over. You have exactly two minutes to leave, or I'll have you dragged out in handcuffs."

Reaching over, I give his tie a little tug. "Kinky."

He swats my hand away. "Don't say I didn't warn you." He digs inside his pocket for his cell phone, but I shove him against the nearest wall and place my forearm over his throat, keeping him there.

"Careful, Carter." Leaning in, I graze the shell of his ear with my teeth. "You don't want to cause any waves before the election."

"I think all the time you spent on that tropical island reduced your brain cells. You're in no position to come here and try to intimidate *me*, asshole."

"Kept tabs on me, have you?" I get close to his face. "Who says I came here to intimidate you?" I lower my gaze to his zipper before meeting his eyes. "Maybe I'm here to hang out with my new friend. We have so much in common. So many things to bond over."

His eyes narrow and I can see those wheels of his turning.

He knows I wouldn't be here if I didn't have something on him. *Something that would destroy everything.*

He bares his teeth. "Where is Eden? What have you done with her?"

"Your little lamb will be staying with me for the time being."

His brown eyes turn black with rage. "Like hell she will."

Removing my arm, I straighten his collar. "Have a good evening. I know I will."

"I'll call the police," he barks when I open the bathroom door.

"That's a good idea." Looking over my shoulder, I flash him a spiteful grin. "*You* obviously don't have what it takes to protect her. Otherwise I wouldn't have stolen her from you."

With that, I walk out.

Cain's hot on my heels as I stride down the empty hallway. "Release Eden and leave town, or I'll hand over the tape to the authorities, Damien. I mean it. Don't *fuck* with me."

"It's not you I'm fucking this time, Carter." I spin around to face him. "You can do whatever you want, but be forewarned I'll tell everyone— including your darling Eden—the truth." Reaching between us, I find his testicles through his pants and give them a sharp tug. "So, unless you want everyone to find out who the *real* Cain Carter is, consider these mine for the foreseeable future. Because our little game isn't over until I fucking say it is."

He scowls. "I'm not interested in playing your stupid game."

"You know as well as I do that games are only fun if you have an opponent."

He bares his teeth. "It would be more fun to see you locked up in a jail cell."

"Unfortunately for you, that's not going to happen. Not after I tell Ed—"

His fist connects with my face. "You hurt her, or tell her anything, and I swear to God I'll kill you."

Staggering back, I spit the blood forming on my bottom lip at him. "That would bring your body count to what? F—"

"Cain, honey," a voice at the other end of the hall interjects. "Is that you?"

"Fuck," Cain mutters before he clears his throat. "I thought you went home, Margaret."

"Looks like you have a stalker," I muse as she starts walking toward us.

He starts to say something, but Margaret picks up her pace.

"You were right, Cain." I reach for her hand and give it a kiss. "She is stunning."

"Thank you." A blush creeps up her cheeks as she looks between me and her fiancé. "I don't believe I've met your friend before."

"You haven't," he grits through his teeth. "He's only visiting for a short—"

"Margaret—oh, what's going on down here?" Governor Bexley questions, his jolly frame marching down the hallway.

Cain looks like he's about to bust at the seams.

I let go of his daughter's hand and extend mine to the governor. "Nice to meet you, Governor Bexley."

He promptly shakes it. "Likewise…" His voice trails off, waiting for me to fill in the blank.

"Damien King. I'm an old friend of your soon-to-be son-in-law."

The governor shifts his stance uncomfortably, clearly caught off guard. "I—uh. I see." He lowers his voice a fraction, like he's about to tell me a secret. "I knew your father. He was…"

"So ruthless he made the devil look like a humanitarian?" I finish for him before winking at Margaret who hasn't taken her eyes off me. "Well, you know what they say—like father, like son."

Cain snorts and we all turn our attention to him.

"Sorry." He pounds on his chest and coughs. "Must be coming down with something."

The governor nods. "Margaret said you haven't been feeling well since last night." He levels him with a look. "Do you think you can pull it together for the next hour? There are some important associates of mine waiting for you in conference room B."

Cain looks like a kid caught with his hand in the cookie jar. "Of course. Let's go." He starts walking but pauses. The smile on his face is about as fake as the governor's toupee. "You said you were leaving, right?"

"Indeed." My expression hardens. "I have something very precious waiting for me back at home."

Governor Bexley and Margaret exchange a bemused glance.

"Home?" Margaret questions. "I thought Cain said you were visiting?"

"I am. But like I was telling Cain earlier, I'll be dealing with some important business matters this month, and since I detest hotels, I decided to purchase the Vanderbilt Castle."

Cain makes a face, but he quickly recovers when the governor whistles. "That's quite an investment for such a short visit."

Cain checks his watch. "We should probably get going."

"How long are you in town for?" Margaret asks as we begin ambling down the hallway.

"That all depends on how well my new associate cooperates with me." I slap Cain's shoulder when we reach the atrium. "However, if I'm still in town for the election, I'll make sure to vote for you."

The look Cain gives me could kill a dead man.

And the look I give him…warns him this was only round two.

Chapter 11

EDEN

"*W*here is he?"

The guy...servant...whatever role Damien hired him for—which apparently includes being at my beck and call —pays me no mind as he continues hunting through the closet in this God-forsaken prison cell of a bedroom.

"Found it," Geoffrey declares triumphantly, holding up a black dress. "This is what he requested you wear for the funeral." Before I can protest, he shoves it at me. "Put it on."

"No."

Pinching the bridge of his nose, he sighs deeply. The action makes him appear much older than his estimated twenty-five years.

It's kind of strange he's wasting his youth working for a ruthless asshole like Damien King—but I have more important things to worry about.

"Where is Damien?" I ask again, sharper than before.

Geoffrey shrugs. "Not in here." He picks the dress up off the floor and hands it back to me. "Now get dressed."

My blood is boiling like lava, but it's obvious fighting with the help isn't getting me anywhere.

Given Damien instructed his servants to keep me locked up like a prisoner, it's time for Plan B.

I shimmy out of my silk sleep shorts and yank the matching tank top over my head. Biting my lip, I meet his gaze as I toy with the clasp of my bra. "Are you going to keep watching me?"

His cheeks take on a tomato color, which would almost be adorable if he didn't work for the enemy.

Faster than lightning, he skedaddles to the door. I hear the sound of his key entering the lock a moment later.

"Ouch," I shriek.

As expected, Geoffrey comes rushing to my aid. "Miss, are you—"

I don't hear the rest of his statement because I make a mad dash for the door.

I have no idea which of the many rooms down the hall belongs to Damien, but if I had to take a guess, it would be the one at the very end.

The one with the balcony.

Geoffrey calls my name and his footsteps get closer, but I pick up my pace, ignoring the shocked look another servant gives me as I pass him.

A few seconds later, I turn the knob...and barrel right into a woman wearing a maid uniform.

Given her hair and makeup are perfect, and her uniform is crisp and spotless, it doesn't look like she does much cleaning around here.

She closes the door behind her and pops a hand on her hip. "Can I help you?"

The way her expression contorts into disgust has me feeling all kinds of self-conscious. Especially since I'm standing here in nothing but my underwear...and she looks like she just walked out of a magazine titled, '*Better Homes and Sexiest Housekeepers.*'

"Sorry, I must have the wrong room."

"You're not permitted to roam around the castle," Geoffrey scolds when he catches up. "It's against the rules."

Rules. Annoyance bubbles in my throat.

Had I known this *deal* with Damien involved taking away my basic human rights—I would have hurled myself off that balcony.

I miss Cain. The thought makes me feel stupid, given the circumstances—but it's no less true.

I miss my life. I miss my home.

I miss being able to walk into the kitchen to get myself a goddamn glass of water.

Cain never treated me like a hostage.

The maid smiles coldly and flicks a hand in my direction. "Too-da-loo."

"Have I offended you in some way?"

I have no idea what I could've done to make her act like I'm worse than the dirt on the bottom of her shoe.

She looks past me to Geoffrey. "How much longer—" she starts to say, but the door behind her opens.

"Get back to work," Damien barks.

Geoffrey takes off like a bat out of hell, but *she* saunters backward down the hall, pouting at Damien. "Will I see you later?"

A weird mixture of suspicion and what feels a whole lot like jealousy slams into me.

It's now crystal clear why she's not too fond of me, but what's not clear is why the thought of Damien sleeping with someone else feels so…unsettling.

I mean, I certainly don't want him. For one fleeting moment, I thought I was attracted to him and that there was this unfathomable connection between us. But then reality came crashing down— around the same time he left me bound, hungry, groggy from the drugs he gave me, and locked in a room until Geoffrey found me hours later—and I came to the sobering conclusion that the man is a psychopath.

Needless to say, Damien screwing another woman should be the least of my worries. If anything, I should feel relieved he's set his sights on someone else.

And yet…there's a sliver of resentment making its way through the hollow space in my chest.

The one created by another man.

I don't have time to digest all these bizarre feelings though, because Damien turns those sinister blue orbs my way.

A wave of heat courses through me as he rakes his gaze up and down my body meticulously, lingering on my panties before meeting my eyes. "Get in here."

My windpipe feels like sandpaper as he opens the door wider and I tread past him.

I let out a heavy breath the moment I'm inside, feeling like I made it past the lion's den. However, I suck it right back in when Damien begins to corner me.

"You're out of your room."

His eyes narrow as he inspects me. I do the same to him, taking in his black t-shirt and gray sweatpants. His casual appearance throws me, but not so much that I miss his damp forehead or the faint smell of sweat…no doubt due to his morning *workout* with the maid.

"Looks like I'll have to find someone who isn't so easily seduced to look after you."

"I didn't seduce anyone," I fib as my back hits the wall. "I pretended to be hurt so I could escape." Fearing he'll hire that maid to do the job, I add, "It wasn't Geoffrey's fault. He was only trying to help." I jab his chest with my finger. "For what it's worth, I don't need anyone to look after me."

"Says the girl who marched down to my bedroom in her underwear."

"I needed to talk to you."

"Well, you've got my attention." He places his arms on either side of my head. "Now, I suggest you tell me what the problem is…or do something else with that pretty mouth of yours before I lose interest."

"What's the matter? Your bitch of a maid didn't do a good job?" I snap before I can stop myself.

"Your little kitty claws are adorable." I want to bite his mouth when it curls into a mocking grin. "Don't bother wasting them on me, though. Save them for someone who actually gives a fuck."

With that, he turns and walks away.

I follow him into the bathroom. "You want to know why I'm so fucked up, but I think we should start with *you*, Mr. Damien King."

Paying me no mind, he turns on the shower.

"Why are you such an asshole?"

There's nothing but silence as he slips his t-shirt over his head.

Anger churns in my stomach, picking up speed with every passing second, like a boulder rolling downhill.

I'm prepared to deal with nearly anything he throws my way, but I can't stand being blatantly ignored.

And I know Damien's only doing it to get under my skin.

Maybe I should return the favor and push a few of his buttons.

It's not like Damien will kill me.

You don't assassinate someone you deem indispensable.

"Let me guess, Mommy and Daddy spoiled you." I take a step closer, watching the muscles in his broad back tense up. "Which would explain why you reek of entitlement and take things that don't belong to you."

He slides off his sweatpants next, but I don't miss the slight tic of his jaw in the mirror.

I creep up behind him, trying not to get lost in the giant reflection staring back at me. Damien might be the Devil, but his body is a temple. Golden skin, abs harder than granite, well-defined muscular arms, and an ass you could crack walnuts on.

A face so perfect your heart skips several beats.

I'm not sure how, but he manages to look both downright menacing and utterly beautiful.

It makes me wonder if he uses his striking appearance as a weapon against people...or as armor because the distraction keeps them at bay.

Perhaps both.

I leisurely run my finger from one of his shoulder blades to the other.

Damien watches me like a hawk in the mirror.

"It's often said that bullies terrorize others as a way to cover up for their own insecurities and pain."

The steam from the shower fills up the room as I trail my hand down his abs, stopping right above the waistband of his boxers. "Is that it, Damien? Did someone hurt y——"

I don't finish that sentence because he spins around with a force so powerful I lose my balance.

For the briefest of moments, I see a flash of something in those stormy baby blues before he forces me to my knees and lowers his boxers.

I attempt to get up, but he grabs a fistful of my hair and stands directly in front of me, trapping me between his body and the wall.

I watch as he wraps his hand around his erection, feeling grateful I didn't see it before it was inside me. The wide mushroom head is slick and demanding...as is the rest of his thick and veiny shaft.

His cock is every bit as dominating as he is.

Fisting it tighter, he holds it out to me. "Open."

The vindictive bite in his voice sends a shiver up my spine. I'm seriously regretting pushing him so far.

"No."

He plugs my nose, forcing my mouth open. My stomach rolls with a violent lurch. I can practically smell the scent of her on his dick.

I clamp my mouth shut and shake my head. His maid looked at me like I was lower than scum before. I'd rather have nails drilled into my eyeballs than lick her off of him.

My head whirls as panic sets in. I only have another few seconds left before my mouth will open involuntarily and he'll shove it inside.

Saying please is moot at this point, because he doesn't want me to beg.

What he really wants...is my cooperation and for me to uphold my end of the deal.

"I'm sorry I made you angry, but please don't make me do this." I look up at him. "If you let me go, I'll get ready for the funeral."

We stare at one another for what feels like an eternity...until finally, he relents.

I make my way to the door on shaky legs but pause before exiting. Damien doesn't strike me as the type of man to give a shit about other people, but the impulse to share this with him is too strong to tamp down.

"After I caught them together...Cain..." *Jesus*. Just saying his name takes the breath right out of me. "He wanted me to finish what Margaret started." My cheeks are damp when I turn to look at him. "People in this town have said some horrible things to me and about me, including my own mother, but I've never felt lower or more disrespected in my entire life than at that moment."

His dark brows knit together as he studies my face, probably wondering why I bothered to tell him that.

I shake my head, feeling stupid. "Enjoy your shower."

"Eden."

"Yeah?"

"*You* didn't make me angry." The glare he aims my way is so ominous my knees wobble. "And I sincerely hope for your sake you never do. Because I won't just disrespect you...I'll fucking *annihilate* you."

Chapter 12

EDEN

I'm shaking so hard my teeth chatter as we make our way toward the funeral home.

The nasty things the maid whispered under her breath as I was walking out to the car echo through my head, muffling the clack of my heels on the pavement.

I'm not sure who she is, but she seems to know all about me and my past.

There's no escaping it. I'll always be known as the town slut who tried to ruin a good man and a happy marriage.

Bile rises up my throat as we pass through the front doors. A few people are gathered in the lobby conversing. It won't be long before they begin speculating and whispering. "I'm sorry, Damien. I can't do this."

My head spins like a carnival ride and my throat constricts when I realize people are starting to look in our direction.

My therapist was right. Normalcy isn't something I'm capable of achieving. I need to focus on small goals: like walking to the mailbox.

I need to stop trying to run when I'm barely able to crawl, because I'm only setting myself up for failure.

My breathing accelerates as I hightail it for the door.

A sharp tug on my arm yanks me back. "Eden."

Oh, God. Damien's saying my name. *Everyone is going to know who I am.*

I clutch my stomach when it rumbles. Damien's speaking, but it sounds like he's a million miles away.

My face feels wet and I don't know if it's from tears or sweat, but it doesn't matter. There's only one thing on my mind.

I have to leave.

An overwhelming feeling of doom surrounds me like a viscous black fog, and I claw at my neck with my free hand, desperate for air.

I'm moving fast but in the wrong direction. The exit is the other way.

I fight against Damien's hold, but it's useless because he lifts me off the ground.

"No."

I need to get out of here. Bad things happen when I leave the confines of my home.

Lives get ruined. People die.

"Goddammit," my tormentor growls. "I told you I won't let anyone hurt you."

Cain said that, too. For all I know, Damien made a deal with him as well. It would explain why he's so insistent on me being here.

This must be the drop off.

A sardonic laugh bursts from me. A funeral home. How convenient.

Then again, Cain's always had a knack for details.

My maniacal laughter about my demise turns to sobs as Damien sets me down. "For fuck's sake. Stop crying."

"Medication," I croak as I take in the table displaying mass cards and the few rows of chairs in the otherwise unoccupied room. "If it's all right with you, I'd like something to take the edge off before I meet my maker."

"Eden, look at me." When I do, he says, "*No one* in this town is going to fuck with you once they know you're mine." He inhales deeply. "Where's this medication of yours?"

"In my purse."

After inspecting the pill bottle, he places a tablet in my hand. "How long does it take to kick in?"

I debate telling him at least fifty years, but given it's a fairly common medication for anxiety and panic attacks, the information is readily available on the Internet. However, he'll likely be even more of a brooding ass if I tell him to Google the answer.

I need to choose my battles wisely with this man.

"About fifteen to twenty minutes."

"Fine. We'll just hang out here until you're ready to go in."

I search his face for signs he's joking, but there are none.

"I don't think you understand—"

"No," he sneers, getting close to my face. "You're the one who doesn't understand. I'm not the kind of man who negotiates, but I did earlier." Anger radiates off him as he continues. "We had a deal and I expect you to keep your word. You're attending this funeral and whatever the hell else I want you to for the next month, and that's final."

My only option is to level with him and try to explain that social situations—especially those involving anyone from town—are a severe trigger for me.

"I know you think I'm being silly and immature, but I'm not. I have a legitimate condition and I can't be in a room full of people—"

"You were in a room full of people the other night."

"It's not the same and you know it. Even my therapist—"

"Your shrink is a quack who deserves to have his license revoked and shoved up his ass."

I'm honestly offended. I've made amazing progress this year thanks to him...and Cain. "You don't even know hi—"

His hand clamps my jaw. "I need you to try." His grip grows tighter, causing me to wince. "You have to try to conquer this. Not for me and not for Cain, but for *you*."

83

It's not so much his words, but the conviction behind them. It's almost like he wants this for me even more than I do.

It's also the first time he's treated me like I'm not part of whatever his agenda with Cain is, but an actual person.

"I might have another panic attack," I whisper, shame coating my insides. "I've already embarrassed us both once today and—"

"I'm not embarrassed." He dips his head slightly and my heart rate quickens, gaining momentum by the second. "You can do this, Eden. But you won't know unless you try. You have to want it."

I do. *I want to be normal so bad I can taste it.*

"Swear you won't leave me in that room all alone? Because I don't think I can handle—"

"I won't leave your side unless you want me to."

"Okay," I breathe. "I'll do it."

In the grand scheme of things, my life can't get much worse. Not only is a ruthless asshole holding me captive, the man I love is marrying someone else…and the happy couple wants me dead.

I might as well throw another log on the fire and go out in a blaze of glory by attempting to conquer my anxiety disorder along the way.

Take some control back over my life.

Easier said than done. Because I know once I'm in that room I'm going to want to run for the hills again.

And I have absolutely no idea how I'll remain intact once I see him.

Correction…*them.*

I rub the knot forming in my chest. *God, it hurts.* Whenever the anger I'm harboring for him eases up the slightest bit…a swell of pain comes rushing in to seal the void, filling all the crevices of my broken heart.

I wish my resentment and hate could wash out *all* my feelings for Cain.

But that's not the way it works.

Love isn't powerful because it builds and restores.

It's powerful because it survives destruction.

"I forgot to give this to you in the car." Much to my bewilderment, Damien shoves a small velvet box in my hand. "Put it on."

I open it cautiously, fully anticipating whatever's in the box will bite my finger off. I honestly wouldn't put it past him at this point.

However, what I uncover is…far more perplexing.

Confusion fills me as I stare down at the large opal stone surrounded by tiny diamonds in a halo setting. The ring is gorgeous, but I'm stumped as to why he's giving it to me.

Damien folds his arms across his chest, seemingly annoyed with my silence. "It's opal."

"I know. It's—"

"Your birthstone." I'm not sure what to make of the expression on his face. "Someone once told me opal was good luck for those born in October. Helps ward off evil spirits or some shit."

I fight back the urge to inform him that this one must be defective given he's still here, because I'm still having trouble understanding why he would do something so nice for me. "Why—"

"I'm leveling the playing field." With a huff, he takes it out and slips it on my left ring finger. "As of this moment, you're officially my fiancée." There's a mocking glint in his eyes as the corner of his mouth curves up. "You're welcome."

I feel like someone just poured a bucket of ice water down the front of my dress. "I'm not marrying you."

"You'll do whatever the fuck I tell you to do." His teeth flash white. "Your fifteen minutes are up, Mrs. King."

"I don't recall Satan ever having a wife," I mutter under my breath as he takes hold of my arm.

And if the Devil was even half as cold-hearted and mean spirited as Damien King is…it was for the best.

"That's because he tossed her off the balcony and cut his losses when he had the chance. Now start walking before I drag you in there."

I hate him.

I hate them both.

My legs shake as we make our way past the lobby and into a

much bigger room holding at least half the town. Due to the large line forming at the front, the people entering are all packed like sardines in the back of the room—which is fine by me.

I look down at my shoes. If I keep my head down the entire time maybe it won't be half as bad as I imagined.

"Stop staring at the floor," Damien hisses in my ear. "Hold your head high and make every last one of these motherfuckers eat shit."

That's easy for him to say, he walks into a room commanding respect and people hand it right over.

People like me aren't as fortunate. *No one respects the home-wrecking town whore.*

Even when she's not…because perception is everything.

"I'm just trying to get through this the best I can," I whisper to my unassuming black heels, my voice cracking.

"Look at me."

Lifting my head, I meet his eyes. His expression is full of disdain, but for once, it's not directed at me.

"There's not a person here who would dare to disrespect you. Not in my presence." Those blue orbs are like laser beams zeroing in on potential targets as he looks around the room. "And if by chance someone is stupid enough to test that theory, I'll shove my cock down their throat and make them choke on it."

The tiny hairs on my arms rise. Damien is out of his mind, but there's something strangely appealing about his no fucks given attitude.

He lets go of my arm and snatches my hand as a large group of people shuffle past us. Now that it's not so claustrophobic and I'm no longer staring at my shoes, I can see the casket in the front of the room.

"Don't funerals usually take place at a graveyard?"

My heart lurches as my thoughts flicker to my mom's. I could only stomach the first few minutes before I had to leave. Fortunately, Cain was prepared and had a driver on standby, ready to take me back home.

"Funeral, memorial. Same shit." Damien lifts a shoulder in a shrug. "They're roasting him after we leave if that's what you're wondering."

The people standing next to us bristle.

I open my mouth to speak, but the couple paying their respects to the dearly departed turn around and the entire room sways.

I watch in agony as Cain drapes his arm around Margaret, gently leading her away. They look so comfortable together—it's almost as if they've been an item for years.

Tears well in my eyes when I notice the black silk tie he's wearing. The one I got him for his last birthday. He looks as handsome and distinguished as ever.

Without a care in the world.

"I'm leaving." I don't care if Damien tries to punish me or how angry he gets. The organ in my chest can't take the sight of him with her.

"Like hell you are," he seethes in my ear.

"It's too hard."

I try to untangle my hand from his, but Damien clutches it tighter. "Look, Eden, there are two types of people in this world. Those who are capable of greatness, but don't bother trying. And those who still try even though they're not capable of greatness. Which one are you?"

His words root me to the spot. Not because they're inspiring... but because I've heard them before.

"I...wh—" My voice stalls as Cain and Margaret start walking toward the back of the room.

The look on Cain's face when he spots us is like nothing I've ever seen before. And when those irate brown eyes land on me, I can't help but notice a hint of something simmering beneath the surface.

Something I never expected to see, given the circumstances ...*betrayal.*

Damien smirks as his glare locks with Cain's. "It's showtime."

Chapter 13

DAMIEN

*O*ne of my favorite things to do is watch my piranha right before mealtime.

I admire the way he examines the pretty fish diligently, his gaze never wavering. How he never gets impatient or tries to rush the process. Quite the contrary—he appears tranquil. At peace.

Because he knows mealtime is only a few short minutes away.

And even though the other fish might fool themselves into thinking the divider is there to protect them...he knows the truth.

The divider is only there so his food can get comfortable in their habitat and be at ease...right before he strikes.

That's why he's so calm. It's easy to remain composed when you're the one in control and you have all the power.

It's easy to deceive others when you know you'll always have the upper hand.

After Cain pulled the rug out from under me, I used to spend my time wondering why he took it so far.

Why he used me and then turned on me when he was the one person I would have done anything for.

However, as time passed and my obsession with getting even grew, I stopped wondering.

Because I understood.

When someone strips you of your dignity—when they take away your power and control...

When they hurt you so much you no longer register pain.

You'll do anything to get your humanity back.

Including destroying others...through whatever means necessary.

It's an intoxicating, primitive feeling, realizing you're in complete control of someone's last breaths. That you and you alone are responsible for every last morsel of life seeping out of them.

But you don't always have to commit murder to kill someone.

You just have to plant a few seeds...and wait for them to bloom.

Chapter 14

EDEN

*N*o one says a word as Cain and Damien continue staring each other down. The hatred between them is so thick I can taste it. Which can only mean one thing.

Whatever their issue is—it's personal. Not business like I originally suspected.

Cain's eyes narrow when he looks at me again. I can practically feel the words burning on his tongue before he speaks.

"Are you okay?"

I glare at him. Why would he give a shit about my well-being when he and his fiancée want me dead?

"You're kidding me, right?" The spite in my voice surprises me, but there's no way I'm going to apologize for it. "You're lucky I don't have you arrested."

A flash of confusion sweeps across Cain's expression before he pales. "I know you're angry with me, but don't make up lies—"

"Is there a problem here?" Margaret questions, pursing her lips.

The way she's sizing me up makes it clear her question is directed at me.

It's all I can do not to punch her in the face.

As if on cue, my limbs start shaking and my vision becomes

hazy. A public confrontation at a funeral for a beloved member of Black Hallows is the last thing I want.

A spike of adrenaline shoots up my spine, urging me to run out and go somewhere safe, but I'm so tired of hiding from my problems.

I'm tired of being someone's dirty secret. I'm tired of not confronting people for their horrible actions.

I'm tired of the man I love using me for his own needs and then tossing me away like garbage.

And I'm not going to stand here and let Cain's latest whore hire someone to hurt me, preen around town on his arm like she's the best thing that ever happened to him, and then speak to me in a condescending tone.

They thought it would be easy to take my dignity as well as my life—but fuck them both, because I'm taking them back.

Steeling myself, I hold her stare. "Don't you *dare*—"

"Eden," Cain hisses at the same time a heavyset man approaches our little circle of hell. "Don't do this here." His brown eyes soften. "Please."

My heart twists and I have to remind myself the only thing he's worried about is the stupid election.

"It's a shame they don't serve booze at these things," the portly man joining us declares with a wry smile.

It quickly fades when none of us return it.

"Eden?" Margaret asks, looking perplexed. "As in Karen's daughter Eden?"

The woman couldn't put more distance between me and her new man if she tried.

"Yes, Margaret," Cain replies, sounding exasperated.

For a woman who went through the trouble of hiring a hitman to get me out of the picture, you'd think she'd do some research on her target.

Either that or she's just super convincing.

"Well, pardon my confusion, Cain," she drawls, giving me the side-eye. "Last time I checked, you said she didn't leave the house due to her *mental issues*."

My cheeks flame as embarrassment courses through me. It would be more humane if she took out a gun and shot me in the face.

I look at my shoes again, wishing the ground would open up and swallow me whole.

"I suggest you both stop talking about my fiancée like she's not standing right in front of you," Damien says, pinning Cain with a malicious smile. "Unless you want to join Covey in that casket."

"Fiancée?" Cain spits, his expression darkening.

"Mazel tov," the man next to him declares and Margaret smacks his shoulder.

"The man just threatened your daughter, Daddy," Margaret mutters. "Don't *congratulate* him."

The man tsks. "As usual, you're not seeing the bigger picture. Just the other night we were discussing where to send the girl so Cain would no longer be burdened with her after he wins the election." He gestures to Damien. "However, it seems she's no longer our problem. Therefore, congratulations are certainly in order."

Every cell in my body screams in silent agony as I glance up at Cain. "That's why you want to get rid of me?" I whisper, my voice quivering with unshed tears. "Because I'm a burden?"

Cain shakes his head. "No—"

The governor clears his throat loudly, cutting him off. "Ah, the priest has arrived. The service will be starting any minute, so we better take our seats."

Damien starts to speak, but the governor ushers Cain and Margaret away. He gives his daughter's arm a gentle squeeze as they make their way to the chairs on the other side of the room and she beams at him.

Cain might not have wanted me gone...but they certainly did.

Beside me, Damien's jaw works. It appears he didn't much care for the governor's rude exit.

Good. Maybe now he'll understand what it feels like to be a fish out of water.

"Are you happy?"

His lips press together in a tight line as he escorts me to the last row of seats in the back of the room. "About?"

"You knew they would be here and yet you still forced me to come today." We take our seats as the priest ambles up the aisle. "You said no one would disrespect me if I was with you, but they did."

It's all people ever do.

I rise from my chair. They already won, but I refuse to give them the satisfaction of seeing me cry.

"Where do you think you're going?"

"To the bathroom."

Damien stands, but I hold up a hand, halting him. "The least you can do is grant me five minutes to myself so I can cry in peace."

I stalk off before he can argue.

I'm wiping the smeared mascara from under my eyes at the bathroom sink when the door opens.

I don't think anything of it until I hear the faint click of the lock followed by swift, hefty footsteps—like someone's on a mission.

My stomach contracts when I look up at my reflection and see Cain standing behind me.

The moment our eyes connect in the mirror, his become tiny slits. He looks more enraged than I've ever seen him.

A scream lodges itself in my throat, but he slams a hand over my mouth.

I struggle against his hold as he drags me backward, but he's double my strength. It's not long before he shoves me against a bathroom stall, pinning me there with the force of his arms.

94

"How the fuck could you do this to me?" He compresses my wrists so hard I yelp. "Damien fucking King."

"I didn't do anything to you," I croak, breaking out in a cold sweat. "*You're* the one who hired him to kill me. You and your new fiancée."

Cain's eyes widen in disbelief and he gives his head a shake. "Is that what he told you?"

More like confirmed it, but that's neither here nor there at this point.

"I'm sorry taking care of me was such an inconvenience, but I thought—" I choke back a sob. "Jesus. I *loved* you, Cain."

I still do.

And in the end, it's my love that will be responsible for my death.

God, what a sad, pathetic, tragedy I turned out to be.

The slap of my hand across his face shocks us both, but I'm too worked up to stop myself.

It wasn't supposed to be like this.

He swore he'd never leave me. He vowed to always take care of me.

He promised not to hurt me…and I stupidly believed him.

I slap his cheek again, harder than before. "I hate you."

Falling in love with Cain Carter was the best and worst thing that ever happen to me.

"I *hate* you," I rasp, my vocal cords ripping to shreds. "I hate—"

He catches my wrist before my hand connects with his cheek a third time.

"No, you don't. You hate how much you love me." My tears fall faster, and he cradles my face in his hands. "Do you honestly think I could ever hire someone to kill you?"

I don't give him an answer. I can't. I never thought he would hurt me like this, and yet here we are.

"Look at me."

I try to turn away, but he won't let me. "Goddammit, look me in the fucking eyes, Eden."

My gaze rises to those intense brown orbs of his that are swirling with so much emotion my breath catches.

"No." I swallow, and it feels like glass going down. "I thought Margaret did, and you went along with it because of the election and—"

"Fucking hell. No. *Never*. I would never let anyone take you from me." My heart squeezes when his lips find my jaw. "Do you have any idea how much I love you? How special you are to me?"

Tears prickle my eyes for an entirely different reason. "I'm sorry. Damien—"

His lips capture mine before I can get the words out. For a moment, I'm too stunned to move.

Cain's never kissed me before. Not like this.

I whimper into his mouth when our tongues brush. He's so gentle and tender with me, like I'm made out of porcelain.

His hand slides down my neck. "Fuck. I love you so much, Eden."

And just like that, my heart blooms back to life like a rose after a long, cold winter.

My toes curl when he groans and deepens the kiss. It's forbidden, frantic, and intense...it's everything we are.

Everything I always wanted us to be.

I want to pinch myself to make sure this is actually happening and I'm not imagining things.

He pivots his hips, digging his erection into me. "Did you like the way he fucked you?"

There's no mistaking the lethal edge to his harsh words or the sheer jealousy shading his eyes. But even more concerning is that he *knows*.

"How—"

He fists the neckline of my dress. "Are you really so naïve? No way in hell would he keep you in his home or declare you're his fiancée without fucking you first." Snarling, he tugs on the material, jerking me close to his face. "Did you enjoy it?"

I give him the truth. "It hurt. But not nearly as much as your betrayal did."

He laughs but there's not a drop of humor. "Want to know what else hurts? Spending the last two nights worried sick about you. Wondering where the hell you were and if you'd ever come back to me." His voice drops to a whisper. "Wondering if you would ever forgive me."

The tightness in my chest turns to flutters when he drops to his knees. "You're the last person in the world I want to hurt. You know that, right?"

I don't even have to look at his earnest expression to know he truly believes that.

But Cain's intentions have never been the problem...it's his actions. How far he'll go to reach his goals. *The people he'll hurt in the process.*

His hands slide up my thighs and he hooks a finger into the band of my panties. "Let me make it better."

My breath comes out in ragged gasps as he kisses my torso and the delicate lace falls to my ankles.

"My beautiful, innocent, Eden." He bunches the hem of my dress in his hand, exposing me. "Such a shame this little cunt of yours will never taste as sweet as it used to."

His words sting, but I know it's all the anger he's harboring over me having sex with someone else.

It must make me an awful person, because deep down there's a part of me that enjoys seeing his pain.

Not because I want him to suffer...but because it means what he feels for me is real.

I want him to hold on to it so tightly it can never escape.

I want it to haunt him just like it haunts me.

"Did you think about me when he fucked you?"

I nod.

I thought about how much I loved him. How angry I was about his engagement to Margaret. How much he hurt...

I cry out when he rams two fingers inside me. "Shh, sweetheart." He removes his fingers and shoves them into my mouth. "Cain's gonna take care of you." He maneuvers his head between my thighs. "I'll fix you, just like I always do."

I grip his hair as he drags his tongue across my slit. "I love you."

Even when I should hate you.

He's like poison pumping through my system. The more I absorb him, the sicker I get.

I jolt against his mouth as he speeds up his movements.

Every flick of his tongue along my clit is a lashing. A brutal reminder of every ounce of pleasure he's ever given me...

Followed by every piece of my heart he's incinerated.

"I love you so much."

So much I hate myself for it.

Tears drip down my cheeks and onto my chest like a river with no end. Freedom from the prison he keeps me in is so close I can taste it, yet I'm too scared to leave.

Cain's all I've ever had. All I've ever known.

And you can't escape when you have nowhere else to go.

Chapter 15

CAIN

*E*den's orgasm is as fiery and turbulent as she is. My chest swells with pride as she comes with tears trailing down her face and my name on her lips, her svelte, curvy body shaking with the force of it.

It's a vision if I ever saw one.

Too bad it's a tainted one.

I nip her little clit as she spasms. "It's too much."

It's not enough. It will never be enough.

I seize her wrist when she tries to push my head away and repeat the action. She doesn't get a say in this.

I control her pleasure and her pain.

And unfortunately, her pleasure will come at a price.

Eden has to pay for sleeping with the enemy. *After she helps me keep him at bay.*

I suck and bite her soft flesh, ignoring her whimpers and pleas for me to stop.

I'll never stop. Not when it comes to my Eden.

Not when I need her now more than ever.

"Good girl," I soothe when her body goes slack and I'm certain the fight has drained out of her.

I give her cunt one last kiss, then walk over to the sink so I can wash my hands and face. I don't want to chance what will undoubtedly be a ghastly fallout if Margaret smells another woman on me.

When I look in the mirror, I notice Eden's still propped up against the bathroom stall. Her red lipstick is smeared, her once pristine face is marred with black streaks, and her dress is ruffled.

A long sigh leaves me. My former innocent girl now resembles a cheap hooker you'd find down an alley in a bad part of town.

Fortunately, her appearance is now Damien's problem. Not mine.

Something my nemesis failed to realize when he came back to town and declared war.

I'd send him a thank-you note for taking the *hot stepdaughter* obstacle plaguing me out of my way during the election, but the moron probably has the reading level of an elementary student.

I eye her in my peripheral as I rinse off my face. "Now that we've kissed and made up, I need a favor."

She gives me a wary look as I walk over to the paper towel dispenser. "What kind of favor?"

Dabbing my chin, I turn around to face her, making sure my expression conveys exactly what I need it to.

Fear. Vulnerability. Need.

All the things that will get Eden to agree to help the love of her life.

"I'm in trouble."

My gullible girl's brows pinch in concern. "What's wrong?"

"I didn't hire Damien to kill you...but that doesn't mean he's not dangerous."

She doesn't look fazed by my statement. Probably because Damien isn't exactly Casanova. The barbarian wouldn't know how to treat a woman—hell, a *human*—if his life depended on it.

Especially someone like Eden.

Eden's like a delicate flower. She needs to be watched and cared for just so. This way you've already earned her trust and she'll be none the wiser when it's time to tear her from the soil and rip her pretty petals off.

"I don't understand why he'd make me think you hired him to *off* me, or why he would bring me back to his home."

Eden's also like a small child. You have to explain simple things to her like you would a toddler.

Lack of experience with the world will do that to a person.

"He did it to trick you, sweetheart. He took you as part of his revenge against me. He knows how much I love you and that makes you an important person to target."

She closes the space between us. "Why does he want revenge?"

I cup her cheekbone. "We were good friends in high school. Until he did something unforgivable. I was going to tell the authorities, but he fled the country. This is the first time I've seen or heard from him in eleven years."

She worries her bottom lip between her teeth. "What did he do?"

I grip the back of my neck. "You know what? Forget it. I shouldn't be discussing any of this with you. I'm gonna set you up somewhere safe for the time being." When her eyes go wide, I add, "Don't worry. I'll make sure to put things in place so you'll be well taken care of after I'm gone."

"Gone?" Her face turns ashen. "What do you mean, gone? What the hell is happening, Cain?"

I rub my forehead. "If I tell you this, you have to swear you won't tell a soul."

She palms my cheek. "Your secrets are safe with me."

"I know they are." I kiss the inside of her wrist. "Sometimes I feel like you're the only person in the whole wide world I can trust."

"I feel the same way."

I pull her close. "I'd never betray you, Eden. I might do some things I don't want to and make choices I'm not proud of—like marrying Margaret in order to help me win the election. But you and me? We're the real deal."

She places her head on my chest. "We're family."

"That's right. And family doesn't turn their back on one another." I kiss the top of her head. "Want to know what my biggest goal is?"

"Becoming President one day?"

My girl knows me well. "No." I trail a finger down her arm. "It's us. More specifically, our future. After I serve my two terms as President, I want to spend the rest of my life making love to you. I want to die old and gray in your arms, Eden Williams. I want to take my last breath looking into the most beautiful eyes belonging to the most beautiful girl I've ever known. The only person I've ever truly loved."

I inhale her sweet scent. As many lies as I've told her, this isn't one. Eden's my end game. Always has been. Always will be.

I'm livid as hell about her sleeping with Damien, and she'll get punished for it—but I'll never love anyone the way I love her.

She sees the best in me. Even though I know she can sense the evil lurking within.

She gives me my humanity back.

She's a reminder of my past...and my North Star guiding me toward my future.

"I don't want anyone to hurt you." She looks up at me. "Tell me what's going on with Damien. Tell me why he wants revenge. Tell me everything so I can help you."

"You'd really help me after everything I put you through?"

I should be nervous when she doesn't answer immediately. But I'm not. If anything, it tells me she's carefully considering her answer and the one she gives me will be set in stone.

"You're the only one..." Her lower lip trembles. "You're everything to me, Cain. I wouldn't know what to do without you. I wouldn't even...I need you."

I give her a big smile.

Love is a capricious thing—it can change with the wind.

But dependency is constant. Resilient. *Permanent.*

It can bend, maybe even chip. But it never fully breaks.

I make a mental note to phone her shrink and psychiatrist later so we can discuss the new game plan since Eden's no longer living with me. I doubt Damien will welcome either of them into his home with open arms, so we'll have to figure something out sooner rather than later.

Damien's already managed to get her outside of the house. Once she realizes the world isn't so big and scary...or worse, that she's capable of handling it when it is—my butterfly might use her newly discovered wings to fly away.

I can't let that happen.

Eden doesn't belong to the world. She belongs to *me*.

But first thing's first. I have a bomb to drop.

"You know how my family died in a fire when I was a teenager?"

Sadness colors her features. "Yeah."

"It wasn't accidental like everyone thinks. It was Damien who caused it." I hold her gaze. "He killed my family, Eden."

Her eyes become saucers. "Oh, my God. You have to call the police. He shouldn't be walking the streets—"

"I know, but I can't."

"Why not?"

"He's blackmailing me. I can't get into it right now, but there are some things I did when I was a kid that I'm not proud of. Nothing close to what he's done, of course, but things that might ruin the election for me if they get out. I can't go to the police until *after* I secure my win. This way I'll have a bit more control over what the press does with the info."

It's not exactly a lie given the fucker is threatening to tell Eden and the entire town about my past if I don't go along with his stupid game.

Hope he enjoys the bone I'm throwing him by letting him borrow Eden for a bit.

"I'll go to the police," she whispers. "This way you're safe."

"You were only seven when the fire happened. They'll all laugh at you."

"Not if I tell the police he held me against my will in his home."

Her trying to come up with a plan of her own is nothing short of adorable, I'll give her that. However, it will serve me better if she keeps her pretty mouth shut while I call the shots.

I grind my molars.

Damien wanted to play a game…well, he's got one.

But I've got home court advantage.

"Sweetheart," I say slowly. "I don't want to be rude, but I—"

"They won't believe me because of what happened with Mr. Delany." Her face falls. "Yeah, you're right. It was a dumb suggestion."

"Not dumb," I assure her. "Just not what I really need."

"What do you need?"

"I need someone I trust to keep a close eye on things…and distract him for me. Just until the election is over."

"Can't you hire a private investigator for that?"

"A private investigator can't get into his home…or his bed."

Her face screws up. "Let me get this straight. You were angry with me for sleeping with him…but now you *want* me to sleep with him?"

"Hardly. But we can't unring a bell, now can we? Therefore, it's in our interest to use the best arsenal we have. This way I stand a chance at making it out alive." I blow out a breath and look up at the ceiling. "If you're not up for the task I understand. I'll just have to figure something else out."

"No." She shakes her head. "I—uh. I can do this." She wrings her hands. "Only thing is, he doesn't talk much, so I doubt he'll be confessing any plans to harm you to me."

"Perhaps he'll open up more if you find some common ground."

"What kind of common ground am I supposed to find with a murdering psychopath?"

I shrug. "Beats me, but you're a smart girl. I'm sure you'll figure out something." I slam my eyelids shut and take a deep breath. "My life depends on it."

"I know it does. I won't let you down."

I edge a finger under her chin. "You're the best thing that's ever happened to me. I—"

A knock on the bathroom door cuts me off.

"Hey, other people have to use the bathroom. Unlock the door."

"Shit," I mutter under my breath. "Okay, I'm going to lock myself in a stall. You go out first so they don't suspect anything." I give her a quick kiss. "I'll touch base with you later."

I start to walk away, but she reaches for my arm. "You can't. I don't have my phone."

I raise a brow. "But you texted me at the ball."

"I know. I had it for most of the evening, but I put it down on a bench later that night. He must have swiped it then." She sighs. "I'll find a way to get it back."

"Fine. Just make sure you edit my name to something less conspicuous and erase our future texts as soon as we're done talking."

I'm not dumb enough to disclose anything serious over a text message, but she might be.

She gives me a strange look. "Wouldn't it be easier for us to talk over the app?"

It's all I can do not to roll my eyes. Eden knows I don't keep up with whatever the latest teenage fad is.

"I have no idea what you're talking about. What app?"

I'm not sure what to make of the expression on her face. "The temp—never mind. It's not important. I'll text you."

"That's it. I'm calling security," the woman on the other side of the door yells.

I bring her hand to my lips. "This is only temporary, Eden. You'll be back with me the moment I win the election." I grimace when I spot her poor excuse for an engagement ring. "Asshole didn't even get you a diamond."

Chapter 16

DAMIEN

*M*y patience is dwindling as the priest continues prattling on and on about Heaven and God and whatever else people like to hear in order to cope with death.

It's almost comical how people have this need to be pacified about the unknown. How quick they are to believe a book, a priest, or any other virtuous entity about what happens in the afterlife when there's never been any tangible proof.

Then again, faith and fear are powerful manipulators.

Some people need something to believe it. While others need something to run from.

I glance at my watch as everyone bows their heads in prayer. Out of the corner of my eye, I see Cain get up from his chair and slink out of the room.

I eye the empty seat next to me.

Such a pity they're going to miss the eulogy.

~

"I tried knocking, but she hasn't come out yet," the woman standing outside the bathroom door says as I approach. "Are you sure she's in there?"

Positive.

I slip her a hundred-dollar bill. "Thank you. Now get lost."

Leaning against the wall, I fish my cigarettes out of my pocket and light one.

She's got about two minutes left before I bust through the door and interrupt their little reunion.

My jaw tightens as I suck the cancer stick down to the filter and light another.

I'm on edge. I've been on edge since the moment she stepped under my roof.

I fucking hate it.

My ears perk up when the bathroom door opens. A second later, Cain's little lamb steps out.

"Ready to leave?"

She jumps at the sound of my voice. "Jesus Christ. You scared me."

I stub my cigarette out on the wall. "You were in there awhile."

The next words out of her mouth will determine what happens between us from here on out.

"I—um. I needed a moment." She swallows hard. "Had to clear my head."

There's something different about the way she's looking at me. I don't like it.

"The bathroom door was locked."

"Was it?" Her shoulders rise in a shrug. "I must have locked it by mistake."

It's all I can do not to shake the shit out of her. *She's a terrible liar.*

I shouldn't be surprised since most people are, but disappointment flickers in my chest anyway.

I thought Eden was different...but she's not.

And I won't waste my time and energy on someone I can't trust. *Not again.*

I drag my thumb across her bottom lip. "Your lipstick is smeared."

"I was crying."

Her pulse quickens as I slide my thumb down her throat, pausing when I reach the first two open buttons of her dress. "What happened here?"

She inhales sharply. "I don't know what you mean."

I graze the lace of her bra. "They were closed before."

"Oh. I needed air." Her eyes dart to the bathroom briefly before they lock with mine. "Speaking of which, I thought we were leaving."

"Sure. I just need to ask you one more question."

"Okay."

"Did your stepdaddy use a condom when he fucked you in the bathroom, or did he pull out?"

"Wha—"

I shove past her. "The seats in my car are leather so keep your legs closed. I don't want a mess."

Chapter 17

EDEN

*T*he silence is almost unbearable on the car ride home.

Home. I shake the thought out of my head. His castle isn't a home...it's a prison.

I study his profile, trying to wrap my head around everything Cain told me.

What in the world would possess Damien to kill Cain's family? It doesn't make any sense.

Then again, I don't know a thing about him. Only that he hates my stepfather. *Hates him enough to kill.*

A shiver runs up my spine. I can't believe I slept with a murderer. A murderer I felt some unexplainable connection to for about two seconds of my life.

God, I feel sick. Sick and mad as hell. He intentionally deceived me by making me believe Cain and Margaret hired him to get rid of me. There was no reason to go to the extra lengths he did. Just his threat to hurt Cain would have been enough to get me to comply.

Instead, he made it seem like he was on my side.

He glares daggers my way. "Stop staring at me."

I feel like a volcano ready to erupt. I can't take it anymore.

"Why did you tell me Cain and Margaret hired you to kill me when they didn't?"

Holy hell. I'm a piece of work. The man has the blood of Cain's family on his hands, yet I'm offended that he wasn't honest with me. As if *that's* the biggest issue here.

"You're the one who came to that conclusion. I didn't bother to correct you because time was of the essence and your cooperation was more important than the truth." His jaw clenches. "But since we're on the subject of lying. Why did you lie to me earlier?"

I shrug. "Because what happened in the bathroom is none of your business."

That's my story and I'm sticking to it. He doesn't deserve honesty, not until he can give me some.

He lights a cigarette. "Fair enough."

I wave the smoke away and roll down the window. "I know Cain didn't hire you, but do other people hire you to kill?"

"What do you think?"

"What I think is irrelevant. I just want the truth."

He takes a long drag off his cigarette. "I'm not a hitman."

I look out the window as my brain searches for a kernel of something that makes sense.

Perhaps he's a drug dealer and Cain owed him money? Cain couldn't pay in time, so Damien killed his family to settle the debt. Cain said he did some things he's not proud of in the past. Things that could impact the election. Plus, it doesn't take a genius to figure out Damien's loaded. All his money has to come from somewhere.

"What about drugs? Do you work for the mob? The cartel?"

"I work for myself." He peers at me out of the corner of his eye. "My business doesn't involve drugs. It involves computers and other forms of technology."

I bite my lip. This is so frustrating. "Why do you hate Cain?"

He smirks. "None of your business."

"It kind of is when you're keeping me hostage."

The tires screech as he slams on the brakes. "Get out."

I balk. "What?"

"You said I'm holding you hostage. If you really feel that way, then here's your chance to leave."

My stomach twists. "What will happen to Cain if I do?"

"For fuck's sake." His hand tightens on the steering wheel. "Do you think Cain would ask the same question if your roles were reversed?"

"I don't know," I whisper, despite the little voice in my head protesting.

He hits the gas. "Guess I'm not the only one you lie to then."

Geoffrey places my phone on the nightstand. "As you requested."

I eye it warily. Call me crazy, but it seems too easy. "So he just gave it to you?"

He nods. "Yes."

"Did he say anything?"

"No." He begins clearing my dinner tray. "They'll be announcing his candidacy in the morning. I'm afraid his focus is elsewhere for the time being."

"Oh."

I didn't realize it was tomorrow. My stomach lurches and I sit up in bed.

I never told Cain. Between all the apologies, promises, and secrets he told me, it completely slipped my mind.

I go to pick up my phone but pause. "Where is he now?"

"Downstairs in his office."

Perfect.

Geoffrey's eyes are practically burning a hole through me.

"Can I have some privacy?"

He bows. "As you wish."

He's halfway to the door when I stop him. "How long have you worked for Damien?"

He thinks about this for a moment before replying. "Six years."

That's even longer than I thought. "Have you ever…" I stall

113

mid-sentence, trying to figure out the best way to ask this. "Why do you work for a man like him?"

There's not a lick of hesitation before he answers. "He helped me get back on my feet when I had nothing. Two days after my nineteenth birthday, a hurricane hit the island my family and I lived on." Sorrow lines his features. "I was the only one of my family members to survive…but, in turn, I lost everything."

My heart squeezes. It's all I can do not to run over and wrap my arms around him. "I'm so sorry."

"Me too." He blinks rapidly and clears his throat. "But to answer your question, Damien walked by me while I was passed out on the street. I was injured and too weak to gather food, so I asked him for some. I thought he was going to ignore me, but he asked me if I wanted a job instead." He stands up straighter. "I've been with him ever since, and I'll stay with him for however long he'll have me."

To say I'm surprised would be an understatement. His story makes me even more curious about the enigma that is Damien King.

A cold-blooded murderer with a heart.

"Has he ever kept a girl against her will before?"

There's a hint of humor in his expression. "You're the first." He heads for the door. "His previous companions have all begged to stay."

Good for them.

I reach for my phone after he leaves and check my messages… but there are none. At least, nothing recent.

The last message I have is from Cain, informing me he was having a driver take me home from the ball.

Obviously, Damien responded to him and pretended to be me, but there's nothing after that.

Not even a phone call.

My hands shake as I open the *Temptation* app. Cain had no reason to pretend not to know about the app earlier, but maybe he felt it was necessary for whatever reason.

That weird feeling forms in the pit of my stomach again as I search through the messages in the app.

Nothing.

No phone calls, no messages, no voicemails, and no emails. *Absolutely nothing* from the man who claimed to be worried sick.

His world kept turning just fine without me in it.

Before I can stop myself, my fingers dance across the keyboard.

Angelbaby123: Do you have a second to talk?

Briefly, dots appear on the bottom of the screen before they disappear.

Angelbaby123: It's about the election.

His response is almost instant.

Devil: What about it?

I roll my eyes. If I had any doubt it was Cain before...I don't anymore. It's all he cares about.

I get off the bed and walk around. I agreed to help keep Cain alive...not get involved in the election. I'm not telling him a thing until he gives me some answers.

Angelbaby123: If you were so worried about me, how come you never once called or messaged me while I was gone?

I close my eyes. Tell me Damien erased your messages. Tell me you were so caught up in grief you couldn't think straight.

Tell me you love me.

Devil: Got to go. Have work to do.

My heart folds in on itself.

Angelbaby123: Wait. I just need a few more minutes.

I miss talking to Cain—the Cain on this app. Up until the night of the ball, I spent the last few weeks talking to him about everything. My feelings, my therapy, my favorite movies and songs, how much I loved him…
I need that Cain back.

Angelbaby123: It's so lonely here. I don't have anyone to talk to. Everyone in this house, with the exception of Geoffrey, is an asshole. There's a rude chef who won't let me enter the kitchen for a glass of water. There's also a bitch maid who likes to whisper mean things to me whenever I walk outside my bedroom. They all suck. I can't take it, Cain. I want to come back home. I miss you.

The dots appear, then disappear again…and then his screen name turns gray.

I'm all but clawing at the window when I hear a knock on my bedroom door.

"Go away."

"I'm afraid I can't," Geoffrey calls out before the knob turns.

I raise an eyebrow as he waltzes in with a bowl of popcorn and two sodas.

"I've been instructed to *hang out* with you tonight," he says dryly, looking less than thrilled.

"By who?"

"Who do you think?" Rolling his eyes, he sets the food down on the nightstand. "What kind of movies do you enjoy? And so help me God, I will hang myself with your bedsheets if you expect me to sit through a chick flick."

"I don't really like to watch movies," I tell him, reaching for the remote.

He looks relieved. "Thank—"

"I much prefer reality television."

He looks up at the ceiling. "This is going to be a long night."

Chapter 18

EDEN

*T*wo hours into our reality television marathon, a sleeping Geoffrey snores peacefully in the chair beside my bed while my mind continues to spin.

Five minutes after I sent my last message, Geoffrey appeared to keep me company.

Coincidence? I think not. Which leads me back to that weird bolt of intuition I had in the bathroom.

Cain's lied to me before, but he had no reason to lie about the app.

Damien's also lied to me once before, and he has every reason to lie about the app.

There's only one way to prove what has now become glaringly obvious to me.

Angelbaby123: Hey, I know you're busy, but I have a quick question.

I'm surprised when he responds so soon.

Devil: Go ahead.

Angelbaby123: Do you remember that thing we talked about earlier?
Devil: Can you be more specific?
Angelbaby123: In the bathroom.
Devil: I remember our conversation. Yes.

He skated right past that one, so I go in a different direction.

Angelbaby123: What about after it?
Devil: Is this a trick question?

That's exactly what it is.

Angelbaby123: No. I just want to know if I'm better in bed than Margaret is.

I hold my breath as he types out his response.

Devil: Self-doubt is an unattractive quality.

Dick. I try again.

Angelbaby123: Sorry, I don't feel so good.
Devil: What's the matter?
Angelbaby123: I don't know. Everything is spinning. I feel like I might pass out.

Less than a second later, Geoffrey's phone rings. The poor guy leaps up from his seat like a startled cat as he answers.

"Yes, sir. Hello, sir." He eyes me suspiciously. "Eden is f—"

A bolt of anger strikes through me like wildfire and I run for the door. Eden is *not* fine.

Eden's had enough.

"She's leaving the bedroom," Geoffrey yells, following close behind me.

I charge down the staircase and then another until there are no more steps and I'm forced to enter a dark, narrow hallway.

Damien must have called Geoffrey off because I no longer hear him chasing me as I trek to the end and make a sharp left.

The neon glow from a gigantic fish tank stationed behind a dark mahogany desk illuminates the room.

Damien doesn't turn around as I approach, but I see the hand resting on the arm of his chair tense.

My heart beats faster as I come to a stop at the front of his desk. "You're the Devil."

He doesn't say a word. The stupid fish have his undivided attention.

And while the fish are beautiful in all their bright, tropical glory —apart from the isolated creepy one sanctioned behind a divider— this is far more important.

"For weeks you tricked me into thinking I was talking to the man I loved on that app." I poke the wood with my finger, wishing it were his eyeballs. "I told you things. Personal things."

My stomach sways. *I sent him pictures.*

But it's my next realization that has me reeling.

"You tricked me into going to the ball." I slam my fist on the desk, infuriation streaming through my veins. "You set me up."

You seduced me in a closet.

"Some might say I did you a favor." The arrogance in his tone is sickening. "It would have hurt worse if Cain pulled the rug out from under you, and then lured you back in again and again until he decided he had no more use for you. Trust me."

That may be true, but it still doesn't make it right. "What Cain did doesn't change what *you* did, Damien."

"If you came down here looking for an apology, little lamb— you're out of luck."

"What about an explanation?" I shake my head, feeling so dumb I could scream. There's no reasoning with a psychopath. Someone so evil is already too far gone. "On second thought, save it. Every word out of your mouth has been a lie. Why would this be any different?"

I have one foot out the door when he speaks again. "Not every word."

No. He doesn't get to do that. He doesn't get to screw with my head like this. "Fuck you."

"It's a shame you don't aim all your anger at the right target."

I whirl around at the same time he does. "You're a hypocrite. Cain might be an asshole, but he's *never* done the things you have. And at least when he hurts someone, he's genuinely sorry for it, which is a lot more than I can say for you."

The hardness in his eyes is gone, replaced by something much more appalling. *Pity.*

"Christ. You're pathetic."

"Does it feel good?" I ask, tears stinging my eyes, despite fighting like hell to fend them off.

"Does what feel good?"

"Breaking people down to nothing in such an ugly, heartless way?"

Hell, his other victims were lucky. He had mercy on them and burned them to death. He didn't subject them to this kind of torture first.

As usual, silence is his only response to the questions I want answers to the most.

"That's what I thought."

No wonder Cain doesn't want to be anywhere near him.

Damien King is toxic. *Straight venom to the heart.*

I've barely turned on my heel again when I hear a dense thud.

"I'd say yes, but it looks like someone else broke you first."

Chapter 19

DAMIEN

$\mathcal{I}$ had no intention of showing this to Eden. Not because she doesn't deserve to see it, but because I don't want her to feel worse about herself.

She already thinks she's weak and that she'll never be strong enough to conquer her demons.

And what's inside this folder will only prove her right. Because it's what she was made to believe.

She takes a step closer. "What is that?"

"Your entire psychiatric history, since you were twelve."

Her eyes widen. "How dare you invade my priva—"

"You can harp about that later. There are more important things for you to be pissed about." I slide the folder toward her. "Open it."

I watch her face as she scans through the first few papers. "Congrats, you know I'm a nutcase. I don't understand what the point of all this is."

"Read the therapist's notes from your very first session when you were twelve."

"Consult with patient requested by the patient's mother after the school nurse reported the patient expressed suicidal thoughts."

She clears her throat. "Patient displays symptoms of anxiety and depression. When asked about her home life, her mother maintains everything is fine and her child has a normal upbringing. When I asked the patient how her home life was, the patient apologized profusely for causing trouble and confessed that she didn't want to harm herself, she just wanted attention from her mother." Her lower lip trembles. "When I asked to speak to the patient alone, the mother declined. When I called for a follow-up appointment, the mother declined and said the patient was getting help elsewhere."

"Do you remember this?"

She nods. "Yeah. The school nurse called my mom in and suggested I go to counseling. After we left, my mom got really angry. She said it was my fault for drawing negative attention to us when she was only trying to do the best she could as a single mother. I felt bad because I knew she was working all the time and I messed up. I promised I'd be better after that."

My chest tightens. I know exactly what Eden's feeling. I know how much it can sting when a parent treats you like a problem half the time and ignores you the other half.

Which is why I need her to keep going. "Read the next one."

She flips the page. "Consult with patient requested by the patient's mother after an episode with another student at school. School reports the patient physically attacked another student in the bathroom during lunch. When asked what happened, the patient refused to speak. The other student maintains she did nothing to provoke her and claims Eden assaulted her when she stepped inside the restroom. When I asked the patient about the incident, she refused to talk about it. However, the patient's mother claims her daughter wasn't feeling well and blames the flu for her outburst. When I called for a follow-up appointment, the mother declined and said the patient was receiving help elsewhere."

I fold my arms over my chest. "Do you remember what happened that day?"

"Lenore Mills said the reason I didn't have a dad was because my mom was a dyke." She shrugs. "So I punched her."

"Did you ever tell your mom what Lenore said?"

"I did. She told me if I didn't want to get bullied, I should start telling everyone I saw my dad on the weekends." She looks down at her shoes. "When I told her I didn't want to lie and asked where my father was, she got mad and said if I wasn't willing to do the right thing for our family, then I wasn't allowed to hang out with my friends from school anymore. She said she was trying to maintain a certain image in order to run for district attorney the following year and all of my antics were messing things up."

"Read the next one," I urge because it's where things go from bad to worse.

"Consult with patient requested by the patient's mother following an incident involving a teacher at school. Evidence of an inappropriate student-teacher relationship was discovered after a fellow student turned in a note containing graphic sexual details about the school's English teacher, Mr. Delany, to school administration. The note was written by the patient. Shortly after the teacher was suspended, the patient was discovered at a local park in the middle of the night with Mr. Delany. Patient strongly maintains nothing inappropriate happened between them and insists they were just friends. Her mother believes otherwise and says her child was taken advantage of. When I asked to speak to the patient alone, the mother declined. Mother and patient left my office shortly after."

She trembles. "What's the point of all this, Damien? If you want me to stand here and claim Mr. Delany did something wrong, I won't. He was my friend."

Pointing out grown men shouldn't be *friends* with their teenage students or texting them all hours of the night won't help matters. *Besides, I'm one to talk.* Although there's a world of difference between a seventeen-year-old guy messing around with his teacher versus a fourteen-year-old girl.

"I won't argue with you," I tell her. "I just want you to read the next report. The one dated a few days later."

She huffs out a breath. "Consult with patient requested by

patient's mother. Patient displays symptoms of severe psychosis. Inpatient treatment recommended. Benzodiazepines and mood-stabilizers prescribed."

"What happened between your last therapy session and this one?"

She looks up at the ceiling. "My mom said Mr. Delany was connected to some big-wig politician and he offered to support her while she was running for district attorney as long as she changed her story and took back the accusations about his nephew. The bullying got worse, and a few days later she took me out of school, then took me to a psychiatrist. I was homeschooled after that."

"Did the psychiatrist ever talk to you?"

She shakes her head. "A little. I think. I don't remember much to be honest. The meds he gave me made me really tired."

It's all I can do not to put my fist through the wall. "That's because you were receiving double the recommended dose." I hand her another sheet of paper. "Only, no one ever caught on because your mother was prescribed the same medication you were but got it filled at a different pharmacy under her name."

For over three fucking years Eden was not only given medication I'm positive she didn't need, she was given too much of it.

She snatches the paper from me. "What? I'm sure it's just a mistake."

"It's not. Notice whenever your dose would go up or he changed your medication, Karen's would change too. That's not a coincidence, Eden. She turned you into a zoned-out zombie on purpose."

"I don't understand—why would she do that?"

I don't have to say it, because the heartbroken look on her face tells me she already knows.

Karen didn't want children. She wanted a place filler to make her life seem normal because of her own deep-seated issues. And when Eden caused too much trouble and became a liability to her public persona and her bottom line, she paid a quack to dope her kid full of psych meds and convinced everyone she was a mental case.

She closes the file and places it back on my desk. "I don't think I can stomach anymore." She looks up at me. "I know you hate Cain, but if you're wondering why I'm so *pathetic*, this is why. I love him and I'm loyal to him because he saved me. After my mom died and he became my guardian, he had the psychiatrist decrease all my meds and got me a therapist who actually helped me."

I shouldn't do it. It's cruel to kick someone when they're already down.

But she needs to know. The pedestal she's placed Cain on isn't one he deserves.

"Cain didn't help you, Eden. He just wanted you to think he did."

Chapter 20

EDEN

I watch in confusion as Damien presses a few keys on his computer keyboard. A moment later his deep voice fills the room.

"Start talking, or I'll put your small intestines through a meat grinder—"

"All right," someone who sounds a whole lot like my therapist screams in agony. "I'll tell you the truth. Just stop hurting me."

I narrow my eyes. "Why are you threatening my thera—"

"Cain paid me to provide one on one support to his stepdaughter. However, he had very specific rules I had to abide by." I hold my breath as my therapist continues. "He'd developed an unhealthy fascination with her and that's putting it mildly. My job was to convince Eden she couldn't be without him by using her anxiety disorder against her and making her agoraphobia worse."

"And you agreed to it?" Damien growls. "Do you have any idea how much you fucked her up?"

"I didn't have a choice," he protests. "Cain was blackmailing me with things that would have landed me in jail. It was much easier to do what he wanted than to object. Besides, Eden was already looking at him like he strung up the moon after Karen died, it hardly took any convincing to make her believe Cain was her knight in shining armor. I'm not sure if you're aware of her history, but the girl isn't exactly what you'd call mentally stable thanks to being doped up on meds and cooped up inside all the time with virtually no socialization, attention, or affection. Her mother already put the nail in her coffin with all her neglect. If you want my professional opinion, what Cain wanted was way more humane."

"I don't want your professional opinion, fuckface," Damien snarls low and deadly. "I want you to tell me what you did to her."

"Sure, all right. It was relatively simple. Whenever Eden expressed that she wished she was well enough to go shopping or out to the movies like other girls her age, I'd tell her she probably couldn't handle it because she'd been kept inside for so long. I also reminded her that sometimes bad things happened—like her mother dying in a car accident—when people stepped outside and that she was safer at home. If she seemed like she was going to object, I'd remind her Cain wouldn't be able to protect her if she left. Then I'd suggest we open the front door together or walk to the mailbox—this way, she'd think she was making progress when in reality she was only becoming more dependent on him, and her agoraphobia became worse."

My head feels heavy as he continues.

"If she'd make a comment about how she wished she had friends, I reminded her what her old friends did to her. How they laughed and spread rumors after the incident with her teacher. Or how the entire town called her a slut, and how everyone wanted her gone. Then I'd gently remind her that Cain never thought of her that way because he cared about her and he'd always protect her. I'd reinforce that she was safe with him because he's the one person she could count on."

"And she never protested? Never argued?"

No.

He laughs. "Are you kidding? The girl was so messed up and infatuated with him by then, I'm not even sure why Cain hired me. It got to the point where I wouldn't even have to speak his praises, she was wrapped around his finger so tightly. Her world begins and ends with him, exactly like he wants it to." He sighs. "It's sad. Eden was a beautiful girl. Smart too. She might have really been something if it wasn't for his obsession with her."

He says it like I'm dead.

The room whirls and my chest caves in. *I might as well be.*

"Hey," Damien calls out as he walks toward me, his tone softer than I've ever heard it.

I turn away. I don't want Damien near me. I don't want anyone near me. I just want to lie here on the floor and dissolve into nothing. I close my eyes and hug my knees, curling up into a ball. I want to disappear into thin air, like I never existed…just like my mother wanted me to.

"I tried so hard." My voice is frail and tattered. "I just wanted her to love me. Why couldn't she?"

"The woman didn't deserve your love, Eden." He touches my elbow. "Sometimes people do shitty things we have no control over, and we excuse it because we love them." His hand slides around my waist and he lifts me up. "But that's not a reflection of you. Her problems were just that…hers. You don't have to keep making them yours."

I bury my head in the crook of his neck as he walks us over to his chair and sits.

Deep down I know he's right, but I don't know how to get out of this cycle. I don't know how to conquer my past or my disorders and be my own person.

Because of *Cain.*

I wanted to be loved so badly I ached for it, but I never wanted to be someone's puppet.

Damien was right. *I'm pathetic.*

He runs his fingertips up and down my vertebrae. "It hurts like hell right now, and you might feel like your life is over, but this isn't where it ends. Take your broken pieces and mold them into whatever you want to be. Not what Cain or anyone else wants."

How can I become something else when I don't even know who I was to begin with?

Easy. *I can't.* I don't get to start from scratch, because I don't have anything left that's worth rebuilding.

My pieces are ugly. Used and manipulated for someone else's enjoyment.

And it's not like I can pretend the warning signs weren't there. Cain's hurt me so many times I've lost count. And each time he's cut a little deeper.

It was only a matter of time before I'd bleed out.

"I hate him."

I hate myself for not being stronger.

And for once, my awareness isn't followed by a swell of love or a trail of tears.

Because there are no more tears left to cry. There's no more love left to give. There's no more heart left to break.

There's nothing but emptiness.

Actually, that's not quite right. There's one emotion registering loud and clear.

Rage twists my insides, it's so intense I shake with the force of it.

I want Cain Carter to burn.

But I don't want to stand by and watch the flames consume him. No, I want to crawl inside his soul and light the match. I want to taste his pleads and siphon his last breath.

I want to diminish him to a shell of everything he used to be.

"Damien?"

"Yeah?"

I shift myself on his lap so I'm straddling him. "I don't trust you."

There's no way in hell I'd be stupid enough to trust anyone after this—let alone a man like Damien King.

"But I think it's safe to say you have a partner...for the time being."

He raises a dark brow. "Ok—"

"A partner, not a *prisoner*. I refuse to be confined to my room. I want to be able to go wherever I please whenever I please."

"Fine," he grits through his teeth.

I'm not done yet. "I'll also need money. Cain controls every cent I have, and if you want me to parade around on your arm and be your fiancée, I deserve to be paid."

I might not be street savvy, but I know money is important. Unfortunately, it's something I don't have...and there's no way I can start over without some.

"Consider it done." His eyes darken. "Is there anything else you want?"

I flash Damien a coy smile as I sink to my knees.

I want to ruin his life...like he ruined mine.

Cain wanted my world to begin and end with him...

And so help me God, it's going to.

Chapter 21

DAMIEN

"What are you doing?"

She tugs on my belt. "Just because I don't trust you, doesn't mean we can't have fun."

I've never been one to turn down sex from someone I'm attracted to, let alone drawn to like a moth to a flame, but I don't like not knowing what the other person's intentions are.

Especially hers.

Eden could be on my side one day...then Cain's the next.

I grind my molars. *I don't like it.*

"You should go to bed."

Although she keeps her expression impassive, I know my comment stung. Eden's eyes reveal everything.

They're little oceans of depth. When she's happy, they sparkle. When she's sad, they dim.

And when she's angry—they're sharp like razor blades.

Without a word, she stands, dismissing me and my erection without a second glance.

The bulge in my pants grows as she walks toward the door with her head held high.

She wants to make me eat my words...and it's working. The

confidence dripping from her is an aphrodisiac. One that has me yearning to get under her skin so I can find out what it takes to make her bleed, and then fillet her wide open.

See what she's really made of.

Turning her head slightly, she glances at me over her shoulder. "If you're worried about me catching feelings...don't. The only thing I feel right now is anger." She shrugs. "Having sex with the man Cain hates seemed like a good way to deal with it tonight."

Her words turn my dick to steel, but it's that peek of vulnerability lurking underneath all her bravado that does my head in.

And that alone should be enough of a warning to keep my distance.

My muscles tighten. *She's supposed to be Cain's bait...not mine.*

The sound of her bare feet padding out of my office and down the hall taunts me.

The longer you resist something...the more you want it. That's the way it goes for most people.

But I'm not like most people. I've never been good at denying my urges.

It's far more satisfying to indulge in them.

I'm on my feet so fast I'm certain there's a trail of smoke behind me.

My dick twitches, keeping in time with my rapid heartbeat as I approach my target.

She's almost to the end of the hall when I snatch her arm and shove her against the wall.

"What—"

"I like to fuck on my terms." I tear the thin tank top she's wearing down the middle and push down her shorts and panties. "Not yours."

I suck and lick my way down her smooth body. *Christ.* I should ban her from wearing clothes from here on out. It'd make it easier to taste and fuck all my favorite places.

I bite her hip. "Spread your legs."

Kicking her clothes out of the way, she does what I ask.

"Good girl."

Her breathing becomes choppy as I bury my face between her thighs and proceed to make out with her pussy.

Eden's whimpers fill the space between us as I continue working her over, taking her in long licks that end with a quick flick of her clit.

"I'm coming," she pants, tightening and spasming around my tongue. "Fuck, I'm coming so hard."

My dick grinds against my zipper as her climax fills my mouth and she cries out my name.

I nip and lick my way back up her body, pausing briefly so I can suck those pretty peach nipples into my mouth.

She's still catching her breath when I slide my hands under her ass and stand up.

It's too dark in this hallway. I want to see her deep throat every inch of me.

She wraps her legs around my waist. "Where are we going?"

"Back to my office so you can return the favor."

Heat zips up my spine. Her hot, naked body pressed against me makes the short walk to my chair feel like a goddamn eternity.

I bite her bottom lip as we sink against the cool leather. "Show me what this mouth can do with a cock."

The neon lights from the fish tank illuminate her perfect form as she sinks down to her knees.

She's tugging at my zipper when I notice a wet spot on the end of my shirt.

Slipping my hand under her neck, I draw her attention back to me. "Open." When she does, I stuff the damp fabric between her parted lips. "Suck your cum off my shirt."

A flush creeps up her cheeks as they hollow.

"You like the taste of your cunt?"

Her blush deepens as she nods. However, there's no mistaking the naughty glint in her eye.

A grin twists my lips. "I do, too." Lowering my pants, I give myself a languid stroke. "Now be a good girl and put my cock in your mouth."

I fist her hair as she wraps her hand around my shaft, her mouth hovering over the tip.

"Such a tease," I hiss, tightening my grip. "Keep it up and I'll make you choke on it."

Smirking, she gives the head of my cock swift feather light licks, intentionally goading me.

Fucking hell. She's playing with fire.

Instinct takes over, tossing whatever smidgen of conscience I might have had when it came to Eden out the window.

I sit forward and place both my hands on the back of her head. "Take a deep breath."

That's the only warning she gets before I drive into her mouth so hard I hit her tonsils.

She gags while I fuck her face. The sound is music to my ears.

I grunt as I pick up speed, lashing my dick into her throat with such vigor my balls slap against her neck.

She takes it like a champ though, attempting to suck me through her gag reflex as trickles of saliva dribble down her chin.

She looks so fucking hot and dirty. It takes some serious willpower not to shoot my load all over her face, then make her motorboat my sac before forcing her to lick me clean.

"Fuck." I ease up so I can watch my cock glide in and out of her mouth.

It's not long before my bad girl takes over, sucking me down in deep pulls.

"Faster."

Grunting, I clutch the armrest. If I'm not inside her soon, I'm liable to kill someone.

Peering down, I crook a finger at her. "Get up here and ride me."

She claws at my shirt as she rises, running her tongue over my abs. "I need this off."

I remove it and she climbs on my lap.

"I've never done this before." Her embarrassment is tangible as she straddles me. "I might be bad at it."

"Don't worry, lamb." My hands fasten around her hips, suspending her above my thick crown now weeping with pre-cum. "I'll show you how I like to be fucked."

She wraps her arms around my neck. The position feels intimate. *Too intimate.* But I can't seem to put my foot on the brake.

I'm not sure I want to.

My head swims with greed as I steadily lower her onto my dick.

Eden became mine the night I took her from Cain.

And I have no intention of giving her back.

"Jesus." She rests her forehead against mine. "This is…not like the last time."

It's almost mesmerizing the way her face changes and her breathing picks up with every inch I sink into her.

It's as if she's taking me into her soul rather than her body. Granting me access so I can corrupt and toughen her up.

My lips twitch. We both know I didn't have to fuck her to do it, but this way is much more fun.

She gasps and holds on tighter as I fill her to the hilt, her tight pussy stretching to accommodate me.

"This is mine while you're with me." *All mine.* I kiss the column of her throat as I lift her hips, steering her movements. "No one gets access to your cunt without begging me for permission first. Understand?"

Her eyelids flutter closed as she matches my rhythm. "And if they don't?"

I sink my teeth into her collarbone and thrust deeper, causing her to flinch. "I'll slit their throat…and make you lick their blood off the floor."

I hold her stare as I pump into her harder.

If she thought I was kidding…she doesn't anymore.

Loyalty is the most important thing to me. I refuse to be fooled again.

I pull back and slam into her. "Cross me and I'll spend the rest of my life ruining yours." I grip the base of her neck. "Consider this your only warning."

She swallows. "I won't fuck anyone else without your permission." Her eyes turn hard. "Except Cain."

Jealousy simmers in my chest. I'm a second away from shoving her off me and tossing her into the fish tank when she palms my jaw.

"You're not the only one who wants revenge, Damien."

She has a point. And if I'm being honest with myself, she deserves it even more than I do.

"He'll suffer more if you tease him," I tell her because I know Cain Carter like the back of my hand. "Mess around and bring him to the brink, but don't let him fuck you."

He doesn't get that luxury.

She opens her mouth to speak, but her attention drifts to something behind me.

"Of course you're screwing the town slut," Tanya, my soon-to-be unemployed maid shrieks, as though she has any right to question me about my sex life.

She's been a thorn in my side since the minute I hired her. The only reason I've kept her around is because she's so desperate for my attention she'll do anything for it. And I mean *anything.*

I'm about to tell the scat play princess to fuck off, but then I notice the look on Eden's face.

"You can either stay the lamb...or become the slaughterer," I rasp in her ear. "If you want something, step up and claim it." I lean back in the chair. "Because there's only room for one queen in a castle."

She worries her bottom lip between her teeth. I can sense she wants to tell the bitch to eat dirt. *But she's not ready yet.*

I'll have to handle this for her.

"You need to go——"

"No." Eden's lips curve into a cruel smirk and she rolls her hips in a way that makes me groan. "Let her watch."

Placing a hand on my chest, she eases back slightly...then proceeds to ride me so good Tanya sniffles behind me.

Lust and pride swell in my chest. She's practically glowing as she glares daggers at the maid.

A few seconds later, the basement door slams shut.

Blood boiling, I dig my fingers into the flesh of her ass and stand up.

"Wha—"

Papers and various objects hit the floor as I throw her down on my desk. "Queens get rewarded."

I pin her legs to her chest. "First with my mouth." She writhes and moans as I take turns sucking her pussy lips before giving her clit the same treatment. "Then with my cock." Straightening my spine, I thrust inside her in one fluid motion.

She hisses as I quicken the pace, causing the desk to rock underneath her. "Oh, God."

Her chest heaves, lifting those heavy tits high and I slap one. "That's not my name."

"Damien." Her eyes roll back as I reach down and rub her clit vigorously. "It's...fuck." The swollen flesh pulses beneath my fingertips and I give it to her harder.

A hoarse cry rips from her throat and she jerks violently, clamping my cock like a vise as a rush of warm fluid seeps out of her.

Eden looks mortified, but I shake my head, convulsing as I pull out and spray my cum all over her drenched cunt. "I appreciate a good pussy shower." I reach inside my desk drawer for my cigarettes. "Have a good night."

She fidgets behind me as I settle back in my chair, focusing on the fish tank.

I expect her to complain about me dismissing her, but she doesn't.

She maneuvers herself on my lap and watches the fish.

Chapter 22

EDEN

"*T*oday is important," Damien growls, the deep timbre of his voice going straight to my core.

"I know."

You'd think it would be me giving the pep talk on account it's his big day, but nope. The second we walked through the back doors of townhall, he grabbed my hand and ushered me into an abandoned conference room.

His expression sets. "Put your game face on."

I look him in the eye. "It's on."

"If anyone starts with you, make them eat shit."

I start to smile but hold it in. "I will."

With that, I head for the door.

I'm almost there when he latches onto my waist, steering me until my spine meets the wall.

My pulse accelerates as he takes in my red heels and black dress. It hugs my curves and shows a tad bit too much cleavage, but I chose it because Geoffrey's jaw nearly hit the floor when I put it on.

It made me feel powerful and sexy. *Intimidating.*

The heat emanating from Damien as he lingers on my red lips tells me I chose right.

But I swear to God I'll put up a fight if he insists I change or cover up.

He tilts my chin. "Stunning."

Butterflies swarm in my belly when he closes the distance between us. I'm almost positive he only meant to give me a chaste kiss, but what happens when his lips meet mine is nothing short of electric. And I know he feels it too because he makes a noise deep in his throat as he coaxes me to open my mouth wider, teasing me the way a snake would its prey. Slowly and methodically.

The moment our tongues touch, the kiss turns fervent and reckless. I can feel his erection straining in his pants, desperate to be free as he explores every inch of my mouth and I do the same to him, unable to get enough.

I don't know what this pull is between us and I don't care. All I know is the second Cain broke my heart for the very last time—Damien came riding in on his dark horse, offering to teach me how to build a stronger one.

Still doesn't mean I trust him fully. Not until I find out why he killed Cain's father and brother.

A sizzle of heat zips down my spine when his hand finds my breast and he gives it a firm squeeze. I pant as he sucks the tip of my tongue and walks his fingers down the buttons of my dress... never undoing a single one.

Jesus. His kisses should be deemed a sin.

"Damien—"

The ground beneath me gives way as he lifts the hem and cups me.

Our eyes lock and my breath hitches when he traces the lace pattern of my panties with his thumb, deliberately drawing out my anticipation.

"My mouth will be here later." A tremor goes through me when he moves them aside and slowly circles my clit. "Remember that if you need something to ease your jitters."

His promise does nothing to ease my anxiety—in fact, it only heightens it—but I appreciate the sentiment.

"I will," I tell him coolly.

I'm not dumb enough to think this wasn't a last-minute test to see how I respond under pressure.

Even so, I damn near whimper at the loss when he removes his hand.

Smirking, he licks his thumb. "Let's go."

Chapter 23

CAIN

*E*veryone waits with bated breath for William Anderson—the head of Covey's political party and his former right-hand man—to grace us with his presence and finally announce who my new opponent is.

Why it's turned into such a dramatic song and dance is beyond me. And the fact that Governor Bexley still doesn't know who will be running against me is...worrisome.

The air in Black Hallows Hall—the main event room where we hold public meetings—feels stuffier than usual.

I go to loosen my tie, but Margaret reaches for my hand. I fight the urge to retract it. She's been clingier than usual since last night —when we fucked for the first time. Or rather, I fucked her while she laid limp like a dead fish on my living room couch, criticizing my every move.

Thoughts of Eden seducing me in the very same spot were the only thing that got me through the horrid experience without putting my head through the wall.

The tiny hairs on the back of my neck prickle as the energy in the room shifts. I assume it's because someone spotted Anderson—

the tardy schmuck—but when I turn my head to the left, I see exactly what's captured everyone's attention.

My eyes narrow as Damien and Eden saunter up the middle row. Damien, the cocky showoff, is wearing his usual smart-ass smirk and a dark three-piece suit that cost more than most mortgages, but it's Eden that has people talking.

There's something different about her. Other than her sexy silk dress and red heels that have me scrambling to adjust myself.

She walks with a confident, almost *regal* air—oblivious to all the whispering her appearance has caused.

That's when it dawns on me.

She's in a room full of people. Not crumbling and hyperventilating in a corner somewhere.

Gritting my teeth, I drop Margaret's hand and loosen my tie, eyeing them both as they take their seats on the opposite side of the room.

This isn't good.

Not only did Eden fail to distract Damien and keep him away like I *specifically* instructed her to—he's somehow managed to undo the screws I carefully bolted into place.

I didn't loan him Eden to fix her.

I loaned her so he can see what he's partially responsible for.

I clutch the side of the bench. *Keep your eye on the prize*—I remind myself.

Eden and Damien will have to wait until later. I have more important things to worry about right now.

Like the dumbass reckless enough to try to run against me.

I snort as it hits me. I'll bet my right nut Damien made a large donation to the fool's campaign. Which would explain why he's here.

The motherfucker wants to gloat, but he'd be better off taking his contribution and flushing it down the toilet, where it belongs.

Unless it's Jesus himself taking Covey's place, the people of Black Hallows are already in agreement as to who they want their new mayor to be.

Yours truly.

Just then Anderson—the slow imbecile—makes his way to the podium. "Afternoon, everyone. I know you're all anxious for the big announcement, but first, let's go over some things, shall we?"

I roll my eyes. *Cut to the goddamn chase already.*

The four-eyed asswipe produces a piece of paper from his pocket. "I know some of you were wondering why we chose a candidate instead of holding another primary election, so I want to clear that up. Article Fifteen of the Black Hallows town handbook states that if a candidate dies within ten days of the scheduled election, his political party may nominate a new candidate. And as long as the nominee has the majority vote from the committee, a public vote shall not be required."

He adjusts his glasses. "The handbook also states polling day can be postponed an additional seven days or longer at the committee's request. As you all know, the big day was slated to be this Tuesday, November sixth, but in light of the tragic events, polling day has now been rescheduled for November thirteenth."

"That's not so bad," Margaret whispers. "It's only ten days away."

I breathe a sigh of relief. She's right. Ten days isn't enough time to sway voters.

People tend to stick with what they know...who they're comfortable with.

My gaze drifts to Eden, but it's so crowded all I can see is the back of her head.

Anderson clears his throat. "Due to the election's extenuating circumstances, the schedule will be a bit different. In an effort to help you get to know your new candidate, we've set up a few fundraising events, luncheons, meetings, and of course, a debate between the two candidates over the course of next week." He smiles wide. "The town will also be assembling a masquerade ball the night before the election." We all stifle groans as he adds, "In honor of the late Mr. Covey and his wife's favorite event."

"It's not like he'll be attending the damn thing," I mutter under my breath and Margaret pokes me.

Anderson's expression turns serious. "I was fortunate to work alongside Mr. Covey for the last ten years. I considered him one of my closest friends and one of the best things to happen to politics." He blows out a heavy breath. "I know his death came as a shock, but I need you all to know he never wanted to give up—though his body did. And even as he grew sicker, he never stopped fighting for his town. He knew his time was coming to an end, and his last few weeks were spent searching for his perfect replacement. Luckily, God answered his prayers and he found one in the nick of time."

He scans the crowd in a dramatic fashion before his gaze rests on a small section of people seated on the other side of the room.

"Do you think it's Glen Dickinson?" Margaret hisses in my ear. "He's been acting awfully strange lately. He snubbed Daddy at the funeral."

I look at the white-haired man seated behind Damien and shrug. "He went to school with Covey. Rumor has it they were on the debate team together and stayed close friends over the years. I suppose it's not entirely out of the question."

Competing against Dickinson would be a cakewalk. No one likes the grump.

"I'll admit that given his past, this man may not seem like the best contender for the job," Anderson babbles. "But I assure you he is. Not only is he a powerful businessman with a knack for making tough decisions, but David Covey had the utmost faith in him. So much faith in fact—his very last words beseeched his political party to see to it that this man take his place in the election. We've chosen to honor his wishes. We kindly ask you all to do the same."

"Glen isn't a businessman," Margaret whispers. "He's an orthodontist."

I shift in my seat to face her. "Robert Barnes is next to him. Bastard's been kissing Covey's ass since they were in diapers."

She cringes. "You're right. And technically he did open that shoe store on South Street, so I guess that makes him a bu—"

Her face twists in confusion and I hear a few audible gasps behind me.

Anderson's next words turn my blood to ice.
"Please welcome your new candidate—Damien King."

Chapter 24

CAIN

*M*argaret nudges me. "You don't look too good. Do you want some water?"

"I don't want any water," I bite out.

What I want is to run up to the podium Damien King is marching toward, take a fucking machete to his neck...and then piss down the stump that used to hold up his head.

"I thought you two were friends?" Margaret chirps beside me. "He seemed so nice and charm—"

"You're even more of a moron then I thought if you believe a single thing that comes out of his two-faced mouth," I snap, and she purses her lips.

My head pulses. It's getting harder to breathe. I pride myself on being one step ahead, but I never predicted this.

How could I? Damien has no political ties and nearly everyone in town hates him.

Sure, he's attractive enough to seduce anyone into bed and skilled enough to keep them coming back...but beyond that, he lacks the intellect to do anything worthwhile with his life.

Which I suppose explains why he's here now.

I thought he came back to taunt and provoke me. At worst, threaten to tell Eden the truth, and hell—maybe even try to kill me.

Not actually try to *take my life* and make it his.

But I can't say I blame him. Even with all his father's money, leftover businesses, and castles…he's still worthless.

His obsession with me and the pedestal he keeps me on will always be his biggest accomplishment.

Jesus Christ. *I should have killed him when I had the chance.*

Instead I had a moment of weakness and let him go…and now it's come back to bite me in the ass.

I'm downright seething as Damien switches places with Anderson.

"My father used to tell me opportunity waits for no one," he begins. "That if you want something, you have to be willing to stand up and fight for it." His gaze locks with mine. "Even if it means going up against an old friend."

My blood boils as he continues. This isn't a speech from a newly appointed candidate filled with false promises and oaths.

It's a personal vendetta.

"It's no secret I've known Cain Carter a long time. At one point, we were nearly inseparable. Thick as thieves. One and the same." His teeth flash white. "I know his strengths. I know his imperfections. I know all his secrets. And by the end of this race, I predict you will all know him as intimately as I do." His creepy blue eyes darken. "Truth be told, I never wanted to run against my best friend. I hoped it wouldn't have to come to this. But sometimes it's not about what you want…it's about doing what needs to be done. And I believe when it's time to vote—the people of Black Hallows will see things clearer than they ever have before…and they will elect the very best man for the job."

You could hear a pin drop as Damien backs away from the podium. Even Anderson's mouth is open so wide he's probably catching flies.

"Wow," Margaret says as everyone begins to shuffle into the banquet hall for refreshments. "That was…intense."

No. I glare at the now empty podium. *That was the start of war.*

My nostrils flare when Damien's arm slips around Eden and he starts leading her out of the room. *Attempted theft.*

I wink at my former friend and my beautiful young step-daughter as they pass by.

A ticking time bomb.

Chapter 25

EDEN

"$\mathcal{I}$ think he's waving you over." I gesture to the tall slender guy in glasses. Anderson, I think. Damien briefly mentioned on the car ride here that he was the man in charge of things behind the scenes and the one who kept everything running smoothly.

He also said he was annoying as fuck and needed to get his dick sucked by something other than his vacuum cleaner and a blow-up doll.

Suffice it to say, I didn't ask him to go into any more detail about Anderson after that.

Damien raises his glass and takes a leisurely sip, not looking at all concerned. "He can wait."

With that, he turns away—deliberately ignoring the man.

I have to stifle a laugh because Anderson looks like he's about to have a temper tantrum.

"He's starting to sweat," I muse as the visibly nervous man dabs his forehead with a napkin. "He might even pop a blood vessel."

Damien shrugs. "If it's so important, he can walk over here like a big boy and tell me himself. Covey might have babied him, but I sure as hell won't."

155

I bite my bottom lip as Anderson walks forward before taking a big step back. "He looks like he's dancing."

Damien's lips quirk up. "Give it a few seconds, he'll start pacing and muttering. After a minute or two of that, he'll finally remember he has a set of balls and come talk to me."

If he does, he'll be the first one. It's funny how people in this town prefer to talk about you, rather than *to* you. Damien isn't worried about it, though. He finds all the gossip comical.

The gleam in his eyes ever since we arrived tells me it's not a front either. He's genuinely reveling in ruffling these people's feathers.

Especially Cain...who's standing about fifteen feet away from us...looking increasingly ruffled by the second.

Lucky for him, our paths haven't crossed in the thirty minutes we've been here. The orange juice they're serving is delicious, and I'd hate to waste any of it on his lying, manipulating face.

Forcing in a breath, I stuff thoughts of him down and focus on Damien, who's not bothering to hide his amusement.

"If I didn't know better, I'd say you're having fun."

He downs the rest of his glass. "Anderson's nervous fits are the most interesting thing about him."

"I meant the election. I know you're only doing this to get back at Cain, but maybe it's your calling."

He makes a face. "Fuck that. I have no interest in politics. As soon as this is over, I'm going back home."

Home. On an island. Out of the country.

Far away from Black Hallows.

If that doesn't put things into perspective, I don't know what will.

Damien and I are a temporary thing. It will hurt less after he's gone if I stick to my own revenge plan and worry about myself.

There are so many things I want to see in this world and so much I want to experience.

Freedom is an equally scary and liberating thing.

"That can't be good," I whisper as Governor Bexley and

another man in a suit approach Anderson. "The governor just walked up to your boy and he looks like he's about to piss his pants."

"Fuck." He places his glass on a nearby waiter's tray. "We should go over there."

I grimace. "I'll stay here. I don't want to go anywhere near that asshole Bexley unless I absolutely have to."

Not only is he rude. He gives me the creeps.

"I can stay here." He grins. "Or go over there and shove my foot up his ass."

"Tempting, but I'm pretty sure that would get you canned from the race." I hold up my empty glass. "Go. I need to get more orange juice anyway."

He studies my face intently. I know it's Damien's way of checking in with me to make sure I'll be fine. I kind of love that about him.

"Okay," he says after another minute passes. "I'll be back shortly."

The second he walks away I want to latch onto his leg and beg him not to leave...but I won't.

I've got this. Fuck this town and fuck these people.

Squaring my shoulders, I stroll over to the table of hors d'oeuvres and other refreshments.

I'm in the middle of filling my glass when I feel someone come up behind me.

"Bathroom on the third floor. *Now*," Cain snarls in my ear.

I take a dainty sip of my orange juice and then nibble a cookie.

For once, Cain will have to wait for me. Lord knows I've waited long enough for him.

I take my sweet time walking to the bathroom, knowing the second I enter I'm going to have to pretend I'm infatuated and on his side.

157

I won't accomplish anything if he thinks I'm out to get him. He'll only push me farther away.

Which is exactly the *opposite* of what I want.

I want him so obsessed and distracted he starts screwing up.

And then, after Damien's destroyed him, and Cain's left helpless, feeling like he has no one in the world to turn to but his Eden...

I'm going to crush him like a bug.

No. I'm going to give him some rope and then manipulate the hell out of him until he slowly hangs himself...just like he did to me.

Breathe—I remind myself when I reach the bathroom door.

Breathe and feign innocence.

My hand is steady as I turn the knob. My head is clear.

I've got this.

He's standing by the row of sinks with his hands clenched at his sides when I enter.

"I wanted to tell you," I say as I approach. "But I couldn't get my phone—"

The sting from his hand whipping across my cheek feels like fire.

Chapter 26

CAIN

$\mathcal{I}$ realize my critical mistake the moment my palm connects with her cheekbone.

She's innocent.

With all the rage building in my gut like a skyscraper, I'd forgotten Eden didn't have access to her phone and couldn't contact me to warn me even if she'd wanted to.

Because I sent her away.

And now she's looking at me like I'm a monster...when she was only doing what I asked her to.

If I didn't drive her to Damien's dick before, this will certainly do it.

"Shit." I kick a garbage can, sending it sailing into a stall. "Goddammit."

"I couldn't text you," she states, pressing a hand to her skin. "I—"

"I'm sorry." I rush over and gather her in my arms. "I'm so sorry. I don't know what came over me."

Actually, I do. His name is *Damien King*.

She's silent. Not even so much as a whimper or a cry escapes her.

This isn't like Eden. She's slipping farther away with every second that passes.

And it's all Damien's fault.

Panicked, I drop to my knees and nuzzle her stomach. "Please forgive me."

Fear coils my insides when she doesn't respond. I can't live without her. *I won't.* I'll kill her before I ever let Damien, or any other man, destroy what's mine. *He doesn't get my Eden.*

"I need you to forgive me." Frantically, I pull at the fabric of her dress. "I would never hurt you."

"You just did," she whispers.

Desperate times call for desperate measures. I never wanted to tell her about my father or brother—I wanted her to believe I had the picture-perfect family, before it was sullied by tragedy—just like everyone else does.

But securing her sympathy is the only way to fix this.

Her eyebrows shoot up as I loosen my tie and unbutton my shirt. "What are you doing?"

"Sharing my biggest secret with you. A part of me I keep hidden from the world."

I've never let anyone see these scars. Not since that night.

Her face twists in confusion when I slide her hand to my back. "What happened? Your skin...it almost feels like... burns." Her eyes widen. "I thought you weren't in the house fire?"

"I wasn't." I cradle her face. "They aren't burns. They're scars."

"From what?"

"Belts, a few chairs, cigars. A cheese grater once."

She looks horrified. "Oh, my God. Who did this to you? Why—"

"My father...and on occasion, my brother. It started when I was young, and it only got worse as I got older. As far as why—that's something I'll never know the answer to. Some people are just wired differently than us. They like to cause pain and suffering because they lost their humanity." I breathe her in like air. "They have nothing to pull them back when it gets too dark."

160

They have no Eden's in their life.

Nothing that makes them feel like a savior.

No one who will love them unconditionally.

Her eyes become glassy. "I'm sorry you had to go through something so horrible—"

I shut her up with a kiss. I don't want to talk about my family. I don't want to relive my past.

Life is about moving forward. Working toward new goals. Embracing what's right in front of you.

"It's over now," I tell her when she tries to come up for air. "My life is good now. It's good because I have you." I bury my head between her breasts, sucking the soft skin into my mouth. "I'll never hurt you again, sweetheart. I swear on my life. I won't do what's been done to me."

She starts to speak, but I cover her mouth with mine and force my tongue through her lips.

I can't bear to hear her say she'll never forgive me.

"Whoa—"

I move her panties to the side and plunge two fingers inside her.

She can't escape me. I won't let her. *I need her too much.*

"Cain—"

I don't like her tone, it's not sweet and breathy like it was before Damien—it's resistant.

I push a third finger inside her, hammering her little cunt as hard as I can.

"You like that, don't you?" She whimpers and clenches around me. "There you go, baby. That's it," I murmur, wrapping my other hand around her throat. "Come for me, sweetheart. Cain won't stop until you do."

Infuriation slices through me like a knife through butter when she doesn't. "Did you fuck Damien today? Is that why you can't come? Perhaps I should shove my fist inside you and see if you feel anything then." She tries to shake her head no, but I tighten my grip. "Then come for me like a good girl, Eden. Prove how much you still want me."

Come for me right fucking now, you little slut.

Come for me or I'll choke you, chop your sexy body up into hot little pieces, and make Damien eat them one by one.

The room sways and my head pulses so hard I scream.

I won't lose her. I won't let him have her. She's mine.

Mine. Mine. Mine.

"I can't lose you, Eden," I choke out. "Please, baby. I need you to come for me. I need you to show me how much you love me."

I need to know I haven't lost her.

When she finally does a moment later, it's glorious. Her chest heaves, her cunt clamps my fingers, and she bucks her hips.

"Such a good girl," I murmur as I fix her panties and smell my fingers, inhaling her scent. "Such a good girl."

A lonely tear streams down her cheek. I lick it up when it rolls into her cleavage. "I love you, Eden."

"I love you, too." She kisses my forehead, then my nose, before finding my mouth. "I love you so much."

Relief fills my chest.

This is my peace. *The storm is over.*

Her tongue is urgent and needy as her hand ventures lower. I utter a deep groan when she palms my cock through my pants. "Is this for me?"

"Always." I move the top of her dress until her tit pops out. I lav her nipple with my tongue. "Christ, I can't wait to fuck you tonight. It'll be so good, sweetheart." I suck the pointy bud into my mouth. "I'm gonna take my time and—"

The hand squeezing my dick stops. "What do you mean tonight?"

I give her a smile. "I'm taking you back home where you belong. It was stupid of me to tell you to spy on Damien."

It was a careless mistake on my part. *One I won't make again.*

I'm going to do what I should have done eleven years ago and get rid of him for good.

Problem—each and every fucking one of them—solved.

"What about the election?"

I flick her nipple. "There won't be much of an election after he's gone."

"You're gonna kill him?"

I narrow my eyes. "Is that a problem for you?"

"No. It's just…" She worries her lip. "I'm concerned about your reputation. One dead opponent is bad enough, but two? You know how this town is, Cain. People will talk. And if they start talking…it might impact their votes." She kisses my jaw. "I don't want people thinking you don't deserve to win the election on your own merits, you know?" I close my eyes as she nips my throat. "No one deserves to win more than you, my love. Killing Damien might screw up your big chance."

"It's the only way to stop him from ruining my life."

She has no idea how Damien is. His determination knows no bounds.

The man is senseless and psychotic. A reckless combination.

I moan as she licks my Adam's apple. "Call me crazy, but if he wants to get revenge by running against you—let him. It's not like he poses a real threat to you becoming mayor. *Everyone* loves you. Just let him think he's getting under your skin like he wants, and he'll go away."

"He could tell everyone my secrets, Eden. I can't risk it."

"Then I'll be your eyes and ears. If I sense he's about to pull a fast one on you again, I'll let you know ahead of time."

I stop and ponder this for a moment.

I suppose if Eden wants to know why I murdered my family… and her mother, it *would* give me enough of a warning that Damien's about to spill the beans.

He's a bastard all right, but he wouldn't let Eden find out the truth at the same time everyone else does. Not if he considers her an advocate…or lover. He'd tell her before then. In private.

Fortunately, Eden's feelings for him won't be real, and she loves me enough she would never be able to turn me in.

Not with the bond we have.

She'd give me hell, cry a river, tell me I'm an evil asshole...and then offer to run away with me. *Just like she's always wanted.*

"You don't have a way to contact me."

If this is going to work, I need to keep the lines of communication open at all times.

Her face screws up. "You can sneak me a phone at the breakfast fundraiser tomorrow. Something small and inconspicuous."

"You really think you can handle this?"

She looks me in the eyes. "Absolutely." She leans in, cupping my jaw. "After everything you've done for me, this is the least I can do."

"You realize if you screw up, everything I've worked for will be ruined. I'm literally trusting you with my goddamn life."

"Do you honestly think I would ever let anything bad happen to you? You're the love of my life. I wouldn't know what to do without you—I wouldn't—"

I kiss her tears. "I know, sweetheart. I know." I pull back and look at her. "I'll tell you what. If you do this for me, after I become mayor, I'll get rid of Margaret for good." I kiss up her jawbone, stopping when I reach her ear. "I'll blame it on losing your mother. I'll tell people Margaret's a lovely woman, but I'm just not ready to move on." I squeeze her breast. "But you'll be the one in my bed every night, helping me work through my grief."

People don't put themselves on the line like this unless there's a good enough carrot being dangled in front of them.

And there's nothing Eden wants more than me.

Nothing she wants more than *love*. And I'll give it to her in abundance.

Her smile is so beautiful my chest swells. "You mean it?"

"It will be just us again. Only this time, I'm giving you everything you deserve."

She wraps her arms around my neck. "I love you."

"We just need to get through this little Damien hurdle and we're golden."

"I won't let you down."

"I know you won't. In the meantime, I'm gonna touch base with Chief Trejo."

She blinks. "The chief? Why?"

I smirk. "We're close friends. I'm gonna let Damien run against me like he wants, but then he'll be thrown in jail like he deserves come polling day."

"For killing your family," she says slowly as if it just dawned on her.

Her hair color suits her—because she sure as fuck has enough blonde moments.

I button up my shirt and fix my tie. "Yes." I eye her as she starts putting herself together. "Are you sure you can handle this?"

She fixes her lipstick in the mirror. "Positive."

That hard exterior is back in place. *I hate it.*

"By the way...your dress."

She crinkles her nose. "What about it?"

"It makes you look like the town whore."

Chapter 27

EDEN

---

*H*is words are water. *Let them roll off your back.*

And really, given everything else he's done to me, calling me a slut is at the very bottom of his list of offenses.

I examine my cheek in the mirror. It's a bit red, but it's not too bad.

The soreness between my legs hurts worse.

"I'm gonna go out first." I need to get away from him before I do or say something stupid and blow my cover.

He kisses my forehead. "We'll be together soon, beautiful."

"I'm counting the days."

A twinge of sadness squeezes my chest. There's a small part of me that truly feels sorry for him. Cain being abused is not only gut-wrenching, it makes total sense.

He never took off his shirt. Never talked about his family.

Never let anyone in.

I'm having trouble deciphering the evil man who paid someone to mentally fuck me up in order to make me solely dependent on him, from the man I was in love with twenty-four hours ago.

It doesn't excuse his behavior and certainly not his actions, but it…I don't know. It makes my heart hurt. The old one he broke and the new tougher one I'm building.

No one should be abused. Especially by the people who are supposed to love you.

And maybe in his warped mind, hiring someone to brainwash me was his way of keeping me close because he was too scared to lose me.

Because he loved me too much. A love he didn't know how to express in a healthy way…because no one ever showed him.

I shake my head. *Nope.* I won't go there. I won't even entertain it.

He hit me. He didn't almost hit me and stop himself…he *actually* hit me.

And then he turned right around and hurt me in a different way. I tried to tell him to ease up, that he was being too rough, but I couldn't get the words out.

He didn't give me the chance…or the choice.

He never does.

I take a few cleansing breaths as I walk out the door.

"Wasn't aware they served orange juice in the bathrooms."

I nearly jump at the sound of Damien's deep voice.

My heart pounds when he stubs his cigarette out and comes closer.

"What happened to your cheek?"

"Nothing."

"It looks red."

"You're so handsome you make me blush." I jut my chin toward the hall. "Can we go back downstairs?"

Cain will be coming out any minute and the homicidal look in Damien's eyes is only getting worse.

He needs to remember the end game. Going after Cain now will only get him thrown in jail…which is exactly what Cain wants.

"Eden." There's a familiar dark edge to his tone. The kind that equally seduces and scares the living shit out of me.

"I ended up walking into the bathroom at the same time

someone else was walking out and got bitch slapped by the door. It's really not that big of a deal, so stop freaking out for no reason."

His blue orbs burn with indignation as he grips my chin. "Look me in the eyes and tell me the truth."

I match his glare. "I just did."

"Okay."

The anxiety filling my chest eases. "Come on. We should—"

My mouth drops when he kicks the door open…sending Cain, who was eavesdropping on the other side, flying into the wall behind him.

"Stop," I shout, but it's too late.

Damien's hand is already wrapped around Cain's throat and his other hand is taking jabs at his stomach.

I try to pull them apart, but it's impossible. There's too much adrenaline and venom between them and neither one will back down.

Not even Cain, who's clearly at a disadvantage due to Damien's size and ironclad grip.

That is until Cain's finger catches the corner of Damien's eye and he stumbles backward, forcing me out the door.

"Someone's coming," I tell them when I look down the hall.

I mutter a curse as the figures come into view.

William Anderson looks like he's trying his hardest to get a word in as Andrew Jones—the head of Cain's political party—nods.

While Governor Bexley rambles on and on.

Until he spots me.

"Are you al—" Governor Bexley starts to say, but Damien and Cain tumble out of the bathroom, still going at it.

"Oh, hell."

Anderson and Jones grab each of Damien's arms while the governor picks Cain up off the floor and then plants himself between them.

"Gentlemen, this is *not* how we conduct ourselves in public." He blows out a breath. "I know there's some bad blood—" He doesn't even bother to suppress the side-eye of contempt he gives me. "As well as some pressing family issues, but physical violence between two candidates will not be tolerated. Do you understand?"

"Oh, my God," Margaret screeches, her heels picking up speed. "What happened?"

"Nothing. Just a little disagreement is all," Bexley declares, his eyes darting from Cain to Damien. "But it's over now. Right, gentlemen?"

Cain nods.

"It looks like more than a simple disagreement," Margaret tuts, rushing over to Cain. "Should we take him to the hospital? Get him an icepack?"

"Drop it, Margaret," Cain says at the same time the governor bellows, "Let it go."

Margaret holds up her hands. "Fine." She whips around to face me. "Maybe you should do us all a favor and go back to being a hermit." Her eyes drop to my cleavage and she glowers. "Every time you step out of the house you cause nothing but trouble for innocent men and their families." She folds her arms across her chest. "No one wants you around. Take the hint and get lost."

I have one of two choices. I can either choose to let her words have the intended effect and make me feel bad.

Or I can stand up for myself.

"Wow, that's all you got?" She blinks as I take a step forward. "Listen to me and listen good. I'm not going anywhere. And if you plan on hurling insults at me every time we're in the same room… you're gonna need a whole lot more than what you're bringing to the table, honey, because I've heard them all before. So please, do *me* a favor and use your six-figure college education and that thing between your shoulders and try to be more original." I snort. "Better yet, do yourself a favor and be more than a show dog for your daddy and fiancé."

With that, I turn on my heels and saunter down the hallway.

"Damn," Damien drawls behind me. "Looks like you'll both be needing icepacks now."

The governor starts to speak, but Damien cuts him off, "Have a good evening, *gentlemen.*"

~

"Are you okay?"

His hand tightens around the steering wheel. "Fine."

"You haven't said a word to me since the bathroom incident."

Silence.

I peer out the window. "Your moods are starting to give me whiplash. One second we're a team, and the next you're acting like I don't exist."

"That's because I don't like being lied to."

I throw up my hands. "I was trying to avoid exactly what ended up happening."

"By lying to me."

I roll my eyes. He's missing the point. "Can you look at the bigger picture for two seconds? Cain would have—"

The tires screech. "I don't care what Cain would have done." His gaze slides to my cheek. "He hit you and you looked me right in the motherfucking eyes and told me you walked into a door. Fuck your bigger picture and fuck your excuses, Eden. You lied to protect someone other than yourself, which means you haven't learned a damn thing."

Chapter 28

EDEN

"*H*ere."

I look down at the bag of peas Geoffrey's holding out to me. "I guess it's more noticeable than I thought."

"I've seen worse." He shrugs. "Not that it matters. The intent is still the same regardless if it leaves a mark or not."

"I'm not making excuses for Cain. I was protecting Damien."

"I understand."

"Why can't *he*?"

The moment we came home, Damien locked himself in his office and he's been down there ever since. I get that he's mad about me lying, but his grudge is uncalled for.

I lied for *him*. I can't fathom why he considers it such a horrible violation of trust.

Lying to protect someone you care about isn't wrong.

"Forgive me if I'm out of line, but Damien isn't a stupid man. I think he understands perfectly well what your purpose was."

"Then why is he so angry when I was only trying to look out for him?"

He lifts his shoulder in a shrug. "Sometimes what we dislike in others is the very same thing we loathe in ourselves."

173

After spending the better part of the evening tossing and turning, I make my way down to Damien's office.

Geoffrey's words have been reverberating through my mind all night.

And call it a hunch or really profound intuition...but I'm thinking I know exactly why Damien is the way he is.

During his speech, he mentioned Cain was his best friend and said they were almost inseparable at one point.

I saw the way Damien attacked Cain earlier today after he slapped me. He looked like he wanted to kill him and if the governor wasn't there to break it up...I think he would have.

Just like he killed Cain's father and brother.

He killed them because they hurt Cain.

And then Cain turned around and threatened to turn him in for it.

No wonder Damien has such trust issues. He was betrayed by someone he cared about.

It's dark when I enter his office. The only light comes from the fish tank Damien's chair is facing.

I find his fascination with them endearing. He's always watching them, feeding them, and making sure the water's clean.

I don't know much about taking care of fish, but it seems like he gives them a great life and they're happy.

Well, apart from the big fish he keeps behind the divider. That one reminds me of Damien because he always looks so grumpy and miserable.

I prop myself on top of his desk. "Maybe he's cranky because he doesn't have any friends."

He tilts his head in my direction. "Thought you'd be sleeping by now."

"I can't sleep." I play with a loose string on the end of my pajama top. "I'd say I'm sorry for lying, but that would only be another lie." I wait for him to look at me before I say, "I get why you're upset. I know why you have trust issues. But I'm not Ca—"

He turns his chair around. "You don't know a thing about me, Eden."

"Fair enough, but I know you're a good person."

He laughs darkly. "What makes you so sure about that?"

"If you weren't a good person, you wouldn't have told me the truth about Cain. You also wouldn't be teaching me how to be a stronger person. And you definitely wouldn't have saved Geoffrey, or—"

"Enough." He stands up. "Everything I do has a purpose, and it's always self-serving. I told you about Cain so you wouldn't be in my way when I take him down. I *hired* Geoffrey because I needed a servant and everyone else on the island was either too injured or dead after the hurricane." He places his arms on either side of my body. "And I'm teaching you how to fend for yourself because I can't stand to be around weakness." His lip curls. "Pathetic people *disgust* me."

I swallow hard. I know he's only trying to push me away because I'm getting too close. "I—"

"Don't," he snaps. "Don't delude yourself into thinking I'm something I'm not, or that this thing between us is more than sex and a common goal, little lamb. Trust me, it's not. And the second I'm gone, you'll be grateful for it."

Geoffrey was right. The size of the bruise doesn't matter...it's the intent behind it.

Unlike Cain, Damien didn't have to hit me to leave a mark.

"Right," I whisper, trying my hardest to keep it together because the only thing I have left is my pride. "Now that we got that out of the way, you should know that Cain wants to have you arrested on polling day." I lift up his arm and hop off the desk. "Evidently he's friends with Chief Trejo and he's going to meet with him soon. I'm not sure when, all I know is he wants you in jail for killing his family."

I snap my fingers as I walk toward the door. "Oh. He's also slipping me a phone tomorrow so I can communicate with him. I kindly ask that you don't take it away from me, because I'd really like to not get slapped and finger banged against my will so hard it hurts to walk again."

His eyes narrow. "He—"

"Nope." I hold up a hand. "Don't worry about me, pal. I'm *good*. And now that you've made it perfectly clear what this is and isn't between us. I think it's best you handle your shit with Cain your way, and I handle mine my way. Our goal might be common, but it doesn't mean we have to take the same path and update each other on our journeys along the way."

"Fine." His expression is so hard it could be carved from stone.

"Great." I pause when I reach the door. I hate that his rejection stings so much. "It's a good thing you have your fish. I hope they keep you warm and—" A scream lodges in my throat as I turn around. The big fish he keeps behind the divider is devouring all the other fish. It's the most savage thing I've ever seen.

Damien flashes me a smile. "You were saying?"

Chapter 29

CAIN

*R*eleasing a sigh, I check my watch for the third time.

It's just after two a.m. The chief should be arriving any minute.

Although he should have been here sooner given he lives right up the road from my campaign headquarters.

As if on cue, he waltzes into my office wearing a ratty sweatshirt and jeans.

My stomach rolls. His uniform would have put things into better perspective and reminded me why I'm going to such lengths.

Although *lengths* would be generous when it comes to the chief.

He plops down in a chair. "Sorry I wasn't here sooner. I got caught up watching the game."

I grab the bottle of vodka on the desk behind me and pour myself a drink. I'll need at least three more before the night is over.

The things we do for leverage.

He makes a face. "Never pegged you for a vodka guy."

"It was a Christmas gift from Claudia." I gesture to the extra glass on my desk. "Help yourself."

"Don't mind if I do."

He's mid-sip when I cut to the chase. "I need a favor."

He doesn't look at all surprised. Then again, we've been down this road once before.

"Figured as much. What is it this time? Parking tick——"

"I need you to arrest someone."

"Why?"

"I need him out of the picture. Preferably for the next twenty-five years to life."

He takes a hearty swig of his drink. "Who?"

"Damien King."

He starts coughing. "Are you crazy? Not only is he richer than God, he just donated half a million to the department."

Of course he did. "I wouldn't ask if it wasn't important, Ray."

"All right, I'll bite. What in God's name would you like him arrested for?"

"Murder."

He stands up. "Yeah, you're crazier than I thought. Have a good night."

"Sit down."

Begrudgingly, he plants his ass in the chair. "Look, I know you two have history and he's your opponent. But I'm not gonna arrest a man for murder just because he pisses you off. I'm not a crooked cop, Carter."

I lean against the edge of my desk. "You're a little crooked...if memory serves."

He flushes with embarrassment. "Don't go there. It was a one-time thing. I was drunk——"

"Yadda, yadda." I refill my glass. "How are things with that wife of yours anyway?"

"They're fine," he says sharply.

I shift my stance so I'm standing in front of him. "I have proof, you know."

"Proof of what?"

"Damien King telling me how he planned to kill my family in a fire eleven years ago."

"Video?"

"Audio."

He winces. "Sketchy." He blinks. "Wait a minute. Your teacher killed your brother and father, so why the hell would you have something like that in the first place? And why the fuck are you telling me about this *now* and not eleven years ago?"

I shrug. "I said I had proof, I didn't say he did it."

He scrubs a hand down his face. "Let me get this straight. You want me to open an eleven-year-old murder investigation that was already solved and tell everyone the teacher who ended up getting murdered by her husband was innocent all along and then pin the whole thing on someone else?"

"Yes."

He snorts. "Not only is it unethical, it's the equivalent of opening Pandora's box. The scandal was one of the biggest in Black Hallows' history."

"I need him gone."

"Then find another way. Setting up an innocent man for a double homicide is fucked. Even for you."

I drop to my knees. "Sometimes we all do things we're not proud of." I rub the small bulge forming in his pants. "Don't we, Ray?"

"Stop it, Carter. I told you—" He moans when I tug his zipper down and flick my tongue through the opening. "Fuck, that feels good."

"It could feel even better…if you'd be willing to help me."

He closes his eyes. "It's been so long."

"I know it has." I reach inside his pants. "You deserve someone who cares about your pleasure. Someone to take care of your needs." I tighten my grip. "I can be that person."

"You'll have to do a better job of convincing me."

I smirk. "Take off your pants."

They fall to his ankles. "You gonna take yours off too? Let me fuck that ass again?"

I undo my belt. "I thought it was a one-time thing?"

He strokes himself. "Shut up and suck it."

Stomach churning, I edge forward. "Do we have a deal?"

He grunts. "Let me fuck you and I'll consider it."

"I'll let you fuck me whenever you want if you arrest Damien King on polling day."

"Oh, hell."

"Come on, Chief." I swallow his short, fat dick in one gulp and he hisses. "Besides, it's a little late to turn back now. Especially if you don't want your wife or anyone else to know how much you enjoy this."

"You're a goddamn snake, Carter." He pushes his hips forward. "Suck it again."

"Do we have a deal?"

"Yeah." He grips my hair. "But let me fuck your ass."

Swallowing my disgust, I stand up, drop my pants, and bend over the desk.

He spits on his hand. "She goes to her book club thing every Wednesday at five."

I grunt as he slams into me. "And you're telling me this because—"

"You'll be taking my cock every Wednesday at five from here on out."

"Sure thing, Chief."

The things we do for leverage.

Chapter 30

DAMIEN

"Sure thing, Chief," Cain grits through his teeth as Trejo plows into his ass again.

I snap a few more pictures from my place behind the bookshelf. *Cain's more desperate to get rid of me than I thought.*

However, if he's going to blow and fuck the whole town so he can blackmail them later, he should invest in better security. Or at least check a room after he enters.

It would save me from having to endure one of the most pathetic screws I've ever witnessed in my life.

Cain used to be good at this. Now he's just sad and sloppy.

Not everything gets better with age.

Sometimes they just get dull.

"You like that, you little bitch?" the chief roars.

Chief might look like a bulldog with rabies, but at least the motherfucker's got a kinky side.

My dick stirs to life. Eden's probably sound asleep in bed right now.

I wonder if she's still wearing those little silky shorts that reveal her perfect ass cheeks.

Lust and want battle in my chest.

I should leave her alone. *Stick to the plan.*

It would be much easier that way.

But the thing about plans is…

They never work out like you expect them to.

Because I seduced when I should have abandoned.

I tasted when I should have abstained.

I sinned when I should have atoned.

My muscles clench with need.

And now I'm going back for more…because I can't stay away.

She wakes with a jolt when I creep up behind her in bed.

"Damien?"

I flip her onto her stomach, pressing her face into the mattress.

"What are you doing?"

I peel her shorts and panties down. "Tasting you."

Proving my point, I swipe my tongue over her plump lips.

She props herself up on her knees, exposing her glistening cunt. "You're an asshole."

I chuckle as I spear her with my tongue. *She's not wrong.*

Wet sounds fill the room as I eat her out with greed, spanking and kneading her pert behind.

"I should tell you to go fuck yourself." She grinds that sweet pussy against my mouth, commanding more. "And then make you leave."

I'd like to see her try.

"You should." Spreading her cheeks, I flick her puckered hole. "But you won't."

She groans deeply as I suckle and lick. "That feels so good." Reaching behind her she grips my head, pushing my face where she wants me. "Don't fucking stop."

Lust blazes up my dick as I devour her little asshole.

"I want you inside me."

My body hums with urgency as I reach inside the nightstand for lube and pour it down her crack. She gasps when my finger follows and I push it inside her.

"Relax." I slip my digit out slowly before diving back in. "It will hurt more if you tense up."

I jerk my cock to alleviate the pressure as I add another finger, stretching her. "Good girl." Shifting, I line my tip up with her hole. "Now touch your pussy."

My abs clench as I work my cock head inside her. "Exhale."

"Why—"

I thrust forward, groaning as the cord of tension breaks free, giving way to pleasure. "That." Grunting, I pull back and slam into her again.

Ragged breaths saw in and out of her as she grips the bedsheets with her free hand.

"And this," I rasp, fucking her into the bed with quick brutal thrusts.

Sweat slicks down my skin. My balls draw tight as her sphincter squeezes, sucking me deeper.

"Jesus Christ," I roar as she milks my dick, coming so hard the entire bed shakes.

My cum seeps out, dripping down her crack but I shove it back in with my thumb while I work my way down her body, kissing her spine as she plays with herself. Her little whimpers and trembles tells me she's close.

Turning onto my back, I nudge my head between her parted thighs, giving myself a front row seat to the world's greatest show.

I grab her hips, positioning her pussy in front of my face as she rubs her clit, working herself into a frenzy. "Squirt in my mouth."

Her hips buck and she spasms, moaning my name as she falls apart. I fervently swallow everything she gives me like the glutton I am until there's no more and her body gives out.

"If that's how we make up, I think we should fight more."

My lips twitch as she drapes her body over mine. "Who says we made up?"

"I did." She lays her head on my chest. "I'm not your enemy, Damien."

Reaching down, I fish my cigarettes out of my pocket and light one. "I'm never gonna be okay with you lying to me."

"I lied to protect you. I don't regret it and I'd do it again if the circumstances called for it. No matter how angry you get with me."

Stubborn girl.

She traces little circles up and down my pecs. "Can I ask you something?"

"Shoot."

"Why did you kill your fish?"

"I didn't. The tank is my piranha's home...the other fish are his food."

"Then why go through the trouble of feeding and taking care of all the other fish when—"

"Because of my mother."

She looks up at me. "What do you mean?"

I draw in a deep breath...and then I tell her things I've only shared with one other person before.

Chapter 31

EDEN

"Beautiful," Damien murmurs.

I turn my head at the sound of his voice.

He's leaning against my bedroom door, impeccably dressed in a dark suit, looking good enough to eat.

But it's the devilish smirk on his face that makes my breath catch.

I finish fastening my earrings. "How long have you been standing there?"

His smirk deepens. "A while."

I motion to my dress. "Is this too much for breakfast?"

I chose a simple light pink shift dress, but the heels I'm rocking make it appear even shorter. And it's plenty short already.

His gaze drops to my legs. "It's perfect." His expression turns serious. "I don't want you alone with Cain again."

"That's not gonna work. Not only will it make him suspicious, but he's supposed to be giving me a phone today, remember?"

Those blue orbs darken as he closes the distance between us. "I don't like it."

"I'm not over the moon about it either, but it's part of the plan." I open my closet and pull out a jacket. "Ready?"

"Not yet." He holds up a black object. "I want you to keep this on you at all times."

"What is it?"

He presses a button and a blade snaps up. "A knife." He gestures to the curve. "See that angle?"

I nod.

"It's specifically designed to do some damage. If he ever hurts you again, I want you to use it. If *anyone* hurts you, I want you to use it. Understand?"

"How am I supposed to conceal a knife?"

He grins as he pulls something lacy out of his pocket. "This should do the trick."

Chapter 32

EDEN

"*T*his shouldn't take long."

If I wasn't so nervous, I'd laugh. Most of the week has already flown by without a hitch, but today's the debate.

Something Cain excels at.

And even though I know Damien can hold his own, I don't want Cain to blindside him. And by blindside—I mean get Damien so riled up he beats the crap out of him...*again.*

I'd be a lot less worried if they didn't have to be holed up in a conference room together. However, it's tradition for the two candidates to be secluded without any distractions for a few minutes prior to a debate. It's supposed to make it easier for them to clear their heads and focus.

I can feel Cain's stare boring holes into us as Damien plants a soft kiss on my inner wrist.

The small teasing smile on Damien's lips makes it clear he's doing it intentionally to get a rise out of Cain.

The debate hasn't even started and already it feels like I'm standing in the middle of one.

"Some things never change," a woman behind me drawls.

"Go away, Katrina," Margaret snaps.

I have no idea who this Katrina woman is, but if Margaret hates her, I'm a fan.

Katrina takes a sip of the drink she's holding. "Someone's bitter they aren't the cat's meow." Her eyes ping pong between Damien and Cain. "Or should I say dogs." Her gaze cuts to me. "Fighting over a bone."

Margaret scowls. "Don't make me call security."

Katrina rolls her eyes and holds her hand out to me, ignoring Margaret's threat. "Hi, darling. I've heard so much about you. That article in the newspaper didn't do you justice, though. You're even prettier in person. It's almost uncanny."

Beside me, Damien tenses. Across from me, Cain's jaw tics.

Raising an eyebrow, I shake her hand. "Thanks, I think. And you are?"

"Katrina. I'm Cain's high school sweetheart." She winks at Damien. "And Damien's—"

"I screwed her in a shed once," Damien declares.

Yeah, not such a big fan now.

"Technically it was twice. But who's counting?"

"How's your stepdaughter?" Cain spits.

Katrina flutters her eyelashes. "Oh, didn't you hear? She's been found. Turns out she went to Vegas with a couple of girlfriends." She crinkles her nose at him. "It completely slipped my mind."

"Probably because you're a lush," Margaret chimes in.

"Careful, Margaret. My husband is the assistant district attorney." She looks at me. "My condolences by the way."

"Tha—"

"My father's the *governor*," Margaret squeaks.

Cain pinches the bridge of his nose. "Now that we know everyone's family tree, can you excuse us?" He gestures to himself and Damien. "We have a debate to focus on here."

Damien's pupils harden. "I'm ready when you are."

Anderson, who's getting sweatier by the second in his corner, approaches us. "Debate starts in fifteen. You're supposed to be in conference room A."

Damien looks at me. "Are y—"

"Don't worry about her, sugar," Katrina says. "I'll keep your girl company during your little debate." She winks at Cain. "Or is she your girl? Do you two keep a schedule?"

"Thanks for the offer, but I'm good." I give Damien's hand a squeeze. "I'm gonna go grab a seat. Break a leg."

"Smart thinking, honey," she calls out. "The last girl who got between them ended up dead."

Chapter 33

DAMIEN

"So, pray tell, what have you got planned for us this evening? Another one of your riveting speeches?" Cain quips as we enter the conference room.

"Not sure," I counter. "I was thinking a little blackmail and murder?" I rub my jaw. "You know, the usual...for *you*."

He snorts. "Please. If you haven't said anything by now, it's because you don't have the balls." A peculiar gleam lights his eyes. "Or perhaps it's something else."

He wants a reaction from me, but I won't give him one. Instead, I lean against the wall with my hands in my pockets, silently watching in amusement because he's about to make a fool of himself.

I know Cain better than anyone.

I valued him when I shouldn't have.

I pitied and loved him when he didn't deserve it. *So much I hated myself for it.*

But even more than that—*I've studied him intently.*

Cain Carter is a brilliant man. He's a master at sensing what people need and giving it to them when it suits his needs. Which makes him incredibly clever and charming when he wants to be.

But the emperor has one fatal flaw. A blind spot that everyone else but him can spot from a mile away.

His obsession with himself…and getting what he wants.

There is no pedestal higher than the one Cain puts himself on…

While he pisses on everyone below.

Unfortunately for him, his pedestal is about to come crashing down.

And when it finally does, he'll see me standing there with a smile on my face…while I watch him burn in the flames.

Slowly, he walks toward me. A man on a mission. "I still think about it, you know."

"What's that?"

"Our history." He gets close to my face. "The things we used to do together." His hand descends, stopping on my zipper. "How much you wanted me." He smirks. "Feels like you still do."

What he feels isn't desire…it's anticipation for his downfall.

The sound of him tugging my zipper down is almost obscenely loud in the quiet room. "Is this what you came back for?" Reaching inside my pants, he gives my dick a firm squeeze. "Your sick obsession with me."

I stay silent as he strokes me from root to tip. "It's why I let you borrow her." He laughs darkly. "I thought maybe you'd like to share again. Just like old times."

I keep my expression impassive. "I appreciate the sentiment, but I'm not into sharing anymore." I trace the edges of his lips with my thumb. "I want all or nothing."

"Is that so?" He kneels before me. "What happens after you get it? Will you concede?"

Licking my lips, I wrap my hand around the back of his neck, guiding his open mouth to my dick. "Why don't you find out?"

Moist heat covers my shaft as he swallows me down.

I start to smile…until I see a quick flash of blonde hair through the crack in the door.

Gripping the back of Cain's head, I shove my dick down his

throat as far as it will go. When his gags turn to retches, I release him and give him a swift kick in the nuts.

"When I said I wanted all or nothing, it wasn't you I was referring to."

He rolls backward, grabbing his crotch. "You son of a bitch."

"Enjoy your debate, Cain." I step over him and head for the door. "I enjoyed mine."

"Well, *enjoy* it while it lasts," Cain spits. "Because if I lose Eden…you lose her, too."

"I know."

Therein lies my own blind spot.

The curveball in my otherwise flawless plan.

Chapter 34

EDEN

"*W*hy don't you find out?" Damien advises as he proceeds to lure Cain to his...

Holy fucking shit. This isn't happening.

I slam my eyes shut, convinced I'm imagining things.

But I'm not, because when I open them, Cain's mouth is still wrapped around Damien's cock.

Mind spinning, I back away from the door. I've seen more than enough.

I clutch my chest as an array of feelings hit me in rapid succession, like darts to a board. Betrayal, jealousy, anger.

And one I haven't felt since that night on the balcony. *Fear.*

The last girl who got between them ended up dead.

Katrina's statement was ominous enough, but after witnessing this?

My feet move of their own accord, as if they no longer trust my head to do the thinking for me. And honestly? I don't blame them because I'm having a hard time trusting myself after falling into their *trap.*

Because that's exactly what this is. There's no other explanation.

ASHLEY JADE

If Damien loved Cain so much he'd kill Cain's family...there's nothing stopping him from doing the same to me.

Because I'm in the way. Because Cain wants me *out* of the way.

Jesus. Who knows? They've volleyed me back and forth so much it's enough to drive a sane person crazy.

A horrifying thought hits me. What if Damien's a jealous, manipulative liar? He was definitely threatening my therapist on that tape.

Maybe none of it was real? Oh, God. Maybe Cain's innocent?

His assault in the bathroom isn't something I can excuse, and I won't...but there's a chance I've been on the wrong side this entire time and assisting the wrong man.

Cain said Damien knew things about his past and was using it to blackmail him.

Before now, I couldn't think of a single reason Cain would want to punish Damien for killing the people who abused him. It didn't make sense.

But if Damien and Cain did certain *things* in the past, and Damien's intentionally holding it against him now, while he's running for mayor...I can understand Cain's anger.

Damien warned me he only did things for personal gain and when it was over between us, I'd be grateful.

But he was wrong. I'm not grateful. *I'm fucking hurt.*

Because I made the crucial mistake of catching feelings for a man I shouldn't have...again.

The gruesome feeling in my stomach intensifies. Damien played me like a goddamn fiddle.

Maybe he played Cain like one too? Or...maybe they're both in cahoots with each other and they like torturing women?

No matter what it is, I don't want to stick around to find out.

"Eden," Damien calls out behind me.

I run faster. If I never see him again, it will be too soon.

He wants me gone so badly. I'm gone.

Damien and Cain can have each other. Or fend for themselves. Either way, I no longer give a shit. I'm out. I'm done. I'm through.

196

Fuck Cain. Fuck Damien. Fuck them both.

My heart will heal eventually. Or maybe it won't. It doesn't matter. I only need the physical organ to survive.

I won't end up dead like that woman.

I won't be part of their sick game any longer.

I'm a player, not a pawn.

A strong arm wraps around my waist and a large hand clamps over my mouth before I'm dragged backward.

I sink my teeth into Damien's hand, struggling against his hold as he wrenches me through the open door of an empty conference room, then kicks it closed behind him.

It's a straight-up brawl as we tumble to the floor. One that ends with him on top of me, pinning one of my arms to the carpet.

Too bad he chose the wrong arm.

Damien was right about one thing, the knife he gave me *is* good for self-defense. The sick fuck almost looks proud as I hold it up to his neck...until it dawns on him that I have every intention of using it.

"Give me a chance to explain. If you still want to take a stab at me after, be my guest."

"I don't take orders from you."

Or anyone else. *I never will again.*

"I know what you're thinking. I can't say I blame you, because I'd be thinking the same fucking thing. But I *need* you to listen to me."

"No—"

He places my free hand on his heart. It's pumping so fast it's practically galloping out of his body. "*This* isn't a trick. This thing between us, whatever it is—is real. It might not have started that way, and it sure as fuck wasn't supposed to end up this way...but it's the truth."

Stupid, traitorous heart. "Start talking."

"Cain and I became friends during our senior year of high school."

I should stab him just for thinking I'm that dumb. "What I saw looked like way more than *friendship*."

He nods. "Yeah, it was." His voice drops. "For one of us."

I'm not sure what to make of the expression on his face. There's something breaking through the surface. Something I haven't seen from him before.

It catches me by the throat when it hits me.

Pain. The kind you can't fake. The kind I *know*.

"You love him."

"I did." He holds my gaze. "Not anymore, though. Not since he betrayed me."

I slide the knife back into my garter. His guard is down for the first time since I've known him, and it's compelling enough I'll risk the potential consequence.

"What happened?"

He closes his eyes, it's as if the memory was physically slashing right through him. "Cain fascinated me. Not because he had money or because he was popular. But because I felt something I hadn't felt with a single soul before him."

"What?"

He looks down at me. "A connection."

Something in my chest dislodges. As much as I want to hate him and judge him...I can't. Because I get it. We had a similar upbringing.

And when you spend your life being ignored by the person who's supposed to provide, love, and care for you...it leaves you with a gaping hole inside.

A hole you're equally desperate and petrified to fill. Because the fear of neglect is a living, breathing entity. It lingers in the shadows. Creeps its way into everything you do. It's your only constant companion.

It makes sense now why Damien asked me if I believed in ghosts.

Because that's exactly what it's like. You walk, talk, and breathe, but you never feel. People don't see you and you don't see them.

They become figurines made of glass. Stand-ins made of cardboard.

Touch is cold. Taste is bitter. Air is suffocating.

Because it's all you've ever known. It's what you've become accustomed to.

You wouldn't know *real* if it hit you upside the head with a steel bat because you've never felt anything tangible before.

How could you? You never learned how to form a simple, basic human connection.

Until one day, the impossible happens. Someone comes along, picks you up from the rubble, and dusts you off.

They look into your eyes...and they see you. They see you in a way no one else ever has. No one's ever tried to.

Suddenly, the world is different. Colors are vibrant. Sounds are clearer. Air is sweeter.

The dead thing in your chest starts to beat.

You're alive. For the very first time.

Not wanting to lose that, you hold on to them with everything you have. Hell, even some things you don't.

It doesn't matter. You're addicted. Obsessed. You need them like a heart needs a beat. You need them to function.

You'd do anything and risk everything for them. *Including your soul.*

Cain Carter was that person for me.

But in a strange twist of fate—it turns out he was Damien's person first.

And now here we are...trying to put the pieces together.

Damien's face goes slack. "I thought we were kindred spirits. He did fucked up things and had the same outlook I did. Only, unlike me—he hid it from others and wore a mask. But the only way you'd know was if you watched him closely enough. The way I did for months."

"You stalked him?"

"I did," he states matter-of-factly. "I was intrigued. I'd never met anyone like him before...like *me* before. Up until then, I was a lone wolf." His throat bobs on a swallow. "But the more I watched him, the more the feeling in my gut got worse."

"What kind of feeling?"

"Like he was a bomb about to detonate. The things he did...his aggression was like nothing I'd ever seen. Every day the kid seemed like he was battling an internal war. He was miserable."

"Because of all the abuse."

"Yeah. Seemed that way."

My heart contracts. "So what happened? Obviously, you guys became friends...and stuff."

"I inserted myself into his life. Katrina, the woman you met before, was Cain's high school sweetheart. I fucked her in the shop shed during lunch. Rumors were circulating and I knew he'd eventually stumble upon us...and stumble upon us he did. They broke up shortly after that."

"That's..." I'm at a loss for words.

There's not an ounce of regret on his face. "He didn't love her. She was just another prop in his life. He wasn't even upset." His brows knit together. "Soon after we became friends. I figured if I could help him alleviate some of the anger he had...he'd be better off."

"Alleviate his anger how?"

A small smile unfurls. "I think you know me well enough to answer that yourself."

"You fucked him."

"Not at that point. Wasn't really my thing. Wasn't against it—I just preferred a lot of pussy with a side of dick. I liked sharing. Specifically, watching the chick I was fucking, fuck someone else... while I fucked them. Part of it was the competition. The other part was sheer thrill and my own perversions."

"Okay, got it. You fucked the same girls together," I bite out.

I don't want to crucify him, but it doesn't mean I enjoy hearing about all the girls that came before me. Nerves bunch in my stomach as Katrina's words from earlier flash through my head.

"Did one of the girls die? Is that what Katrina meant?"

The groove in his forehead deepens. "Cain and I only shared one girl. A science teacher named Mrs. Miller. She...I can't really explain it. Kristy was special. Gorgeous and haunting at the same time. But I wasn't in love with her. There wasn't a connection, just a mutual respect for one another. She didn't judge me or try to change me, and I didn't judge or change her. But if I needed someone, I knew she'd be there. With no pretenses or bullshit. In a way, she was probably the closest thing to a mother I ever had."

My stomach rolls. "That's—"

"Disturbing? Yeah, probably. But neither of us cared. It was what it was. I had my own issues and she had hers. Our demons got along well together...until Cain's took over."

"What do you mean?"

"Things started off fun between the three of us. But then it took a turn. A dark one."

"How so?"

His nostrils flare on an indrawn breath. "Cain took it too far. He started hurting her during sex, and not in a good way. He stopped teasing her...stopped caring whether or not she got off. It was almost like he was taking all his anger out on her. At first, I thought he was doing it to validate his masculinity or some shit since we'd started messing around without her. But it was deeper than that."

His statement sits heavy on my chest. "Did you do anything to stop it?"

"I'm not the type of person to babysit others and make decisions for them. I don't like getting involved in people's personal shit. However, I reminded Kristy that she didn't have to do anything she didn't want to...and eventually, I stopped inviting her over altogether."

"You did the right thing."

Even though he didn't want to interfere, it's clear he was trying to protect her from Cain.

"Not really." There's a twinge of regret in his voice. "I wish I could say it was solely for her best interest, but my feelings for Cain were running rampant at that point. It was more than friendship.

More than romance. Hell, more than sex. I wanted to save him from himself. Pull him back from the edge." He averts his gaze. "I thought I was helping him, but all I ended up doing was creating a monster."

"Kind of like Frankenstein."

"Exactly." He props himself on his arms, hovering above me. "But he was *my* monster, Eden. I couldn't turn my back on him."

I touch his face. Damien needs to know Cain's issues aren't his fault. "Loving a monster doesn't make you one."

He turns away from my touch as though I've burned him, then raises one of his arms off the floor. The opening he's granting me implies this is my chance to go if I want.

But I don't. I want to stay right here on this floor with him.

I want him to continue bearing his soul to me…so I can find a way to make it better.

"You're not a monster," I whisper, bringing his arm back down. "Cain might be, but not you."

"Don't fool yourself, Eden. Cain's one level of evil, and I'm another," he rasps, his voice rough. "But you're not. You've never been. And that right there is the monumental difference between us. You're inherently good. But I'm not and neither is Cain."

We'll agree to disagree on that. I've been on the receiving end of both Damien's good and bad side. And while Damien might think he's a monster who's inherently bad…I know he's not.

He's more like a piranha. Scary and deadly? Absolutely.

But he doesn't strike…not unless he's provoked or he's hungry and you get too close.

Or when he's protecting someone he loves.

"For what it's worth, I don't judge you for killing his father and brother. I know you only did it because you thought it would—"

"I didn't kill them."

I swallow. "You didn't?"

It's not that I don't believe him, I'm just…incredibly confused.

There's a storm brewing in his eyes when he looks at me. "Don't get me wrong, I would have. Hell, I even told him how I would do it during a private moment he initiated...if you catch my drift." Anger tightens his features. "Unbeknownst to me, he recorded our conversation and blackmailed me with it. I thought I was getting through to him. I thought we were a *team*. But in the end, he was only seducing me and intentionally leading me on. It wasn't real...*none* of it was real. And he made sure to get rid of me the moment I no longer served a purpose in his life."

He bows his head. The muscles in his nape pull tight with tension. "I loved him...he was my *best friend*, Eden. I would have killed...hell, I would have died for him. But he discarded me like trash...just like my mom. He held a fucking gun up to my face and said my choices were jail, death, or leaving town. My heart wanted death, but my body chose self-preservation, so I left the country."

I blow out a heavy breath as my own heart cramps and twists for him. I knew Cain was fucked up. But this?

"I'm...Jesus. I don't know what to say." I place his hand on my chest, over the organ stinging with injustice. Sometimes there aren't any words to convey exactly what it is you feel, but I try anyway. "It's hurting for you. For what he did to you."

He rubs the spot with his thumb. "I didn't tell you any of this to cause you pain."

"I know." I skim his jaw and he leans into my touch. "But I want it."

Part of caring about someone is accepting their flaws and their pain. Carrying bits and pieces of it with you, so they don't have to bear all of it on their own.

"Eden..." I feel his entire body tense. It's torture for him... being this vulnerable. Being this close to another person after the way his mother treated him, and what Cain did to him.

But I'm not out to hurt Damien. I want to give him what he deserves.

A friend. A lover. Someone willing to take on some of his pain...not inflict any more.

"Damien," I whisper, lightly trailing a finger down his back. "It's okay to let someone in again. I won't hurt you."

They say the Devil was once an angel.

But no one ever bothered to ask the Devil what led to his downfall, or why he became so evil.

No one wants to hear his side of the story...because no one cares.

But I do.

Damien closes his eyes, still fighting it.

He doesn't want to be touched or cared for...even though he deserves it.

I can empathize because I didn't want him to bring me back to life, either...I didn't want to see the truth.

But I'm so grateful he showed me.

The day he contacted me on that app, pretending to be the man I loved...was the beginning of my metamorphosis.

It hurt like hell, but it was worth it in the end. Because now I'm wiser and stronger. I've got scars, but those scars give me tough skin.

All because Damien saw *me*. Not the Eden everyone else saw.

"You don't have to be a ghost anymore." I cup his cheek, forcing him to look at me. "I see you. I feel you. I—"

Snarling, he grabs my wrist. For a brief moment, I think my piranha is going to bite me.

But then it happens. His mouth finds mine and his arms wrap around me so tightly all the air in my lungs rushes out.

His kiss is turmoil and his body is a violent wave, sucking me under.

My insides swoop when he pulls back and looks at me in that way only he can before his mouth dips lower. His stubble prickles my skin as he sucks and bites the tender flesh of my neck.

I grip the back of his head. "More."

Tension in my core tightens when he pushes my dress up and tugs on the fabric of my bra, causing my breast to pop out. Shivers of desire race through me when his mouth descends and he pulls my nipple into his mouth, laving wet circles around the puckered bud before giving the other the same attention.

"Damien," I breathe, pulling off his jacket and then tugging open his shirt so I can feel his warm skin against mine.

His hands tangle in my hair as he maps kisses up my throat before finding my mouth again. His tongue is greedy, urgent.

"Need you inside me." I lift my hips, grinding against his bulge. I know he's trying to take his time and make sure it's good for me… but that's not what either of us really wants. It's not what he needs. "Fuck me."

I spread my thighs wider and his hands pull at my panties until they're nothing but torn scraps. I barely have time to catch my breath before his zipper is down and he's rooted inside me, driving as deep as he can before he stills himself.

"Eden." My name is a dark rumble. A warning of what's to come.

"I want it." I'm a glutton. I can drown in him and still it will never be enough. "I want everything."

A feral groan tears out of him as he starts to move. "Jesus."

I nip his earlobe. "That's not my name."

A small smirk unfurls as he picks up his pace, fucking me so hard against the carpet my back burns. I dig my heels into his ass, spurring him on.

Burn me. Bruise me. Mark me. Cut me.

I'm strong enough to endure it.

Clinging to his shoulders, I rock my hips against his as he pumps into me hard and fast. *So good.* Too fucking good.

My toes curl and I claw his back as I match his savage thrusts. I let out a sharp gasp, pulsing around his cock when he hits a spot so deep, pleasure spikes through me, triggering a full-blown orgasm.

I bite my lip, holding back a scream as the first ripple hits. Damien watches me intently, his hand clasping my jaw as I shake and tremble beneath him.

"Eden." The moan he lets out is guttural, coated in longing and agony as he shudders his own release.

We lay silent for a bit, his head buried in the crook of my neck while I trace lazy circles up his back.

As much as I wish I didn't have to interrupt this moment with him, I have to. A burning question is still lingering between us.

"Damien?"

His breathing picks up, like he already knows what I'm about to ask. "Yeah?"

"If you didn't kill them...who did?"

He doesn't answer right away. Instead, he pulls us into a sitting position, locking his hands around my waist.

"According to the police...Mrs. Miller did."

Why in the world would their teacher—who they were sleeping with— kill Cain's family?

"That doesn't make any sense."

"It doesn't," he agrees. "Part of that is my fault."

My mouth goes dry. "How?"

I watch his Adam's apple bob. "When Cain was called in for questioning, he told the detective—who's now Chief Trejo—that his twin brother Caleb and I were the ones involved with Mrs. Miller. He claimed she started the fire because she didn't want her husband to find out about the affair and Caleb was threatening to expose it."

"That's..." Bile rises up my throat. "Why would he do that?"

I'm not stupid, it's obvious Cain's lying in order to cover up something.

My intuition doesn't just whisper the truth. It slaps me in the face with it.

Oh. My. God.

"Before I get into it, I need to ask you something." He tips my chin. "After you saw us in the conference room, what was your first thought?"

I have no idea why he's asking me this when there are more pressing issues at play, but I answer him anyway. "Pain and betrayal...jealousy. I thought maybe you were both playing me. Then I thought maybe you were manipulating Cain and black-mailing him like he claimed. And then—"

"That's all I need to know," he interjects, cutting me off.

"Are you angry?"

He shakes his head. "No. Like I said earlier, I don't blame you." He sighs heavily. "But it also means I'm not the person you should be asking for the truth."

I raise an eyebrow, not understanding his logic. "You think Cain's just going to come clean about murdering his family?"

He shakes his head. "No. Probably not." His shoulder hitches. "But I want you to think for yourself and come to your own conclusions about what happened. I know what it's like when feelings get in the way...it makes it hard to see things objectively and separate the person you loved from the killer he really is."

He's right, but Cain killing the people who abused him isn't what has me tied up in knots.

It's the backstabbing, manipulating...the innocent people he hurt.

Because deep down inside...that's who Cain is. It's who he's always been.

I'm just finally seeing him without my rose-colored glasses.

Same goes for Damien.

"I believe you when you say you didn't kill them. I can even see Cain seducing you and then setting you up." And ugly feeling crawls up my gut. "The only thing that doesn't make sense to me... is why he pinned it on your teacher when he had the perfect fall guy already."

If Damien helped throw that teacher under the bus for murder in order to help Cain cover it up? Now is his time to come clean.

Because then I'll know for once and all what kind of person he is.

And how this might end for me.

Our gazes lock. "Did you help him set her up?"

My heart stops cold when he falls silent.

"Yeah," he says finally. "I did." He rubs the back of his neck. "Detective Trejo told me what Cain's version of events were when he brought me in for questioning. At the time, I didn't know Cain had secretly recorded me detailing how I would kill his family or that he'd end up blackmailing me with it." His voice is barely audible as he continues. "But I covered for him, I told Trejo it was Caleb and not Cain."

He stands up. "When Trejo said Kristy kept insisting it was Cain...I told him she was only saying that because Cain was alive, and Caleb wasn't. That it was easier for her defense to claim she was sleeping with the twin who still had a pulse."

Jesus. "Dam—"

"I know. Trust me, I know how wrong it was." He scrubs a hand down his face. "I won't ever deny my part in this. I also won't stand here and claim I'm innocent because I tried to throw Trejo off the scent by blaming the murder on her abusive husband...because it doesn't matter. Her piece of shit husband bailed her out of jail... and then she was gone."

He bows his head. "She was my friend. But she died...because I chose Cain." His voice is laced with so much guilt he's practically choking on it. "She was a good woman. A kind, innocent soul who didn't deserve the ending she got. But she's dead, because of *me*." His blue orbs hold mine and he punches his chest.

"And that's something I have to live with. Her death is on me."

"No, it's not," I tell him as I stand up.

I'm not diminishing the role Damien played in all this, but he's taking full responsibility for something that doesn't fall on him.

"Cain told Trejo it was Mrs. Miller, correct?"

He nods.

"And her husband killed her? You said he was abusive and bailed her out of jail, so I assum—"

"That's what they say happened." There's an edge to his tone.

"Look, you already know what you did was wrong. But the way I see it—if you take yourself out of the equation, it still would have happened. Even if Trejo didn't bring you in for questioning, she still would have been in jail because of Cain. And even if she wasn't in jail...it sounds like her husband was going to kill her sooner or later." I palm his cheek. "It's sad and tragic, and you're right—she didn't deserve to die. It sucks that she did.

You might not have saved her, Damien. But you didn't kill her either."

He starts to protest, but I hold up a hand. Damien's going to continue blaming himself no matter what, and we can work through that later. Right now, we have to come up with a plan before it's too late. The election's less than three days away.

Anger races over my skin. "We have to clear your name and take Cain down before he has you arrested for murders you didn't commit."

I don't want Damien to end up like his teacher turned ex-lover did. I don't want to see him in jail. Or worse, *dead*.

I'm not sure what to make of the expression on his face. "What do you suggest we do?"

"I can't tell if you're being sarcastic, or if you actually value my input."

There's a smug smile on his face as he buttons his shirt. "With the way you were going to gut me before, I'd say my little lamb has officially become the slaughterer and should probably take the lead on this one."

I give him a smile of my own. One that conveys how pissed off I am about what I walked in on. "It would do you well to remember that, King. Because the next time I see your dick in someone's mouth without *my* permission—"

"It was a power play. The second he started choking on it, I kicked him in the nuts and found you. I just wanted him to know there were no feelings left over for him on my end...except hatred."

Well, that certainly changes things. "Oh." My pulse quickens when his gaze falls to my torn panties on the floor and he takes a step closer. I have to remind myself to stay focused on the plan and not his sex eyes.

"I wish there was a way to get him to confess so we can record it." I chew my lip as the wheels in my head start turning. "Are we having the ball at the castle again?"

He slips on his jacket. "I can arrange that if you think it will help."

209

"Yes. Home turf is always best." I slide my heels on. "I know I can manipulate Cain, especially if I can get him alone...but not enough to confess to murder. Knowing him, he'll walk out the second he realizes it's a trap."

"What if you tie him up?"

I think about this for a moment. "I don't know. Cain's stubborn. I don't think he'll confess whether he's bound or not."

Plus, if we keep him there too long, people will start to wonder where he is.

Damien's voice jolts me out of my thoughts. "He might if you have proof of something he's done and can blackmail him with it."

"Will recording him having sex with me be enough?"

A muscle in his jaw clenches. "*No.* But someone else could work."

Jealousy flares in my chest. "You mean you—"

"Trejo," he says quickly. "Let's just say Cain and the chief are a little more than friends. I have some pictures of them on my office computer."

My mouth falls open. Although I don't know why I'm even surprised. There is literally nothing Cain won't do to get ahead.

"As far as blackmail goes, that's more than enough." I snap my fingers when it comes to me. "Okay, so here's what I'm thinking. Tomorrow during the charity dinner, I'll flirt with him as usual so he doesn't think anything weird is going on." I circle the room as I continue talking. "The day after that is the ball. I'm going to text him that morning and tell him I found some concerning things on your office computer, but I don't know how to remove them, and I'm afraid to try because I don't want you to hurt me. I'll avoid him for the first quarter of the ball, build up his anxiety...and then text him to meet me downstairs so I can take him to your office in the basement."

His lips compress in a tight line. "I don't want you alone with him."

"You have security cameras in your office, Damien. You can keep a close eye on me."

He grunts. "Fine, but it will be a *very* close eye."

"Then I suggest you close them when I strip off my ball gown and start seducing him."

He frowns. "I don't think——"

"The small couch in the corner of your office——think there's a way I can hide some restraints underneath it?"

"You don't have to."

I roll my eyes. "Look, I know you don't like it, but it's the only way to get him——"

"You don't have to hide restraints under the couch. They're already there."

"Oh." *Of course they are.*

"You're right though," he says, pulling me toward him. "I don't like it...which is why the second he's bound, I'll be coming in and taking over."

"Are you sure? Because I can black——"

"Cain won't break easily, Eden. It's going to require a certain skill set."

"You're going to beat him up?" I don't bother hiding the uneasiness in my tone. Cain deserves everything coming to him, but abusing him after knowing his history just feels...

"If you don't think you can handle it——"

"No." I look up at him. "I can."

"I'd torture him sexually, but not only does he disgust me, I think he'd enjoy it too much."

"Probably." I nod. "I think this plan will work."

Cain Carter isn't the man I thought he was.

And it's time he got a taste of his own medicine.

Chapter 35

EDEN

"*W*hich dress do you like better?"

Geoffrey looks at the ceiling. "You look great in both. Please pick one before you're late and Damien blames me for your tardiness."

I twist my hair up. "What should I do with my hair?"

I shouldn't enjoy ruffling his feathers so much, but he makes it too easy.

"It's lovely," he says tersely. "Now please, take off your clothes —" My eyes widen, and he catches himself. "My apologies, miss."

Geoffrey is way too polite for his own good. "You don't have to apologize."

I look up at the same time Damien enters the room. I expect him to join our little convo, but he hangs in the background, observing the exchange.

It's a good thing Geoffrey's back is to him because he'd probably shit his pants.

I decide to have a little fun. Damien can consider it payback for yesterday.

"On second thought. I hate this dress. Let's go with the dark blue one."

Geoffrey's lips form a tight line. "Of course."

I bat my lashes. "Would you mind helping me out? The zipper on this one is tricky. It always gets stuck right above my butt."

Damien's eyes darken...but there's also a hint of a challenge burning in those baby blues.

One I won't back down from.

Geoffrey's throat bobs as I turn around. "As you wish."

His fingers shake as he clasps the zipper. I bite my lip. He's positively adorable.

"Do you ever go out and date?"

He freezes. "Damien grants me rest hours and permission to leave the grounds."

That was the most proper response to a casual question I've ever heard.

He finishes dragging my zipper down. "May I ask what your sudden interest in my personal life is?"

I slip my arms through the holes and face him. "Just wanted to make sure you were allowed to have fun."

"Well, thank you for your concern but—Oh, my."

Geoffrey turns ten different shades of red as he zeroes in on my bare breasts.

Damien crosses his arms over his chest, and I flash him a smile. Geoffrey doesn't notice the exchange though because his eyes are still focused elsewhere.

"Gorgeous," Geoffrey whispers under his breath. "So perk—"

Behind him, Damien clears his throat.

Geoffrey bolts upright. "My apologies, sir. It shan't happen again."

Before I can blink, he sprints out the door like his ass is on fire.

"Cute," Damien muses as I slip the dress back on. "However, your little stunt almost gave my servant a heart attack."

"He works hard." I motion for him to help me with the zipper. "Just wanted to make sure the poor guy didn't go through life without ever seeing a pair of tits."

My zipper goes up with ease. "Geoffrey's been living with me for years. He's seen plenty. Trust me."

Touché, Mr. King.

"Is that so?"

Pushing my hair out of the way, he kisses my shoulder. "Someone sounds jealous." His teeth sink into my skin. "I told you, if you want something…claim it."

I run my hand over his length through his pants. "I already have." My nipples pucker when it thickens under my touch. "But I might be willing to share this part…on special occasions."

"You don't have to do or share anything you don't want to, Eden."

"I know. But I won't *know* I don't want to do something until I try it." The green-eyed monster rears its head again when I think about the maid. "I can't watch another woman fuck you, though. Hard limit. However, she'd be welcome to watch me fuck you."

His breath tickles my ear. "Can I watch her pleasure the queen after?" His palm slides over my breast. "Demonstrate her gratitude for the sexy show you gave her?"

I suck in a breath. Damien has a way of making everything sound appealing. "That might be fun."

His hand slithers down my torso. "It doesn't have to happen. Just talking about it with you makes my dick hard."

I start to smile…but then a horrifying thought hits me.

"What if I hate something you like? What happens then?"

It's no secret Damien's light years ahead of me when it comes to…well, pretty much everything. He's also not turned off by anything. All of it gets a green light from him…while I'm still exploring what I'm into.

"We don't do it." His fingers dip into the band of my panties. "My sexuality doesn't own or control me. I own and control *it*. If the person I want to fuck isn't into something, we switch gears and go a different route. This way, we both have fun and get off."

"I don't want you to feel like you're missing out if I ever draw a line in the sand."

If we're gonna do this, I need to know I'll be enough to satisfy him.

My eyes flutter closed when he rubs my clit. "How can I be missing out when I have this?" He kneads my ass with his other hand. "And this." He sticks the finger he was touching me with in my mouth, making me taste myself. "This is nice, too."

"If we keep this up, we're gonna miss dinner," I remind him when he squeezes my breast.

"I don't give a fuck," he growls. "I'd much rather eat you."

"As soon as we get home, you can." I pat his dick. "Good boys get rewarded."

With a grin, he tugs down his zipper. "I've never been a good boy." My pulse skitters as he bends me over the dresser and guides the wide head of his cock through my slickness. "It's way more fun being bad."

~

Cain: Sit next to me during dinner.

I knew the evening would suck the moment I received the text from Cain. So did Damien.

And suck it does. Being anywhere near Cain makes my skin crawl.

It's a complete one-eighty from almost two weeks ago…when he was my everything and the highlight of my day was spending time with him.

Shame coils my insides. There's a very small part of me—way deep down—that misses Cain. I'm having a hard time digesting it though because I also fucking hate him. So much so, there's a distinct possibility I'm going to stab his eye with my fork if he touches my knee again.

Deep breaths, sister. You've got this.

Damien said it's normal for me to be experiencing an array of emotions at this stage. He compared it to grieving, because even though Cain is very much alive—I still lost someone I loved.

In a weird way, it makes sense.

Luckily, I only have to play the part of his mistress for another twenty-four hours.

I've purposely avoided drinking any liquids during this dinner so I won't have to run to the bathroom.

Although it might be preferable to hearing Margaret drone on and on about her upcoming wedding.

Pick a topic. Any topic, gentlemen.

Unfortunately, what they all want to talk about is politics, but that's considered poor form at a charity dinner. Especially with the heads of two opposing parties at the same table.

"So, I was thinking we can hold the cocktail hour—"

"What's your opinion on the new legislation that's being proposed?"

Rules were made to be broken.

Eight sets of eyes wake from the dead.

"Which one?" Governor Bexley asks.

I have no idea. "The one regarding taxes."

It's America. Taxes are a big deal to these big wigs.

Margaret huffs out a breath. "It's uncouth to talk about politics at a charity dinner, dear," she says slowly in a condescending tone that grates on my nerves. "Particularly when you're sitting at a table full of politicians."

Everyone but Damien chuckles.

I stab my potato with my fork. "My mistake. I just wanted to *liven* the conversation up a bit."

To the left of me, Anderson coughs, although I'm almost positive it was a laugh in disguise.

Across from me, Margaret tsks, looking around the table. "See, gentlemen? This is a perfect example of why teenagers shouldn't be permitted to attend adult functions." Her stare snags on Damien. "Grown men should find someone their *own* age to play with."

Shots fired.

The governor takes a big swig of his drink. Cain pretends to answer an email on his phone.

Damien narrows his eyes. Anderson starts to sweat.

The other men at the table look down at their plates. *Smart move.*

This lady chose the wrong night to mess with me.

I daintily clean my mouth with my napkin. "You're right, Margaret. I should have asked my daddy's permission before joining you all for a meal." I turn my head to the right, feigning surprise. "Wow, would you look at that? Here he is."

Cain looks like a deer caught in headlights.

Damien was right, it's fun to fuck with people. Especially those who deserve to be fucked with.

"Daddy, my new step-mommy says I can't sit at the big kids' table." I bite my lip innocently and do the sexy, breathy thing with my voice. "But we both know I'm a big girl now, right?"

To the left of me, Damien snorts.

"Okay," Cain warns. "You've made your point."

Margaret's positively fuming. "You're despicable."

"And you're *boring*," Damien bellows. "Something Eden isn't... no matter her age."

My chest swells, but then Margaret opens that trap of hers again.

"Yes, I'm sure she's very entertaining...especially when she's spreading her legs for all the men in Black Hallows."

Here we go again.

"Not *all* the men in Black Hallows." I crinkle my nose. "Just two."

"That's *enough*," Cain hisses.

Something peculiar passes through Margaret's expression. I see the exact moment it hits her.

Those are the very same words Cain said to me when I walked in on them...and he claimed he had no idea who I was.

She blinks rapidly, and for a second, I think she's going to excuse herself so she can cry.

To be honest, I kind of want her to...but not so I can gloat.

I want to tell her she's better off without him. I want to tell her not to marry someone who lies and manipulates. That she shouldn't spend the rest of her life with a man who commits murder and then sets up innocent people to take the fall.

There are better men out there than Cain Carter.

But even if there weren't…she'd *still* deserve better.

Margaret lifts her head and looks at me. "It's a shame your mother didn't teach you how to be a respectable woman with class."

That might be true. But I'd rather be known as the classless town whore…than a miserable bitch who slut shames another woman.

Screw her. I'm a person, not a martyr. She can fend for herself.

"That's quite enough, ladies," Governor Bexley says. "This little feud has gone on long enough. You two are going to have to learn to get along for the duration of the race."

"He's right." I take a bite of my carrot. "I love your dress."

She gives me a tight smile. "Thank you."

"It reminds me of one Claudia has."

Chapter 36

EDEN

"**S**o fucking good," Damien rasps from his spot between my legs.

I'd agree, but I'm too far gone to speak. Hell, I can't even move because the thing he's doing with his tongue currently is...not of this world.

My legs shake as Damien continues devouring me like he's been trapped in the desert and my pussy is the first drop of water he's stumbled upon in years.

His talented tongue pushes against a spot that lights me up like the Fourth of July and I grip the edges of the couch.

"I'm so close," I breathe, writhing against his face. "God, I'm so—"

"They want to know if they can move the—" Geoffrey starts to say before he turns pale, then pink, and finally, vibrant red, in under three seconds.

"My sincerest apologies." He looks down. "I thought you were in here working. I won't disturb you again."

I fix my panties, covering myself as Damien, who looks like he wants to throttle poor Geoffrey, whips his head around to face him.

"What do you want?" he grunts as Geoffrey skedaddles to the door.

He freezes. "The party people are here to set up for the ball tomorrow night. They wanted to know if they could remove all the furniture from the living room again. They said you were angry with them for doing it last time, so they wanted me to get your permission."

Damien sighs, clearly irritated. "I don't care."

"Very well." Eyes still to the floor, he turns to face us. "My apologies again, sir." He bows. "And miss."

As usual, Geoffrey has nothing to apologize for. It's not like Damien's office door doesn't have a lock. We just forgot to use it.

For the briefest of moments, the hardness in Damien's expression eases up a bit. "It's fine, Geoffrey."

Geoffrey practically beams. It's endearing how he holds Damien in such high regard.

And it goes both ways because even though Geoffrey's petrified of him, I've never once heard Damien threaten to fire or hurt him.

"Have you ever…you know?" I ask Damien as Geoffrey walks out of the office.

"Are you asking me if I've ever messed around with my servant?"

I nod.

His lips twitch. "I've let him partake in my extracurricular activities once or twice."

I'm not mad. If anything, I'm intrigued.

"Call him back." Leaning in, I whisper, "I want to know what it's like."

I won't know if I'm into something or not until I experience it. And as nervous as I am, I can't deny my curiosity.

"Geoffrey," Damien barks. "Get back in here."

I crack a smile as I hear Geoffrey's footsteps speed up. He sounds like a horse galloping toward the finish line.

"Yes, sir," he says out of breath as he enters.

Damien stands. "Lock the door."

Geoffrey's Adam's apple bobs as he does what Damien asked.

The energy in the room shifts the second the latch clicks. It's a little darker...forbidden.

My heart speeds up.

Damien crooks a finger at him. "Come here."

Geoffrey's legs shake a little as he walks closer to us.

Feeling hesitant, I look at Damien. I don't want Geoffrey to feel like he's being forced to do something he doesn't want to do, but Damien only smirks.

"He's fine, Eden." He starts circling Geoffrey like a vulture. "Aren't you?"

"Absolutely, sir."

Damien's movements come to a halt behind him. "You saw Eden's tits earlier. I'm curious what you think about them." Geoffrey blows out a breath as Damien reaches around and walks his fingers down the front of the younger man's jacket, stopping when he reaches the top of his pants. "And you better tell me the truth." He tugs his zipper down. "Because I'll know if you're lying."

Geoffrey's ears turn pink. "They're beautiful."

My temperature creeps up a few notches when I notice the outline of Geoffrey's dick getting thicker.

"Would you like to see them again?"

"Very much so."

Damien's gaze locks with mine. "Lower your nightgown, Eden. Show Geoffrey your beautiful tits."

Sitting up, I lower the straps of my black lacy nightie. My nipples pucker as their gazes drop to my chest, lust darkening both their expressions.

"They taste incredible," Damien rasps in his ear as he undoes the button of Geoffrey's slacks. "Every part of her does."

My thighs clench, and I swear Geoffrey whimpers as his cock springs free and his pants hit the floor.

He's not as long or thick as Damien is, but he's not too shabby either. He's definitely packing under that uniform he wears.

A strangled gasp erupts as Damien wraps his fist around Geoffrey's length, giving it one long stroke from base to tip. "Just so we're clear." His gaze lingers on me. "My cock is the only one allowed inside her cunt. It's *mine*. Cross me and—"

"I wouldn't dream of it, sir," Geoffrey utters. The reverence he has for Damien is practically bursting from his chest. "I understand the boundaries."

My heart swells. Not only for how respectful Geoffrey is but from hearing Damien's limit.

I feel the same way he does. I'm down to have fun and explore, but there are certain things I'd like to reserve for just the two of us.

Damien nips his earlobe. "Perhaps I should reward your obedience and let you taste Eden's pussy."

Geoffrey's hands clench at his sides as his chest rises and falls. "Please, sir."

Damien tilts Geoffrey's chin toward him. "Have a taste."

My pulse explodes when Damien opens his mouth and Geoffrey licks his tongue.

It's one of the hottest things I've ever witnessed.

"Oh, sweet mercy that's good," Geoffrey breathes, going back for more.

"Goddamn right it is," Damien grinds out, catching Geoffrey's bottom lip with his teeth. "You want more of my Eden?"

"Please," Geoffrey whispers.

"Then beg me," Damien growls, undoing his belt. "With your mouth."

My breath catches when Geoffrey drops to his knees. "As you wish."

I lean back and watch them, my insides tingling. A rush of heat flits through me when Damien yanks down the waistband of his boxers and his thick cock slaps against his stomach, hard and demanding. Geoffrey wastes no time shoving as much as he can into his mouth.

Damien's hooded eyes find mine as his hand wraps around Geoffrey's neck, forcing him to swallow until the tip of his nose brushes against the short, dark hairs at the base.

Jesus Christ. It's so hot.

I run my fingers down the length of my body as Geoffrey's cheeks hollow out and his head begins bobbing up and down, sucking Damien's dick with such vigor, *I'm* liable to come soon.

Groaning, Damien rasps, "Pull down those panties. Show me how much you enjoy this."

I do one better. I peel both my nightgown and panties off, then part my thighs a fraction, giving him a little peek.

"Christ," Damien grunts, his gaze smoldering. "Look at Eden teasing me with her pretty pussy."

Geoffrey angles his head slightly and his eyes widen.

"Suck me harder," Damien demands.

His servant takes him deeper, giving it everything he's got.

My breathing escalates as Damien threads a hand through Geoffrey's hair, pulling the short, blond strands taut through his fingers. "Good boy."

Slurping and gagging sounds fill the space between us as Geoffrey's movements accelerate. Damien's muscles draw tight, his mouth parting with a groan as Geoffrey tugs on his balls before tonguing those, too.

"That's enough. I need to save some for Eden."

I slide a finger down my center. *Yes, save some for me.*

Geoffrey releases him with a wet pop and looks my way, his breath catching. "She's so beautiful."

Well, shit. Damien better up his game because Geoffrey is sweeter than candy.

Damien holds my gaze. "I know." A slow smile unfurls as he closes his fist around his dick and gives himself a slow stroke. "She's even more beautiful when she comes all over my cock."

"May I have my taste now, sir?" Geoffrey asks, looking up at him for approval.

He nods, despite the flicker of jealousy I see in his expression.

My blood quickens as Geoffrey crawls over and kneels down in front of me, peppering kisses up and down my slit, like the perfect gentleman he is. I run my fingers over his scalp, encouraging him as Damien watches us, his eyes burning like hot coals.

"Show me her gorgeous cunt."

I moan when Geoffrey spreads me with his thumbs and dips his tongue inside my pussy. He's so delicate and tender, a stark contrast to the savage way Damien devours me.

"More," I urge as Damien stalks toward us. "I need more."

His tall form towers over me as he leans down for a kiss, then grips Geoffrey's nape, shoving his mouth into my wetness.

My toes curl as Geoffrey cranks it up several notches and I mewl against Damien's lips before I kiss down his neck, licking the flames of his skull tattoo.

His throat bobs against my tongue. "Eden."

I love the way he says my name. Like it's a prayer and an answer all at once.

His hands slide under my ass, lifting me, then before I can catch my next breath, he shoves Geoffrey aside and pushes inside me, filling me to the hilt before slamming me back down on the couch, pinning my legs to my chest.

Geoffrey, saint that he is, shifts his position and goes to town pleasuring us both, licking and suckling with every thrust. A groan lodges in my vocal cords as I wrap my arm around Damien's neck, holding on for dear life.

"Don't stop," I croak as Damien drives into me faster, hitting all the right spots.

Geoffrey, the trooper, stays with us, his mouth doing delicious things as Damien fucks me so good my entire body vibrates.

"I'm so close," I tell them as pressure builds higher and higher between my legs, turning them to jello. Geoffrey reaches between us and rubs my clit as Damien hammers my pussy, giving it to me just how I like it. The sensation that rips through me is nearly blinding as they wrench my orgasm from me.

"That's it. Milk this cock, Eden. Keep squeezing your tight little pussy," Damien roars, his dick swelling inside me as he pumps frantically. "Now take my cum like a good girl."

I drag my nails up his back, clenching around him as he utters a long, deep groan and his hot cum fills me.

Sated, I fall back against the couch, my eyes fluttering closed.

Liquid spills out of me, trickling down my skin, as a warm hand latches onto my knee, spreading me wider.

"Clean her," Damien instructs, taking a step back.

I mewl and writhe as Geoffrey's face disappears between my legs and he gently laps up Damien's climax and mine.

"That feels amazing," I tell him as he continues massaging me with his tongue, murmuring compliments every so often.

The guy is too selfless for words.

Damien holds his still semi-hard dick out to Geoffrey when he's finished with me, and Geoffrey goes to work cleaning him next, eagerly laving Damien's glistening shaft before slurping up the left-over cum on his balls.

My eyes cut to Damien. "He's been such a good boy."

"A very good boy." He flashes me a quick, evil grin. "We should reward him."

"Your turn," I tell Geoffrey as I slide off the couch and sink to my haunches.

Damien joins me on the floor a moment later and ties Geoffrey's hands with a stretchy band.

When I give him a look, he says, "Don't worry, he likes it. Don't you, Geoffrey?"

"It's wonderful," Geoffrey replies, his dick twitching as pre-cum leaks onto his stomach.

Lowering my head, I scoop it up with my tongue.

Geoffrey hisses. "Oh, mercy."

Feeling naughty, I close my mouth over his tip, sucking it in short, hard pulls.

He trembles. "That's spectacular."

Opening wider, I run my tongue along his length, sweeping over the pulsing veins and ridges. I jolt in surprise when Damien leans in and his tongue brushes mine.

Geoffrey loses his shit as we proceed to work him in tandem. "Fuck me. That's incredible."

Damien gives me a wink before he sucks him down in one languid pull, causing Geoffrey to cry out his name and then mine as I tease his testicles.

Damien's eyes gleam. "Want to cum on Eden's tits?"

Geoffrey's entire body convulses, his lips parting with a husky groan. "Please."

I quickly get into position as Damien begins to jerk him hard and fast.

"Shit," Geoffrey shouts as his cum jets out in quick, short spurts all over my breasts.

Damien holds the bit that got on his hand out to me. I suck his fingers as his lips trail down my neck, his teeth biting at my skin before he licks Geoffrey's release off my nipples then works his way back up to my mouth.

"Did you have fun?"

"So much fun."

"Good," he murmurs, his tongue slashing mine. "Now bend over and spread your pussy so I can finish what I started earlier."

Chapter 37

EDEN

I draw air into my lungs as quickly as I can while Geoffrey helps me with my dress.

My anxiety is creeping in, but I don't want to bother Damien.

Or rather, I don't want him to think I can't follow through with my part of the plan.

I can and I *will*.

I just need a moment to collect myself and put my game face on.

"I know you're nervous, but you look magnificent," he says, zipping up my dress. Although *dress* is a bit of an understatement.

It's a gold, full-length, off-the-shoulder gown made of satin. One I picked out on my own when I went shopping this morning.

Geoffrey hands me a box with a gold bow on it and smiles. "You'll be the belle of the ball."

I don't think so, considering I'll be seducing my stepfather into confessing to murders he committed and is blackmailing Damien with.

I look down at my opal ring. Damien told me opal was good luck, and I'm counting on it. I need all the luck I can get tonight.

My gaze shifts to the elegant box. It's almost too pretty to open.

"Do you know what's inside?"

Geoffrey shrugs. "Damien said to give it to you."

He leaves the room shortly after and I untie the ribbon before removing the top.

A shiver runs down my spine when I read the note on top of the tissue paper.

There's a reason for all the bad things we go through.

Something that makes us realize the pain was worth it in the end.

I found mine.

I hope like hell you find yours one day, Eden.

I already have.

Lifting a finger, I wipe a tear out of the corner of my eye then take out the tissue paper.

Inside the box is a beautiful gold mask.

Geoffrey peeks his head back inside my door as I finish putting it on. "Damien's waiting for you."

My heart beats out of my chest as I walk down the hallway and see him standing at the top of the other spiral staircase.

He looks striking in his tux, despite the black mask covering his gorgeous face.

I give him a smile, but he doesn't return it.

Instead, he stares at me for what feels like an eternity before he speaks. "You're breathtaking."

"So are you." I lift up the bottom of my dress with one hand and hold the railing with the other so I don't fall. "Meet you at the bottom?"

Our eyes lock as we walk down our opposing staircases. An eerie feeling catches me by the throat when I think about the last ball… and how much my life has changed in the short time since.

Damien holds out his arm for me when we reach the bottom. "Ready?"

"Yea—" A camera flashes, taking me by surprise.

"Wow, such a great shot. Can we use this for the local paper?" some woman asks.

"Sure." I link my arm through Damien's. "Let's do this."

Chapter 38

EDEN

Cain: I need to see you.

I dip out from the pillar I'm hiding behind. Cain's standing next to Margaret on the outskirts of the dance floor, looking agitated as his fingers frantically move across his phone screen.

Eden: I'm wearing a gold dress.
Cain: I don't give a fuck what color your dress is. You have to destroy those computer files.

Rolling my eyes. I type my response.

Eden: I have no idea how to do that. I'll meet you in a little while when Damien's preoccupied and take you to his office so you can do it yourself. I don't want to accidentally screw anything up. It's too risky.
Cain: Fine.

After tucking my phone away, I join the party.

Damien—who's ditched his mask—is talking to whom I presume must be Anderson due to the beads of sweat dotting the man's forehead as I walk over to them.

"Having fun?"

Damien's lips turn down in a frown. "Not particularly. You?"

"No. My phone keeps going off every few seconds."

He smirks.

Anderson clears his throat. "Sorry to interrupt, but like I was saying, Damien. You can't—"

Damien ignores him. "Dance with me."

It's not a question.

My mouth goes dry. Not only do I not dance, nor have I *ever* slow danced with someone. There are no other couples on the dance floor currently, which means we'll be drawing attention to ourselves.

I might have a mask on, but I'm almost positive half the people in the room have already figured out who I am.

Not waiting for a response, Damien seizes my hand and starts walking.

"Take off your mask," he says when we reach the dance floor.

Now he's pushing it.

"Then everyone will know who I am," I grit through my teeth, hoping he can take the hint.

"Good." His hands find my waist. "You don't belong under a mask, Eden."

Feeling a little braver, I oblige him.

"Everyone's staring at us," I whisper as the lights dim and the song changes.

He presses his body against mine. "Let them."

I fold my arms around his neck as we begin swaying to the music. "Thank you."

"For what?"

Reminding me I'm no longer that girl.

"Being you." I inhale his scent. "You're the best thing that's ever happened to me."

It's not a lie. I don't know how I'll ever be able to repay him for everything he's done for me.

Everything he's taught me.

His body tenses and he holds me a little closer. "Did I mention how beautiful you look yet?"

I can't help but smile. "When you saw me on the staircase, remember?"

"I do." He turns us around. "And I'm an idiot for not telling you at least a hundred more times between then and now."

My heart flutters. *Who knew Damien King could be such a smooth talker?*

My cheeks heat. "You—"

"I wasn't finished," he murmurs, his lips tickling my ear. "Beauty is only the outside layer of a person, but you're more than that. And if someone tries to make you feel inferior, it's only because you intimidate them. Because they see the same thing I do when they look at you." His blue eyes blaze. "You shine so bright you put the entire galaxy to shame, Eden." All the air gets sucked out of the room when he stops dancing and cups my face. "And don't you *ever* fucking forget it."

The organ in my chest thumps. "Wow, I think I just swooned a little."

"I mean it." His voice takes on a serious tone. "I want you to keep holding your head high wherever you go. And if someone gives you hell, you make them eat shit. Got it?"

I look for signs of humor in his expression, but there aren't any.

A sinking sensation fills my gut. "Damien, what's wr—"

"Nothing." He pulls me close again. "I just wanted you to know how special you are."

No. It's more than that. He's been acting off all day. At first, I thought maybe it was the events that took place last night, but this feels more significant.

He's talking like he's never going to see me again...

"Look at me." When he does, I say, "We've got this. The plan is going to work."

233

"Yeah." He flashes me some dimple. "It will."

The song ends and he pulls out his phone. "I hate to cut this short, but I have to make a call."

He stalks off before I can say another word.

"It should be a crime to leave a pretty girl by herself on the dance floor."

My stomach rolls at the sound of Governor Bexley's voice.

"It's fine. I needed to powder my nose anyway."

I start to walk off, but he catches my elbow. "Humor an old man and give him a dance?"

I'm about to decline because I don't want to be anywhere near him, but then he says, "It will be worth your while."

I'm fairly certain nothing he says will be *worth* anything, but I relent anyway. Mostly because other couples are filling up the dance floor now, and it would be rude of me to dis him publicly.

Plus, there's the bonus of pissing Margaret off. Something I know I'm achieving when I spot her glaring at us as I take his hand.

"So, to what do I owe this honor?" I ask him as another slow song cues up.

He places his hand on the middle of my back as we begin moving. "Trust me, the honor is all mine."

Considering the man has been nothing but rude to me, I highly doubt it.

I'm about to ask him to cut to the chase and tell me what the point of this is, but then he says, "Damien King isn't going to win tomorrow."

Damien was never interested in winning anyway. That's not what any of this was about for him. However, I don't care for the governor's condescending tone.

"Wasn't aware our great governor was also a psychic." I give him a sardonic smile. "Last I checked, polling day doesn't end until tomorrow night...after they tally all the votes."

I cringe when he presses me a little too close. "You're right. But I have it on good authority that Damien won't be around when they do."

My stomach drops. "What—"

His hold on me tightens. "I have a once in a lifetime offer for you and I suggest you take it." Not waiting for me to turn it down, he continues, "You're going to end things with Damien *tonight*. Cain and Margaret will take you in and help put you back together. And after you embrace them as your family and apologize for the disrespect you've shown my daughter, you will be allowed to attend a college of your choice and move on with your life. If you don't, you can look forward to spending your days locked inside a padded room at the Shady Oaks mental institution."

I start to laugh, but his hand dips lower, skimming my behind. "If neither of those choices appeals to you, you can always live with me." His lips hover over my ear. "Cain told me that pretty mouth of yours does lovely things with a cock stuffed inside it, and I'd be lying if I said I haven't been dying to find out for myself."

Disgust and rage zip through me like a live wire and I twist out of his grip. "How's this for an offer? Go fuck yourself."

My voice is loud enough the woman dancing nearby gasps.

Bexley laughs nervously. "Stop being dramatic and making a scene, dear." His eyes narrow. "We haven't finished our dance yet."

He reaches for me, but I back away. "I don't dance with pigs. I don't make deals with them either."

With that, I stride off the dancefloor and take out my phone.

Eden: Meet me at the staircase near the atrium.
Cain: I'm in the cigar room with Johnson, Judge Kennedy, and your fiancé. Give me a few minutes to make a clean getaway.

"Why the fuck does he keep his office in the basement?" Cain questions as I lead him down the dark, narrow hallway.

"I have no idea."

It's on the tip of my tongue to rip into him about what the governor said, but there's no point.

Knowing Cain—he'll either deny it or defend his precious governor and suggest that Bexley only said it because he has a reputation to uphold and I'm making waves.

I don't even know why I'm wasting my energy being pissed off about it anyway. *Cain's not the man I thought he was.*

Nothing he says or does should shock me anymore.

I turn on a light when we enter Damien's office and point to the computer. "It's password protected, but I figured it out."

I didn't. Damien gave it to me so Cain still thinks I'm on his side.

I turn my head to look at him when he doesn't say anything. "You okay?"

His eyes are glued to the gigantic fish tank behind Damien's desk.

There's a hint of amusement in his expression when he finally speaks. "I think that's my piranha." He snorts. "Given there are other fish in the tank, he must not have eaten yet."

"He ate the other night." I gesture to the small leather sofa. "I remember because Damien fucked me right there after."

If my seduction doesn't tempt him, his need to compete with Damien will.

His eyes become tiny slits. "What's the password?"

"Cainisacocksucker1829," I deadpan.

"Goddamn prick," he says under his breath as he marches toward the desk and sits down.

I take the pin out of my hair and reach behind me for the zipper of my dress.

Cain's eyes widen and his face goes slack…but it has nothing to do with me.

It's due to the picture of him with the chief's cock in his mouth.

"This isn't me." He swallows hard. "Fucking idiot can't even manage to use Photoshop correctly. These are *obviously* doctored. Trejo spilled his drink during our meeting, and I was on my knees cleaning the floor."

It actually hurts not to laugh. Unless Cain—who's never so much as put a dish in the sink since I've known him—wanted to be *really* thorough about missing any spots, his little explanation still doesn't account for why he's sucking down the chief's dick like a popsicle.

He sticks what looks like a USB drive into the port. "Just in case anyone is dumb enough to believe that was real, I've not only deleted the file but infected his computer with a virus. Problem solved."

He stands at the same time my dress hits the floor.

"You know, it's a shame it's not real," I say, stepping out of it. "It kind of turned me on."

He crosses his arms over his chest. "The idea of me with a man turned you on? What the hell is wrong with you?"

Trailing a manicured fingernail down my black and gold bra, I bite my lip. "I don't know. It just looked so…forbidden and naughty."

He rakes his gaze up and down my lingerie-clad body, zeroing in on my panties. "Is that so?"

I nod. "You can't deny there's something sexy about doing something…or someone you shouldn't. Maybe it's why we're both so attracted to one another."

"What I feel for you goes beyond attraction. I love you. Always have. Always will."

What Cain loves is the idea of controlling someone who genuinely loves *him* and making them his personal puppet.

Because he knows when love sinks its teeth into someone, it never really lets them go.

It always leaves behind a scar.

I undo the front clasp of my bra, bearing my tits to him.

"I know you love me." His eyes darken as I lick my finger and circle a puckered nipple. "But you can't deny there's also something so tantalizing about forbidden fruit." I drift my gaze to the couch. "Taking something that doesn't belong to you."

The vein in his forehead bulges as he comes out from behind

Damien's desk. "You don't belong to him, Eden. You belong to *me*, goddammit."

"Are you sure about that?" I finger my lacy underwear. "Because I think I might need a reminder."

He's standing in front of me in four strides. "I'll fucking remind you, all right."

I gasp when he plucks the crotch of my panties and plunges a finger inside me.

"Cai—"

He grabs the back of my head and crushes his mouth against mine.

Revulsion works its way up my esophagus, and I have to remind myself to focus on the plan.

"I've missed you so much," I say between kisses.

"I've missed you more." He nibbles my bottom lip. "Have you been a good girl for me?"

Placing my hand on top of his, I grind against his fingers. "The best girl *ever*."

He makes a low noise in his throat as he adds another finger. "Cain should probably reward you then, huh?"

If I keep playing my cards right, Cain most definitely will.

I suckle his earlobe. "Please. I've been so, *so* good."

"Prove it." He tugs down his zipper with his free hand. "Get on your knees."

"Get on the couch." I run my hand over his thickening erection. "I want to suck you off where Damien fucked me."

His face contorts in anger then lust as I remove his fingers from my pussy and lick them before leading him to the sofa.

The moment he sits, I straddle his lap, writhing against his cock. "I love you."

His thumb brushes my cheekbone before making its way down the length of my body. "I love you, too." He pulls his dick out and strokes it. "Now be a good girl and take care of me."

With a coy smile, I sink to my knees. "I'm gonna take care of you so good." Swallowing my disgust, I lap the liquid off his crown.

"I want to savor this fat cock of yours." I lick the pulsing vein as I fish underneath the couch for the handcuffs and rope. "But first, can I try something fun?"

He starts to answer, but I stretch my mouth over his tip, and he hisses. "What's that?"

Pushing his legs together, I suck him down a little farther and tie his ankles together the way Damien taught me to this morning.

"What are you doing?"

He begins to move, but I get on top of him again. "Relax." Leaning in, I kiss his bottom lip. "I just want to see you at my mercy while I drain every drop of cum from your dick with my mouth and cunt."

"Jesus." He grunts when I nip his throat. "Deal. But just my ankles."

I hold up the handcuffs. "But it's more fun this way."

"Eden—" I shove my tits in his face and he sucks my nipple. "Fuck, you're such a bad little girl. Aren't you?"

"No," I say, edging away a bit so he has no choice but to lean forward. "I'm *always* a good girl for daddy."

A strangled groan lodges in his throat. "Christ." He places his arms behind his back. "You better fuck daddy *real* good."

I hold his gaze as I lock the cuffs on his wrists. Damien isn't in the room yet, but my gut tells me he's close.

I kiss Cain's cheek hard enough to leave a mark with my red lipstick. It might not be permanent like the one he left on me, but it will still sting when he goes to wipe it off in his jail cell. "Don't worry. I'm gonna fuck you so good—"

"I'll take it from here," Damien's deep voice calls out from behind me.

Chapter 39

DAMIEN

*T*he look on Cain's face when I walk in and Eden gets off his lap is priceless.

I snap a picture with my phone and smile. "Are you enjoying the party, Cain?"

"What the fuck," he grunts, rocking back and forth in an effort to get off the couch.

I look over at Eden. "You okay?"

She nods as she fixes her bra. "Thanks for coming to the rescue when you did. A minute later and I might have puked." She looks at her ball gown on the ground and frowns. "Think Geoffrey will freak if I ask him to come down here and help me get back into my dress?"

After it dawns on him that I'm planning on torturing and killing my opponent? *Probably.*

I pull off my suit jacket and hand it to her. "Here."

She smiles and it twists the knife a little deeper because I know it will be the last one she'll ever give me. "Thanks."

"You set me up," Cain roars, fighting against his restraints.

I walk over to him. "Let me help you out with those."

Before he can blink, I grab his head and bash my knee into his face. "*Much* better." I step back, assessing the tiny trickle of blood coming out of his nose. "However, I think there's still room for improvement."

Sinking to my haunches, I get more rope from under the couch, dodging Cain's pitiful attempt at a kick. "You never were the greatest athlete, friend." I wink at him as I coil the rope around his calves. "Except when it came to running track. Which is a bit ironic, considering you excel at running away from all your problems." I pull the rope taut and secure it. "Wait, did I say running? I meant *killing*."

I get up and park myself between him and Eden. "Which is exactly what brings us all here today."

"I have no clue what he's talking about." Cain looks at his step-daughter. "I never killed *anyone*. Don't let him brainwash you into believing such bullshit."

If looks alone could kill, the one Eden gives him would do the job in record time. "Damien didn't have to brainwash me. You did that all on your own."

He keeps his expression impassive. "I have no idea what you're talking about." He looks up at the ceiling. "Help!"

I click my tongue. "Scream as much as you want, nobody will hear you. Not only am I hosting a party upstairs, my office is sound-proof. Didn't want to take any chances. Being a man of your caliber, I'm sure you understand."

"I don't know what your objective is, but you'll never get away with it," Cain spits. "People—important people like the *governor*—will be looking for me soon."

I snatch his phone out of his pocket. "Not if you tell Margaret you're going home because you don't feel well." I glance at Eden. "I'm offended he doesn't consider us important people. How about you?"

She thinks about this for a moment. "You know, a little actually."

Cain cackles. "You're officially out of your fucking mind, Damien. No way in hell am I calling anyone."

Blowing out a breath, I look at my co-conspirator again. "We're gonna have to speed things up a bit. He's ruining my grand finale."

Eden shrugs. "Fine by me."

I amble over to my desk and fetch the remote. "By the way, thanks for the virus you put on my computer." I lean against my desk. "Not to be a buzzkill, but it didn't get rid of the array of pictures I have of you getting fucked by Trejo. Quite frankly, I'm insulted you assumed I wasn't smart enough to not only have backup files but to protect my computer."

Reaching over, I turn on my monitor and press a few keys on the keyboard. Cain protecting and serving Chief Trejo's cock illuminates the screen a moment later. "Newsflash, Cain. Technology is a passion of mine. If you invested even a small fraction of your time learning things about me like I did you...you would know that already."

"Those are *fake*. Your Photoshop skills are shoddy at best." He wriggles against his restraints. "Lucky for me, they're on par with your time management skills. Margaret's probably started a search party for me already."

I hold up my remote. "Ah, yes. I appreciate the reminder." I press a button and the base of the tank lowers to pelvis level. *Perfect.*

I walk back over to Cain who looks genuinely scared. *Good.*

"You might want to turn your head for this, Eden. It won't be pretty."

"I'll be fine. In fact, I say we bring the governor down here after this." She gives Cain a dirty look as I wrangle him into a standing position. "By the way, I'm so flattered you told Bexley about my oral skills." She gestures to the computer screen. "Coming from you, I'd say that's a real compliment."

Cain curses under his breath. "I knew that motherfucker couldn't stay out of it."

"Focus, Cain. There are far more important things to worry about than Bexley meddling in your affairs." I drag down his zipper. "Like whose mouth will be on your dick next." I wince. "As chance would have it, my—I'm sorry, *your* piranha—is due for a meal soon."

His face turns white as a sheet. "Wait a minute—"

"Can't. We're running out of time, remember?"

He struggles like a fish on a hook as I lug him behind the tank so Eden can have a front seat to the show. *The irony.*

Grimacing, I grab his flaccid cock. "On second thought, let's make a deal."

Cain looks relieved. "Whatever you want."

I look at Eden. "I need a hand."

She scrunches her nose. "Ugh. I dealt with his dick once already toni—"

"I need you to hold the phone so he can call Margaret and tell her he's not feeling well."

"That I can do."

After swiping his phone off my desk, she joins us at the tank.

I grip Cain's face. This is important so he needs to pay attention. "Tell her anything and the shriveled-up chunk of skin that's attempting to crawl inside your body right now—otherwise known as your penis—will be piranha food. Got it?"

He swallows thickly. "Yes."

"And don't even think about using a code word."

He nods and Eden presses a button.

A moment later, Margaret's voice filters through the speakerphone. "Hey, I've been looking all over for you. Where are you?"

"I've been holed up in the bathroom. I'm not feeling too well."

"Oh, no. Which bathroom? I'll come find you."

I tilt Cain toward the tank.

"I'm not in the bathroom anymore. I'm in the car heading home."

"You mean you just left the ball without telling anyone?"

Cain rolls his eyes. "I'm telling you *now*. Like I was saying, I'm not feeling well."

Margaret tsks. "Nervous about the election, huh? If you want, I can leave and bring you some soup?"

244

"No," Cain says quickly. "I think it's best I relax and clear my head before the big day. Talk to you tomorrow, okay?"

No, you won't.

"Sure. I'll text you when I leave to see if you changed your mind about that soup."

The woman can't take a hint for shit.

Cain hesitates briefly and I kick him.

"Fine, but if I don't answer, it's because I fell asleep."

She sighs. "Okay. I'm probably leaving in a little while anyway. Daddy said the food gave him some bad reflux, and we're both tired of looking at your trampy stepdaugh—"

Eden disconnects the call and drops the phone in the tank. "Oops." She walks over to my office chair and sits. "Just out of curiosity, Cain—did Margaret ever confront you about our *close* relationship after dinner last night?"

Cain clears his throat. "She did."

Eden crosses her legs. "And what did you tell her?"

Cain averts his gaze. "I handled it."

"Right." Pain slashes across her face. "And by *handled*, you mean you put it all on me. Because God forbid you take responsibility for anything."

Cain, relentless bastard he is, tries to pry his way through an opening that isn't there. "I'm sorry—"

"No, you're not." She looks right through him. "If you were, you would have stopped hurting and using people a long time ago."

"Eden—"

"Enough, Cain," I sneer. "You're losing focus again."

I position him so the tip of his dick drapes over the tank. "Look, I'm not gonna make this complicated. Consider this my special version of a lie detector test. For every question you refuse to answer or try to lie your way through, your cock goes in the tank. I should warn you though, my patience is wearing thin. I suggest you do yourself a favor and only tell the truth."

"That's your big plan?" He snickers. "For the record, Brainiac, forcing a confession from a person under duress is inadmissible in court."

"Fortunately, I'm not interested in a judge or jury hearing the truth, I only care that Eden hears it."

Confusion spreads across Eden's face. "I already know the—"

"Not all of it. There's more than Cain killing his family and blackmailing me."

Cain shakes his head. "That's not true. I *never*—"

"And in the tank we go," I interject. "Boy, that didn't take long."

"Wait," Cain shouts. "Okay." He looks at Eden. "I did it. You said I had to tell the truth, right? Well, here it is. They abused me for years." He inhales a ragged breath. "I finally had enough of it, so I killed them." His eyes become glassy. "I couldn't take it anymore, Eden. If that makes me a terrible human being, so be it."

"That's not what makes you terrible," Eden says, jabbing her fingernail into my desk. "Blaming the murder on an innocent woman and then blackmailing Damien when he was only trying to help you is."

"You're right. But I was young and scared. I didn't want to go to jail. I wanted the future I planned for myself. The one I worked my ass off for." He sniffs. "You don't know what it's like to have someone you love treat you like you're lower than dirt and control your every move. You don't know what it's like to have all this fury and pain building up inside you, waiting to erupt every time they hurt you. It eats away at you, Eden. Just like poison—it kills every good thing inside you. And every single fucking day they look you in your eyes, *taunting* you as they cut you deeper. But you can't make it go away and you can't stop the bleeding because you're not strong enough. So, the monsters continue to win…continue destroying you little by little. Until one day you just snap…because you've finally had enough."

Eden stays silent, but I see the pain flashing in her eyes. She knows exactly what it's like.

Because Cain is her monster.

He tilts his head toward me. "For what it's worth, I'm sorry. It took me eleven years to say it, but I truly feel horrible for what I did to you. You were a good friend, we had a bond...and I took advantage of that. I'm so sorry."

"No, you're not." Cain can't fool me anymore. "The only thing you're sorry about is the position I have you in now."

The one I've been pining for all this time.

I fish out my cigarettes with my free hand and light one. "Now that we got the first two murders out of the way, let's jump to the next notch on your list. Shall we?"

He struggles against me. "There is no other notc—"

I lower his dick into the water, and he starts to scream...until he looks down and realizes he's on the side with the good fish.

But the thing is, most fish tend to get curious about new friends in the tank. Especially when you haven't fed them much for the past few days...in preparation for this moment.

Cain exhales, looking relieved...until some of the fish start nibbling.

"Fuck." Eden looks away. "That's gross."

Stubborn bastard he is, Cain withstands the torture for the better part of a minute before he whispers, "Karen."

"Sorry, man." I cup my ears with my free hand. "You're gonna have to speak up if you want the love bites to stop."

"Karen," he grits through his teeth and Eden gasps. "I killed Karen."

I tug him back so he's out of the water. "See? That wasn't so hard, was it?"

Eden bolts up from the chair. "You *killed* my mother?"

"Yes," Cain says with more vigor. "What she was doing to you was abusive and I couldn't take it anymore."

For a moment, I think Eden's going to fall for it, but she shakes her head. "Yeah, so abusive you waited four years to do it, and then *paid* medical professionals to brainwash me." She starts pacing the room. "Christ, what is *wrong* with you? I know she was a bitch, but she was the only family I had. You had no right to take that from me."

"I'm so—"

"She might have come around." Eden folds her arms around herself. "She was cruel and mean. But maybe we could have had a relationship in the future. Now I'll never know...because of you."

"I was doing what I thought was best," Cain snaps. "And that includes hiring professionals to treat you. With all of Karen's neglect and mistreatment, I needed you to learn to trust someone first before—"

"Shut the fuck up," I growl. Every word he says brings me that much closer to the end of my fuse. And I'm sure as fuck not going to stand here and let him manipulate Eden into thinking he did this for her benefit when he only did it for his. "You make me *sick*."

"Funny," Cain muses. "Your fascination with me always made *me* sick." He turns his head to Eden. "He's been obsessed with me since high school."

"I know," Eden informs him. "Damien told me everything about your history."

He snorts. "Sweetheart, the fact that you're still standing here helping him tells me he did not."

Her red lips part in surprise as her gaze flits to me. "What's he talking about?"

"Come on, Damien," Cain sneers when I don't answer. "Don't leave us in suspense."

Rage lights me up and faster than the flip of a switch, I kick his legs out from underneath him and plunge his head into the tank.

Cain's not running the show this time, I am.

He thrashes against me as I drown him, but I don't let him up for air until his movements slow down.

He wheezes, gasping for air. "Damien helped me set up the teacher we were having sex with for the murder of my family." He winces, preparing to be dunked again. "Damien might have you fooled, but trust me he is far from innocent. He could have saved her and told Trejo the truth during his interrogation, but he didn't."

"I already know about Mrs. Miller," Eden says. "Like I said, Damien told me everything, including the part he played in it."

Cain's eyebrows draw together, and I can see those psychopathic wheels in his head turning.

I don't want his wheels turning, though. What I want—is to hear him admit the one thing I haven't been able to prove, but feel burning in my gut every time I think about it.

"So, you know she was his friend? The one who introduced me to her—or should I say, presented her on a platter to me to use and take however and whenever I wanted. He took an abused woman and manipulated her into doing whatever he wanted, and then betrayed her when it suited his needs. He's no different than I am." He holds Eden's gaze. "And if you don't believe me. Just ask yourself this question, sweetheart. If he could backstab his friend…a woman he claimed to care for, what's to stop him from doing the same thing to *you* one day?"

Eden opens her mouth to speak and then clamps it shut. She wants to argue but she can't.

Because as much as the both of us hate to admit it…

"Cain's right."

My feelings for Eden are real…but it doesn't change what I did. Or the truth I've been concealing from her so I could keep her a little longer…like the selfish bastard I am.

I might not have murdered all those people like Cain did, but I really am no different.

There are different shades of evil, but in the end, it doesn't matter whose shade is darker—we're both still villains.

Eden's eyes grow bigger. "What do you mean he's right? I don't—"

"You will." I grip the back of his head. "But first, I need something from Cain."

"I'm not doing shit until you—"

I immerse his dick in the tank and lower my lips to his ear. "Did you kill her?"

"Who?"

"Don't play fucking stupid. *Kristy*. Did you kill Kristy?"

"No, you idiot. Her hus—" He flinches when I press a button on the remote, lowering the divider. "Damien, don't do this."

Oh, I'm gonna.

"Two hungry piranhas can never coexist in one tank, Cain," I grind out, repeating his own words back to him. "Therefore, I suggest you speak now and admit what I already know, or so help me God I will make you suffer far worse than you made that poor woman suffer."

Hell, I plan on doing it anyway.

A guttural scream erupts from Cain as the piranha munches his way through the fish closest to him first. He's got about two seconds left before the piranha comes over to this side of the tank and he loses his favorite appendage.

"I did it," he screams. "I killed Kristy. *Fuck.* I'll tell you everything, Damien," he screams. "I'll tell her the *truth*, I swear. Just take my dick out—" He sucks in air, wheezing as I yank him back. "Thank you."

"Don't thank me, motherfucker. This is far from over."

"You killed her?" Eden whispers. "How could you—"

"I'm sorry," Cain croaks, hanging his head in defeat. "I'm so fucking sorry, Eden."

He knows as well as I do this is it. The final showdown.

And for once, it's no longer about our feud or revenge.

It's not about winning either...because the last round ends in a draw.

We both lose her.

Eden's eyes ping pong between us. "Why is he apologizing to me?"

The muscle in my chest squeezes, reminding me I have a heart deep down...one that's breaking for her.

I've spent my whole life not giving a fuck about other people, or my actions. But if there's one major event I could ever take back. One *wrong* I could undo...it would be saving Kristy.

But I can't. The only thing I can do is tell Eden what she never could.

What she never got the chance to…because of me.

"Because he killed your mother."

"I know," she says, not understanding. "Cain confessed before."

"He confessed to killing Karen before." I look her in the eyes because it's the least you can do when you're about to rip someone's entire world out from underneath them. "Karen wasn't your biological mother. Kristy was."

Chapter 40

DAMIEN

Past...

"You ever wonder what your life would be like if it weren't for one major event?"

"Sure." I rake my gaze up and down her naked body before I grab my cigarettes off the nightstand. "Just today I thought about all the good sex I'd be missing out on if I didn't bend you over the table in the science lab that day."

She smiles and lets out a small laugh, causing those big tits of hers to jiggle with the action. "I was being serious, Damien."

I light a cigarette as I think about her question. We don't usually get into such weighty conversations, but I don't mind talking to her.

Mrs. Miller's not only hot. She's chill as fuck.

"Sometimes I think about what my life would be like if my mom didn't die."

I hate the pity shadowing her blue eyes. "I wish I knew what to say."

Sometimes there isn't anything to say. It just is what it is.

"She was a junkie who preferred drugs to her kid." I take a long drag of my cigarette. "I'd say her death was upsetting, but you can't lose something you never had, you know?"

"Yeah." She winces. "Can I ask you something kind of messed up?"

"Shoot."

She props herself up on her elbow. "If your mom wanted forgiveness for not being a good parent, would you give it to her?"

"Depends."

"On?"

I shrug. "Why she wanted it. Was it because she's truly sorry, or because she wanted to make herself feel better about being a shitty mom?"

"The first," she whispers.

"Then yeah. We all make mistakes. Some worse than others, but who the fuck am I to judge?"

"I wish there were more people in the world like you."

That gets a laugh out of me. Usually people are wishing they don't run into someone like me ever again.

I lean back against my headboard. It's obvious she's got some shit going on in her life and needs someone to lay it on.

"What's your big event?"

"My daughter."

I expected her to mutter some shit about marrying her husband, or maybe even fucking a student, but not this. She never mentioned kids before.

"You have a kid?"

"Yes...no...not exactly." She looks at me. "It's complicated. Promise you won't judge me when I tell you this?"

"Like I said before. Who the fuck am I to judge?"

She sits up in my bed. "I ended up getting pregnant when I was twenty-one." Her forehead creased as she continues. "Here's some irony you'll appreciate. I was sleeping with my teacher." She exhales a small puff of air before she continues. "My very hot, very married professor. I went to his office after class one day to get extra help and he came on to me. It was dirty and wrong, but after fumbling teenagers and drunken frat boys, it was nice to have sex that actually ended in an orgasm."

I can't help the cocky smirk I throw her way. She already knows not to paint me with that same brush.

The tip of her mouth crooks up briefly, despite her serious tone. "It's all fun and games until someone gets pregnant. I still remember the look of sheer terror on his face when I told him. The next day after class he said it was a huge mistake and he couldn't lose his family." Her eyes closed and a flash of pain pinches her features. "He told me to get an abortion... gave me three hundred bucks and an A for the semester and that was that."

"Shit. Talk about leaving someone high and dry."

"Yeah. I was scared and on my own, so I did what any girl would do, I called my mom...mistake number two. I knew better. My family was overly religious. Not the real kind where you accept everyone and help people in need. They were the hypocritical kind that only cared about appearances and judging people. When I told her I was pregnant, she said I was an embarrassment. When I told her who the father was, she declared my bastard baby and I would burn in hell and as far as she was concerned, I was no longer her daughter."

I blow out a breath. "Sounds like your mom cast a few stones in her picture perfect glass house."

"Yeah. Nice, right? At that point, the only thing I could think to do was call my cousin. She was four years older than me and had left the church the second she turned eighteen." Reaching for my cigarette, she takes a deep drag and slowly exhales. "She doesn't freely admit it to outsiders because she's pursuing a career in law, but she's gay. Which is the reason she was also kicked out of the family. I thought if anyone would understand, it would be her."

She tucks a strand of long blonde hair behind her ear. "Anyway, I asked her if she could drive me to the clinic. She said yes, and that I could stay with her for the week to get my bearings. My spring break was coming up so I took her up on the offer. When I got there, I started getting cold feet. I wasn't ready to have a baby, but…"

"You didn't want to have an abortion either," I finish for her and she nods.

"Exactly." Her eyes become glassy. "It's funny, you never really know how you feel about something until it happens to you."

She wipes her tears with the back of her hand. "That's when my cousin asked if I would consider letting her keep the baby. She said she always wanted to be a mom but in vitro or adoption were her only options. If she adopted my baby, not only would they be family, she assured me I could see him or her whenever I wanted, and I'd know my baby was being taken care of." She smiles, but there's no humor in her expression, only pain. "I liked the idea. I knew Karen was in a much better position than I was and would give my baby a good life."

"I'm sensing a but coming up."

"But then I made mistake number three."

I wouldn't call anything she did a *mistake*, so much as being young and naive, but I digress. "What happened?"

"I trusted Karen. When my semester ended, I moved in with her for the summer. She took care of the medical expenses, bought baby stuff, drove me to doctor appointments. Basically everything I had hoped my own mother would do." She looks up at the ceiling. "She was a lawyer, so it never occurred to me to have the adoption papers looked over before I signed them. I did ask her what a closed adoption was, and she said it meant that no one but the two of us would be able to find out she adopted my daughter."

There's despair in her gaze when she looks at me. "I had a minor complication when I gave birth, something to do with the iron levels in my blood. They wanted to keep me an extra night for observation, but my daughter was discharged. Karen and I decided she would take the baby home and come back for me the next day. I hugged my little girl, kissed her on the forehead and handed her to Karen."

This time, she makes no attempt to wipe away the tears rolling down her cheeks.

"But Karen never came back. She didn't answer her phone, either." She presses a palm to her stomach. "I took a taxi to her house, but it was empty. When I went to her office, they told me she had given notice and left her job three weeks prior. She was just...gone." She clenches her fist. "She didn't have any friends that I knew of, and I didn't have any money to look for her. God, I just remember the panic of thinking I'd never see my daughter again."

"Did you call the police?"

In my experience, cops are usually nothing but assholes, but not when it comes to children.

She nods. "I did. Unfortunately, the state we lived in had restrictive adoption laws. I could only reverse consent for the first three days and I had already missed that window. My only other option was to take her to court, but in order to do that, I'd have to find her and come up with the money to hire a lawyer. I had no job, no money, and no help. So I gave up."

Damn. That seriously sucks. "I'm sorry."

"Me too. But, it forced me to take a good look at my life and I made changes. I finished my degree, became a teacher, fell in love." She looks down. "Imagine my surprise when I moved to Black Hallows last year and saw a gorgeous little blonde girl with bright blue eyes in the parking lot of a grocery store next to my cousin Karen. Did I mention I named her Eden? After the garden in the Bible? It was perfection on earth...and so was she."

"Are you gonna try to get her back?"

She shakes her head. "I went home and told my husband. He didn't know about her, but I wanted her back so badly, it didn't matter. I wanted to fight for her. I figured he'd understand, and maybe even be happy since we were talking about having children." She swallows hard. "But that was the first time he ever..." She trails off, but she doesn't have to finish that sentence.

I already know where the road ahead leads.

His fists.

"Let's just say he made it clear that trying to get her back was not an option…" She averts her gaze. "Things went downhill at home. I mean, it's not like they were great before, but it got bad. I stalked Karen for a bit after I knew where to find her, but Eden looked happy. She was smiling and gorgeous and well taken care of. I couldn't…"

"You don't want to bring her into this."

"I'd rather die than see my daughter be abused." She snorts. "And with the way his temper's been escalating, hell I just might."

"I can take care of him."

I've offered once before, but she declined.

She cups my cheek. "You're sweet. But it's my mess. I'd never forgive myself for getting you involved and possibly ruining your life."

She gets off the bed and starts getting dressed. The bruises on her body make my blood boil.

But it isn't my life, it's hers. I have to respect her decisions.

"One day I'll leave him." There's a hint of determination in her eyes. "I've been trying to store some cash away, little by little whenever I can."

"I can give you money."

"No, honey. I appreciate it, but you're still a kid. I won't let you get involved in this."

Her life. Her choice. I remind myself.

"Offer stands whenever you want it."

"I know." She grabs her purse. "I have to get home to make him dinner."

I hope she puts arsenic in it.

I nod. "See you at school tomorrow."

She fidgets, which is odd since she's usually in a rush to get back home to her piece of shit husband.

"Promise you won't laugh?"

"No."

She rolls her eyes before her expression turns solemn and she holds up her right hand. "See this ring?"

Jewelry isn't really my thing, but it's nice. "Let me guess, it's an *I'm sorry I beat you* last night gift from your prince charming."

I'm being a dick. I promised I wouldn't judge her and yet here I am.

It just pisses me the fuck off that she won't accept my help. I know to her I'm just a teenager, but I'm more mature than half the adults my age and have the means to make her life better.

Hell, I could probably teach her a thing or two. Make her stronger.

She closes her eyes. "I'm gonna go."

"Wait," I say when she starts to turn around. She has no one to listen to her. I know this because she once confessed that her husband made her kick all her friends to the curb. The only reason we're able to hang out is because he's under the impression she stays after class to tutor students. "Tell me about the ring."

Her face lights up. "Eden was born in October." She comes closer and points to the large center stone. "That's opal. It's her birthstone. Tradition says you're not supposed to wear it if you aren't born in October, but I wear it for her because it's supposed to bring her luck. Some even say it wards off evil spirits." She swallows and points to the circle of tiny stones around it resembling a halo. "And these are diamonds."

"Is that your birthstone?"

"No."

"Oh—"

"But diamonds don't break." Her gaze sharpens. "They're strong and resilient. Just like I want her to be." Her voice cracks. "Even though I'm not." She sucks in a breath. "I *will* be one day, though."

"I know."

I believe it.

She kisses my forehead. "Thank you for being you, Damien."

"Hey, Kristy," I call out when she opens the door.

"Yeah?"

"For what it's worth, you would have...will be...a good mom. I hope you and your daughter get to talk one day."

She gives me the brightest, most beautiful smile I've ever seen. "Me too."

It's a smile I've never forgotten.

Chapter 41

DAMIEN

"So, my mom... Karen, was Kristy's—my biological mother's—cousin?"

Her eyes search my face, looking for a kernel of something tangible to untie all the knots she's in.

Eden wants answers, and she's entitled to them. Unfortunately, I only have the bare minimum...because the pieces of the puzzle were stolen by a psychopath.

And he's the only one who can put it back together for her... which is the *sole* reason he's still breathing.

"Yeah. That's what Kristy said." I already told her everything I know. I wish I had more to tell her. Something to make this a little easier to process.

She sits back down in the chair and draws in a few deep breaths. Her anxiety must be at an all-time high right now. Her universe has just been permanently altered.

And yet, she's staying strong...when she has every reason to break.

I'd be proud of her...but I no longer have that right. Not after Cain's confirmation.

There was a small glimmer of hope when Eden told me she

believed Kristy's husband still would have killed her despite what I did. As fucked up as it is, I was hoping she was right...but that ship has sailed.

Because nothing will ever take away from the fact that I introduced Cain to Mrs. Miller. I was the one who presented the forbidden fruit on a platter and told him to take a bite.

I told him how satisfying it was.

And then I protected him when he swallowed it whole.

It's easy to absolve someone for having a hand in the death of a woman you've never met. It's a different ballgame entirely when that woman is your own mother...and a mother's love is all you've ever wanted.

There's no forgiveness for me, and I'd never expect it or manipulate her into giving me any.

I've earned my throne in Hell, and I will gladly burn in the flames...I just want to make sure Cain's roasting in them first.

"How long have you known?"

I assume Eden's question is directed at me because she hasn't looked at Cain since I told her the truth.

"I was seventeen when she told me——"

"No." She glares at Cain. "How long have *you* known I was her daughter?"

He doesn't answer. *Bad fucking move.*

When I start pushing him forward, he shouts, "Wait. I'm going to tell her the truth, goddammit."

"You better," I seethe. "Or I'll make sure your death is even more brutal than the one you deserve."

He inhales sharply. "I've known about you the whole time."

"The whole time," she repeats, her tone flat. Void of any emotion. "Okay, well, I already know you don't feel bad—so I guess that just leaves me with one more question."

"I *do* feel bad, E——"

"Piranha," I hiss in his ear. "Just give her facts, not another load of your bullshit. Fuck knows she's had more than enough of it already."

"Why did you marry Karen?" Her lips purse. "If you knew she adopted me and was Kristy's cousin…" Her eyes widen. "That's why you killed her, isn't it? Because she found out you murd—"

"No," Cain says sharply. "Karen already knew what I did. She was working as one of the assistant prosecutors for the district attorney when Kristy was in jail." He shakes his head. "Hold on, let me start from the beginning. When I set Mrs. Miller up for the murders, I hired a private investigator to do a little research and dig up some dirt on her. He didn't find a whole lot…except that she'd given birth at a hospital in Florida. I found it odd, given she didn't have any children, so I had him dig a little deeper. He found out she gave her daughter up for adoption, and the adoptive mother's name was Karen Williams. Her cousin."

He shrugs. "I didn't think anything of it until I received a list of employees from the prosecutor's office and saw Karen's name." His jaw tics. "I got scared, I figured her working for the prosecutor meant she had enough pull to throw the case for her cousin. I decided to approach her in a parking lot one night when she was working late and ask her point blank if she knew Kristy. When she refused to answer, I threatened to turn her in for working on a case with an obvious conflict of interest."

A smile stretches across his lips. "She called me a punk kid and said she would report me if I didn't leave her alone. Then I asked her how her daughter would feel if she knew her mommy was helping to put her *real* mommy in jail." He rolls his eyes. "We went tit for tat for a while until she finally admitted she wanted Kristy gone for good. She'd only recently found out Kristy lived in Black Hallows and didn't want her making any waves. She had plans to become District Attorney in the next ten years. Last thing she needed was a family member dragging her to court, claiming she was a baby stealer."

Eden's brows knit together. "I guess after that, you two started dating secret—"

Cain chuckles. "We never dated. Never even so much as kissed

263

apart from the wedding day. We both liked pussy. In fact, it was the only thing we ever agreed on."

She worries her lower lip between her teeth. "Then why did you two get married?"

"Because she did me a favor, one I promised to repay one day. And I did, years later when she ran for district attorney."

"What kind of favor?"

Dread punches my gut. *Favors* for Cain are never the good kind.

Cain falters. "Damien? A word please."

"Sure, step into my office. Oh, look. We're already here, shitbag."

"Listen, I don't think telling Eden this part will help matters," he whispers harshly. "In fact, I'm positive it will only make things worse."

For him or Eden?

"Don't you dare," Eden says, slamming her hand on the desk. "Don't either of you treat me like I'm a child. Not when you—" She points to Cain. "Killed my family. And you—" She points to me. "Lied to the police to protect *him*, and then kept the truth about my birth mother from me." Her nostrils flare. "Tell me what happened, Cain. *All* of it. It's the least you can fucking do, you murderous, manipulating, piece of shit."

I jut my chin toward Eden. "You heard her. Start talking."

His expression hardens. "Perhaps I should take my chances with the piranha."

"Fine by me—"

"No," Eden yells. "Tell me the truth." Desperation shades her eyes. "Please, Cain."

Frustration skitters up my back. Even now he's somehow found a way to control her.

Give him an inch, and he'll wrap a mile's worth of vile around your throat.

"Of course, sweetheart. Whatever you need." The groove in his forehead deepens. "I asked Karen to talk to Kristy's husband." He looks sheepish. "I wanted her to persuade him to bail Kristy out of jail. I had her tell him that if he did, I'd write him a check to cover the bail, plus another forty-thousand after I received my father's life insurance policy. It was no surprise he agreed. After he found out his wife was cheating on him with not one, but *two* teenage boys, his ego was bruised. He wanted her gone more than I did. He thought I was doing him a favor."

The muscles in my chest tighten when Eden makes a painful sound deep in her throat. "And so her abusive husband became your perfect fall guy."

Cain nods. "Not that it matters in the grand scheme of things, but I killed him, too."

Considering Kristy was beaten to death, and all her scumbag husband got was a shotgun to the head, I'd say he got off way easier.

"Before or after you killed her?"

I'm not sure what difference the order makes, but Eden lurches up from her chair. "Did you kill him before or after you killed her, Cain?"

Then I realize. She wants to know if Kristy got to witness his murder before she died. If Cain granted her a moment of peace before he took her life.

"Before," he whispers. "I figured it was the least I could do."

"Why'd you have to kill her?" Her face contorts in agony and for a moment I think she's going to cry, but she keeps it together. "You could have let her go to jail. You didn't have to——"

"I couldn't take that risk." He releases a long sigh. "I had no idea I'd end up falling in love with you, Eden. I suppose it's my karma."

No, his karma's going to be hand delivered by me.

Eden laughs...so hard she shakes. "God, I don't even know what to say to that." She looks at me then. "What's next? You gonna tell me you helped him bury the bodies? What other secrets are you hiding from me, Damien?"

"None." I hold her gaze. "I wasn't sure Cain killed Kristy until now, I only suspected. I couldn't prove it."

"But you obviously knew Kristy was my mother."

"I did, but to be honest, I didn't start putting the pieces together until Cain married a lawyer named Karen from Black Hallows. That's when it mattered to me."

I'm not some white knight. Far from it. At the end of the day, I'm just as selfish and manipulative as Cain. Only difference is, I don't deny or hide it.

Pressing my knee to Cain's back so he stays put, I light another cigarette. "After the guilt started settling in, I tried to look for you on social media, but you didn't have any accounts. I hired someone to check the local high school for me and found out you were no longer enrolled."

The tightness in my chest is back again. "I couldn't find you, Eden." I take a long pull off my cigarette, let it burn my lungs. "I stalked Karen for a bit, even sent her some anonymous notes warning her about Cain. I thought she wasn't getting them until she went on a business trip and I watched her rip one to shreds with my own eyes. She was getting them all right, she just didn't give a fuck. Now, I know it's because she was corrupt, too."

I swallow my rage. "After Karen died suddenly, I started to get worried. I figured if he hadn't killed you yet, you were next on his chopping block. I knew Cain wanted to run for mayor, and the last time he had a big goal." I glare at him. "He went on a murdering spree."

I stub out my cigarette. "By then, I had found an email address for you, not that it mattered at that point. You were still a minor and Cain was your guardian. I had no choice but to wait until your eighteenth birthday so I'd be in the clear." I gesture to my computer. "I had to be meticulous though. If I struck too soon, you might slip up and tell Cain about me. If I waited too long, I could lose my window, and I needed to know everything about you before I made physical contact."

My breath catches, just like it did the first time I saw her. "I ended up getting a copy of the local paper when you did your first interview. They put your picture in it. You're not identical, but you do look like Kristy...so much so I'm certain it was a big part of Cain's sick fascination with you."

"Pot meet kettle," Cain grits through his teeth.

I cast him a dirty look. "Anyway, a few weeks before your birthday, I contacted you on the *Temptation* app. You fell for the bait. I was positive you were messing around with Cain after our first conversation, but I also needed to find out other things about you." I slap Cain's shoulder. "So, I hired Katrina's stepdaughter, who wrote for the gossip column, to conduct another interview and report back to me. The rest as they say...is history."

"When did you contact my therapist?"

"After you mentioned him on the temptation app. Contacting him led to me finding out everything else about your past."

Her forehead wrinkles. "I gu—"

My phone rings, cutting her off. I'm planning to ignore it, but my office phone rings next. Geoffrey doesn't call both phones unless it's an emergency.

I answer my cell when it rings again. "This better be import—"

"Something's wrong with the governor. He collapsed on the dance floor. I've already called an ambulance, but I think you need to get up here now," Geoffrey says out of breath before he hangs up.

Shit. "I have to go."

Cain perks up. "Leaving so soon?"

I pull out a stretchy band from my pocket. "Get on the floor."

"Absolutely not—"

I kick him in the nuts. "I don't have time for your shit. There's an emergency upstairs."

"What kind of emergency?" Eden asks as I maneuver Cain to the floor and hogtie his ankles to his cuffs.

"The governor collapsed." I walk over to the couch and get some more rope before fastening Cain to the base of the fish tank. If he squirms too much, he'll have a few hundred gallons of water and a piranha to deal with. "An ambulance is on the way now."

"Shit," Cain mutters. "This is gonna fuck up the election."

I survey him, wondering how someone with an IQ of a hundred eighteen fails to realize what's blatantly obvious.

"Don't worry. I'll do you a solid and kill you before then." I point to the tank when he starts twisting against the restraints. "I wouldn't do that if I were you."

His body goes slack.

I take hold of Eden's elbow and steer her out into the hallway, ignoring the feeling rising like a tidal wave in my chest.

The one telling me not to let her go. I have to. It's time to set the butterfly free. God knows she's earned it.

"I'd ask if you're okay, but—"

"It would be a stupid question."

"I'm sorry I didn't tell you sooner."

She crosses her arms over her chest. "Why didn't you?"

If I was ever going to tell her how I feel about her—this would be the time. *But I'm not.* Eden doesn't need an anchor. She needs to fly.

The hardest part of loving someone is knowing it won't last forever. *Sooner or later, one of you will have to let the other go.* Because all things, good and bad, come to an end at some point. That's the way shit works.

I point to the pocket of my jacket she's still wearing. "There's a check made out to you for twenty-five million. There's also a first-class plane ticket to Spain. Your flight leaves tomorrow."

I could walk the planet a thousand times and back again, but I'd never find someone like Eden. Kristy was right, she is perfection on earth...and I want her to get out there and explore it.

She looks at me like I've sprouted another head. "Twenty-five million? Spain?"

"If you want more money, it's yours. If you don't want to go to Spain, I can have Geoffrey book you a flight to somewhere else. The tropics are beautiful this time of y—"

The sting from her hand slapping my cheek is well deserved.

"You drop this bomb on me...and now you're leaving when I need someone to help me pick up the pieces?"

"Technically *you're* the one who's leaving. And you don't need anyone's help, Eden. You can pick up the pieces yourself this time."

"Fuck you." She jabs her finger in my chest. "Fuck you for making decisions for me without asking. Fuck you for not even giving me *a second* to wrap my head around everything that's happened tonight before sending me packing. Fuck you for making me have feelings for you and then abandoning me. Fuck you, Damien."

She needs to understand the road we walked down was never an ongoing one. And for once, I'm not hurting her because I want to… I'm doing it because I have to. Because it's the right thing to do.

I can't take back what I did to Kristy. I can't undo the role I played in her death. Therefore, I'll never be able to take away Eden's pain.

I've earned my life sentence in purgatory, but Eden hasn't.

And unlike Cain, I won't make her serve the time with me. It's not fair to her.

She shouldn't have to live the rest of her life with a constant reminder of what she's lost. *What she never got the chance to have.*

And quite frankly, I'm fucking tired of living with the guilt. My penance to Kristy has been served.

Eden's strong and resilient—just like Kristy wanted her to be. Mission accomplished.

I prop my arms on either side of Eden's head, caging her against the wall. "Tell me it doesn't hurt to look at me now."

As predicted, she averts her gaze. I don't blame her.

"I can't." Her hand finds my jaw. "But that doesn't mean it will always be this way."

She doesn't get it. "The best you can ever hope for with me is to become numb and desensitized. You'll have to shut off parts of yourself." It takes every ounce of willpower not to close the distance between us and bury myself balls deep inside her. "You'll be a ghost again."

We both will.

"I'm not ready to lose you."

"Tell me it doesn't hurt to look at me," I repeat, punching the wall with my fist. *The more she protests, the harder this is.*

"Tell me you don't love me," she counters.

Jesus. I'm hanging by a thread. One of us has to be the strong one here, and it has to be me.

"I could...if the circumstances were different." I kiss her tear-stained cheek. "But they're not."

They never will be. *Not in this lifetime.*

I start to pull away, but she catches my wrist. "I still love you despite the circumstances, Damien."

When an animal is wounded beyond repair, you should do the righteous thing and put it out of its misery. Same principle applies here.

"You know as well as I do, you can love someone with everything you have, and it will never be enough to make them love you back." I pin her with a look of disgust. "I thought you learned that lesson already. Do yourself a favor and stop making the same mistake."

She lifts her chin. "Right."

"I have to handle the shitstorm upstairs, but you're welcome to spend the night." I start walking down the hall. "Geoffrey will drive you to the airport tomorrow."

Her expression turns to stone so fast it's almost jarring. "Thanks." She gestures to my office. "I'm gonna grab my ball gown. I'll be upstairs in a few."

I start to object, but my phone rings. "I know, Geoffrey. I'm coming."

With a grunt, I walk out the door and up the stairs. It's not like Cain can get to Eden the way I left him.

Chapter 42

CAIN

The fat fuck better not die. I've put in too much time and effort with Bexley and his irritating daughter for things to go to shit now.

Blowing out a breath, I remind myself I need to use my time wisely. Damien will presumably be coming back at some point.

If I can bash this tank against his desk and somehow manage to knock the phone down, I can use my nose to call for help.

It's not a foolproof plan, but it's the best one at my disposal.

Sweat drips down my back as I fight against the restraints, trying my hardest to get the damn tank to move. I curse when it doesn't budge.

I search my brain for a Plan B—but there isn't one. There's nothing I can offer Damien at this point. Nothing he doesn't already have, given he's stolen everything of mine.

My election, my Eden…my goddamn piranha.

He's even managed to secure blackmail as a parting gift. Fucking stalker.

I could almost respect the lengths he went to if his intent was to elicit my confessions in order to go public so he could win the election, but it's not.

271

ASHLEY JADE

There's only one thing he cares about…Eden.

I grind my molars. Motherfucker's gone soft. I loaned him some prime cunt with my name stamped on it and suddenly he's developed a conscience. A guilty one at that.

This is a perfect example of why you should never let anyone borrow your things. *Especially your most prized possession.*

I knew better. I fucking knew better and still I let her trick me into staying with him.

Eden's been yanking my dick this whole time. *Little backstabbing whore.*

I should have left her the medicated, drooling, zombie she was when I found her. Instead I fixed her up and cared for her. *Killed* for her.

All so my loyal pet could turn around and bite me when I needed her the most.

I loved her. I loved her more than I thought I was capable of loving something.

And there was a time she lived and breathed for me as well… but those days are gone. *Treacherous slut.*

It's disappointing how little it took to sway her perception of me. For Christ's sake, it's not like the people I killed were saints. Quite the contrary. If anything, I'm a goddamn hero for taking them all out of the universe.

The only innocent one in this whole ordeal was Kristy, and she wasn't all that virtuous considering she was cheating on her husband with two high school students and gave her kid up for adoption. The world didn't mourn her loss. *Just Damien.*

That alone says a lot about her character.

I could understand Eden's outrage if Kristy had raised her. But Eden didn't even know she existed until ten minutes ago. That's hardly enough time to form any kind of attachment and declare the man who's done nothing but care for you a villain.

My chest aches. I *never* should have set her free. I lent Damien a jewel he didn't deserve…and now she's ruined. Because that's what Damien does. It's all he knows how to do.

272

For a moment I think I'm seeing things and do a double take when Eden walks back into the room...sans Damien.

She's upset. More than upset. She's been crying. Given she hasn't looked at or said a word to me, it can only mean one thing.

Damien hurt her. God, I'd laugh if she didn't look so sad. Did she really think Damien King was the type to settle down? Or that he cared about her more than he cared about getting revenge against me?

No. A leopard doesn't change its spots. He might have felt bad for her, but there's only one person on earth he's ever loved.

Me.

Poor, naïve, Eden.

"Let me guess," I say as I catch a peek of what looks to be a plane ticket in the pocket of the jacket she's still wearing. "Either he's leaving, or he wants you to leave?"

She doesn't respond. Sometimes my girl is stubborn like that. Unfortunately, this is the only opening I may have before Damien returns and I end up fish food.

Eden's my only hope.

"You're too good for him, sweetheart. A man like Damien doesn't know how to love."

Finally, she glances my way. "I guess you two have something in common."

Fair enough. "He and I have a lot in common actually. The only difference is, I'd never send you away because my feelings for you have always been genuine. You're not a game to me, Eden. You never were."

She opens her mouth and then clamps it shut. *Dammit.*

"Don't worry. Even though you hate me, I'll make sure I avenge you."

"I don't want you adding any more names to your body count because of me."

"Then what do you want?"

A scoff pushes through her lips. "From you? Nothing."

"That's a shame because I'd give you anything. *Everything.*"

273

"You didn't give me *everything* when you had the chance, why should I believe it would be any different now?"

Hmm. It's not a large window by any means, but with enough finesse, I might be able to wiggle my way through.

"We all make mistakes. Some of them are worse than others. However, when Damien kills me, my biggest regret won't be killing my family or Karen…it will be not treating you the way you deserved."

Her face screws up. "You really think Damien's going to kill you?"

I think he's fighting with his conscience over it, but in the end, his dark side will win. "I have no doubt these will be my last few minutes on earth." I give her a small smile. "At least I get to spend them with you. The only person I've ever loved."

She closes her eyes. "I—you. I can't believe everything that's happened."

"I know it's a lot to digest, sweetheart, but you're strong. You've *always* been strong. You didn't need Damien or anyone else to validate it."

Her eyes become glassy. "Can I ask you something?"

"You can ask me anything." *Just make it snappy.*

"Did you ever think about telling me the truth? Or ever feel guilty for taking my mother away from me?"

I don't know why I'm compelled to give her honesty, but I do.

"No." When she glares at me, I add, "Telling you what happened would mean losing you. That's not something I was ever willing to do given you hold my heart in the palm of your hand. As far as guilt goes—the more time passes, the more complacent I got…because I'd gotten away with so much already. It's hard to feel guilt when you're happy someone is dead. Kristy was the only one who didn't deserve to die, but she never gave me a reason to feel remorse either. We weren't friends like she and Damien were. Whenever we were together…she treated me like I was a second-class citizen. It was clear she only put up with me because Damien wanted her to."

"Oh," she says softly.

"It hurt," I whisper. "Feeling unwanted. Rejection, no matter what form it comes in, always stings. And I've had a lot of it throughout my life."

She draws in a slow breath. "It still doesn't excuse anything you did, but at least I can kind of understand it now." She looks toward the door. "I should probably get going."

Fuck.

"Wait," I call out. "I know I have no right to ask you for mercy, considering all I've done, but please give me just a few more minutes." I exhale heavily, blinking back tears. This is my only chance to save myself and possibly get Eden back. "Damien's gonna kill me. I know it and you know it. I just need a little more time with the most beautiful girl I've ever known."

"Cai—"

"Please."

"Okay." She kneels down next to me. "Um...your pants are still down."

"Would you mind pulling them back up? Giving me a little dignity?"

I'm shocked when she does. "Better?"

It would be better if her mouth was on my dick, but at least the draft is gone.

She worries her lip between her teeth. "Cain?"

"Yeah?"

"Did you ever think about killing me?"

"No," I say quickly. "You're my everything. I knew the second I saw you—you were it for me."

She looks down at the floor. "I was really out of it the first time we met."

"I know." I crane my neck to get a better look at her. "I remember you were sitting on your bed...staring into nothing. You didn't even realize I'd entered your bedroom until I said your name. And then you looked at me...and I was a goner. I swore right then and there I'd find a way to rescue you...and I did." I hold her stare.

"I know you're angry about the therapist, but it was the only way. You were so mentally fragile, I had to put you together piece by piece. But in order to do that, I needed you to learn to trust someone first. Karen had neglected you for so long…" I shake my head. "It doesn't matter. She's gone. I killed her for you. Because no one hurts my girl."

I narrow my eyes. "And don't you worry, sweetheart. Damien will get what's coming to him. It may not be my doing, but trust me when I say there's a bullet with his name on it coming straight for him."

The first day he showed up in town, I took measures to protect myself. Or rather, to make sure he follows close behind in the event he takes me out first.

I was trying to be *nice* and send him to jail for the rest of his life…but obviously that just won't do anymore.

Damien no longer deserves my mercy. He only got it because he loved me so much…it made him special. *Just like Eden.*

She draws her knees up to her chest and I let my gaze roam to her panties. If the silky fabric moves to the left a little, I'd catch a peek of one of her soft pussy lips.

If she moves up several inches, I'll have my face between her thighs. I close my eyes and inhale. *She's so close but still too far away.*

"I'm gonna miss you, Cain. And I don't know how to feel about that because you've done so many bad things."

I swallow hard, pulling out all the stops. "Someone once told me it's not the number of bad things a person does…it's the number of bad things they do to you. For what it's worth, I've always loved you. Always tried to do right by you."

"I know," she whispers. "That's what makes this so hard. The Cain I fell in love with isn't the Cain sitting in front of me now."

"I'm still the same Cain." I press my cheek to the hardwood of the floor. "What's your favorite memory of me?"

She's caught off guard by my question. *Good.*

And then it happens. She smiles. "The day you told me Karen was dead. You came into my room late at night, crawled into my bed, and held me. You promised me you'd always take care of me. You said we were family." A tear falls down her cheek. "I felt *loved*... for the first time in my entire life."

"I'll always love you. Even after I'm gone."

"Part of me doesn't want you to leave."

We're so close. "You could set me free. Let me turn myself in."

She makes a face. "We both know you wouldn't."

"You're right. You know me better than anyone."

She looks pensive. "Let's say I did let you go. What would happen? Would you kill me like all the others?"

"God, no."

"Not even after I betrayed you?"

"I can't kill what I love. Hell, I'd probably ask you to run away with me."

"Where would we run to?"

"Anywhere you want."

"Damien got me a ticket to Spain."

"I prefer France."

She laughs. "You mean it? Me and you?"

My heart thumps against my chest like it's trying to break free. "Swear it."

She raises an eyebrow. "No more killing?"

"I'll never kill again," I lie. *Damien King is a dead man walking.*

"I'm scared of you," she whispers. "I love you, but you petrify me."

Good. However, that won't help me now. "I'd never hurt you."

"Promise?"

"You have my word."

She shifts so she's on her knees. "There's a small storm hatch behind you we can crawl out through."

"Perfect. But let's work on untying these, first. Shall we?"

"Oh, right." Her hands tremble as she undoes the ropes on my legs before moving to the ones on my wrists. She pulls out the key for the cuffs...then pauses.

"What is it?"

"Where are we going after this?"

It's all I can do not to roll my eyes. "Wherever you want."

"I'm not doing this until we have a plan."

She's turned into quite the demanding little thing. "I figure we'll go back home, get some sleep—"

"You said we were leaving town. If you're just using me—"

"I'm not." Christ almighty. *She's so needy.* "We'll spend the night at the house. Then we'll head for the airport at the break of dawn."

There's a smile on her face as she undoes my cuffs. "Okay."

I stand up, and she tenses, as though expecting me to hurt her. "Come on, sweetheart. Let's go home."

So I can fuck your little whore cunt…and then kill you.

Make you both pay for your sins.

Chapter 43

DAMIEN

"*P*arty's over," I tell Geoffrey as the ambulance drives off with the governor and Margaret. "Kick everyone out."

Turns out Bexley's years of bad food and no exercise caught up with him and he suffered a massive heart attack while eating an eggroll. The EMTs are trying their best to keep him alive, but they don't think he's going to make it to the hospital.

Looks like karma is catching up with everyone tonight.

Geoffrey bows. "As you wish."

"Wait," I bark before he scurries off.

"Yes, sir."

"I want you to spend some time with Eden tonight. She's...just hang out with her. Do whatever it takes to make her happy. I'll be in my office for the remainder of the evening. I don't want any interruptions."

I have an opponent to torture and kill.

"Of course, sir."

The heaviness in my chest eases as I make my way down the stairs.

Revenge is so close I can taste it.

My heart beats like a drum as I walk down the dark, narrow hallway leading to my office.

Tick tock, Cain Carter.

I've been waiting to do this for eleven long years. It's better than the last bite of a decadent dessert.

Hell, it's almost better than sex. My dick gets hard just thinking about slitting his throat from ear to ear.

My lips twitch as I enter my office. The evil, vile things I'm going to do to him.

"Time to rock and roll, Cai—"

My heart stops cold. *No.*

Dread crawls up my throat, squeezing like a vise.

How does a man who's cuffed, hogtied, and fastened to a tank...get up and disappear?

Easy. He doesn't. Not without a lot of help.

I check my office phone. It doesn't look touched. The tank is fine. Eden's ball gown is still on the floor. Everything other than Cain not being tied up looks exactly the way I left it.

Pressure tightens against my ribs.

Eden's ball gown is still on the floor.

My insides twist into something dark and vicious. The thing currently beating out of my chest tells me not to believe it, but the writing is all over the wall.

I brace my arms on my desk and blow out a heavy breath. *She let him go.*

Why the fuck would she do something so stupid? I know I hurt her—but Cain. It doesn't make *any* sense.

Eden was in the clear. She never had to see or hear from him ever again after tonight. Hell, her plane was leaving...

The anger in my gut takes a sharp turn, propelling up my esophagus before surrounding the vital organ she snuck her way into.

That fucking bitch. *I trusted her.* I thought she was playing Cain...not me.

Not only does Cain win the girl, but he also gets twenty-five million dollars of *my* money to boot.

Christ. When she demanded money, I didn't question it.

Faster than my brain can catch up with my reflexes I rip the cord of my lamp out of the wall and raise the steel base over my head.

Then I bash it against the fish tank.

The first crack is small—they usually are.

There's damage. Water is trickling out. But it's repairable if you patch it up in time.

But my mother didn't give a fuck.

The second crack is worse—it's deeper. Bigger. Water isn't trickling anymore…it's pouring out onto the floor.

The damage is too significant to repair. The only thing you can do is take the chunks left behind and turn them into something else.

Something stronger.

So you can get your vengeance.

Until that third crack—because that third one is catastrophic damage. Nothing is salvageable.

Nothing matters anymore. You've lost everything.

Including the piranha flopping on my office floor. The one you're currently beating to death with a lamp because Cain's no longer here to take the years' worth of payback you've saved up for him.

Because Eden let him go.

She took my heart, my money, my plane ticket, and my revenge…

And then she betrayed me…just like everyone else in my life.

I should have known something was wrong. The way she looked at me. The way she went from spilling her heart out and crying while proclaiming her love…to becoming a stone in the blink of an eye.

It's like nothing I've ever seen before…

I drop the lamp.

Not since Cain told me his father and brother died.

Chapter 44

CAIN

I take a deep breath, letting the crisp air fill my lungs as I pull up the driveway. *Freedom.*

"Home sweet home."

Eden sighs as she steps out of the car. "Feels like forever since I've been here."

I follow behind her as she ambles up the walkway. "I'm glad to have you back."

You won't be leaving again.

She opens the front door. "Can we relax a little before we start packing?"

I flick on a light. "Whatever you want."

Turning to face me, she palms my cheek. "I missed you."

I kiss the inside of her wrist. "Missed you more."

Her palm drops to my chest and she comes closer, pushing me against the door.

Christ. She's so fucking sexy, it's almost enough to give me second thoughts.

Loose ends are trouble—I remind myself. You granted someone mercy before, and look what happened?

Talk about irony. If Damien really wanted to help Eden, he should have left her alone.

History always repeats itself.

Eden's kisses are soft and sweet like cotton candy. I want to gorge on her until she fills my bloodstream, but I can't. My baby's toxic.

Tainted by Damien King.

Our kisses turn frantic and I slip my hand between her legs. *My little Eden.* She's wet for me.

Bile works up my throat. *Wet from Damien's cock.*

No, this simply will not do. I need to fix her. Make her better. *She deserves it.*

My temples throb so hard I wince. *I want to be inside her before she dies.* And maybe again after. Just to see what it's like.

Fucking hell. It's been a long time since I've felt this powerful and in control.

She mewls when I slide a finger inside her. "Take your tits out." Not willing to wait, I pull her bra down. Suck the hard pebbles into my mouth.

Eden has nice tits, just like her mother did. Almost too big for her perfect frame but not so big she looks disproportionate.

Her cunt is tighter, though. Then again, my angel hasn't taken the number of dicks her mommy did.

I'm preserving my little cherub.

I give my precious girl a smile, then kiss her lips and her cheeks as I remove my hand from between her legs.

Every killer keeps a souvenir. A little token to remind them of their favorite victim.

Eden's mine.

And I want this to be special for her. *For me.*

It'll be less messy if we do it in my office. The rug is small and cheap. And hideous—thanks to Claudia's terrible fashion sense.

It will be easy to discard.

But I'm getting ahead of myself. That comes later.

First, I want to light some candles and pour a little alcohol. Show her how special she is. *Celebrate this monumental occasion.*

It's going to be so hard watching her leave me. Almost impossible to ever unravel the knot she's tied my heart in. But I'll always remember her.

Because she's mine. And now she always will be. *Forever.*

"Wait for me in my office," I tell her as I give her a kiss.

She starts to walk away, but I halt her.

"Would you like something to drink? A little wine? Perhaps some whiskey? A little something to relax?"

It'll help with the pain.

"I'm not old en—"

I place my finger to her lips. "Shh, sweet angel. There aren't any rules tonight. It's just me and you."

She blushes a beautiful pink, the same color as the inside of her pussy. She's perfect. *Simply perfect.* Perfection on earth.

It's a shame such beauty has to die. It's not fair.

Damien shouldn't have fucked with her. With my humanity.

But he did. The bastard made her taste the fruit like the snake he is. He made her see what it was like to be without me...and now she has to pay the price.

I can't possibly be her everything when she allows him into her head, heart, and body.

No one else should come before me.

I deserve every perfect inch of her. And tonight, I will have it.

I'll have her last heartbeat and her last breath while I'm rooted deep inside her. Plucking my pretty flower from the earth's soil.

After fetching my supplies, I join my angel in the office.

She's so obedient, already bending over my desk for me with her pert little ass in the air.

"Gorgeous."

I place my glass of whiskey on the desk after I take a sip. Not too much though. I don't want to get sloppy. I'll be drunk enough on this experience.

I scratch a match against the box and light two candles then place them both on my mantel. This is a spiritual experience for me. *My version of church.*

"A little ambiance to help set the mood."

If Eden turns out to be a fighter like her mother was…things will get messy. I'd rather keep it contained in one area.

I should bind her wrists, but I'd rather have her follow my orders like the good girl she is. It's much more satisfying that way.

I wince when my head throbs. Harder than before.

When the migraines start, I know there's no going back. *What needs to be done will be done.* It's a calling. A need I can no longer control.

I run my hand down the curve of her ass. Beautiful.

I think Eden will be better than her mother. She's courteous and young.

She's respectful just like my Damien was. I shove my hand down my pants and fist my erection. He got on his knees for me. Bowed before his god and vowed to do everything I wanted him to.

I was going to piss in his dirty mouth, and he was going to drink it all up and ask for more. You can't fake that kind of devotion.

Perhaps I should grant Eden the same privilege and see how much she loves me. Yes, yes. I think I will.

After moving her panties over, I spread her with my fingers, take a look at her insides. So pretty. Like a blooming flower…right before it perishes.

"Would it be easier if I took them off?" my angel questions.

So considerate. Unlike her mother.

"No, baby. It's better like this. Just lean over a little more."

Yes, just like that.

I close my eyes as I brace my dick with both hands. I'm hard as fuck and I'll spray everywhere instead of my intended destination. I want her to take all of me. I want her panties soaked in my fluids. Her hot pussy filled with my piss and cum.

"Almost ready," I whisper. Then, "Oh, no."

Her breath hitches. "What's wrong?"

"I have to pee."

She tenses. No, Eden. *Stay strong.* Take all of me.

"You don't mind, do you?" If she does, it's too late. I'm already sticking the head of my cock inside her panties like a hose.

She doesn't make a sound as it runs in rivets down her perfect pussy, thighs, and legs. She takes my golden nectar like the good girl she is.

"Such a good girl. Cain can't wait to be inside you."

This is the last time I'll ever see her alive. I don't want her back to me. I want to see her face as I pump inside her. I want to see her neck swell as I put my hands around it and squeeze. I want to see the moment life leaves her beautiful blue eyes.

"Eden, sweetheart. Turn around so I can——"

Chapter 45

EDEN

a stream of blood squirts into the air, flashing like lightning during a storm as I drag the curve of the knife along his throat, cutting through tendons and veins.

The best way to make someone pay for their sins...is to strike when they least expect it.

Cain makes a gurgling noise, his eyes widening in horror as I shove the knife into his chest and begin twisting. Drilling a hole right where his heart was supposed to be.

I want to take my last breath looking into the most beautiful eyes belonging to the most beautiful girl I've ever known.

A slow smile spreads across my face as he collapses on the floor, clutching his neck.

I should feel something. There should be remorse. A touch of sadness. An ounce of regret...

But there's nothing.

Because Cain Carter's taken everything from me...

And the people most important to me.

It was only a matter of time before the evil he projected onto others would catch up with him.

Sooner or later everyone pays for their sins.

I peer at his face as his body goes limp. Watch the venom and poison ooze out of the gaping wound on his neck as his eyes begin to dim.

I no longer see the man I loved. The one my heart beats for.

Because a heart can't continue to beat when it's no longer intact.

Vengeance always comes at a price.

And I have every intention of paying it...

I just need to say goodbye to someone first.

Chapter 46

DAMIEN

*A*drenaline courses through my limbs as I speed up the walkway, masking the panic burning a hole through my chest.

He didn't lock the front door behind him. *Because he knew she wouldn't run.*

I take a heavy breath, pushing down the dread as I twist the knob.

The house is eerily quiet when I enter…never a good sign.

"Cain," I call out. *No response.*

There's an ominous tug in my gut when I check the kitchen and see the bottle of whiskey on the counter. The cap is off. *He was impatient.*

Bracing myself, I walk past the living room, following the small beam of light coming through a crack in the half-open door at the end of the hall.

The sick feeling in my gut intensifies with every step I take.

I never should have let her go back to get her dress.

I never should have abandoned her when she was so vulnerable.

Eden wasn't ready for the truth. She's strong, but she wasn't strong enough.

Regret and remorse pump through the organ currently beating like a jackhammer in my ribcage. *I should have told her I loved her.*

The foul stench of death fills my nostrils as I push open the door.

Tiny hairs on the back of my neck stand on end, and pure shock roots me to the spot as I take in the sight.

Cain's blood-soaked body lays stiff on the floor of his office. His flaccid cock hanging out of his pants. The tip of the knife I gave Eden is sunk into his chest, straight into his black heart.

I walk a little closer and smile. *After she slit his throat.*

Pride starts to swell...until the awareness of it all plummets like a boulder in my gut. *She killed him.*

I check my watch. It's almost midnight.

If I don't act now...it will be too late.

A smug smile pulls at my lips. I wish I could have seen Cain's face the moment he realized his little lamb had officially become the slaughterer...and she was out for his blood.

But as Cain found out tonight, we don't always get what we want. Sometimes you just have to make the best with what you have.

I quickly survey his office, taking in the surroundings before I zero in on the full glass of whiskey on his desk.

I'll start there.

After extracting the knife from his chest, I drizzle some of the amber liquid over the wound before doing the same to the gash in his throat. I pour the rest around his body, pausing when I notice a wet spot on the rug by his desk.

I grimace as I inhale. *Urine.* Son of a bitch.

Swallowing my rage, I remove one of the candles from the mantel and put the flame to the end of my cigarette.

I step back as I take a long drag, examining his body. His brown eyes are fixed and dilated. His body is drained of color and stiff as a board. However, it's his mouth that draws my attention. It's hanging open...as if she took him by complete surprise.

The muscles in my chest draw tight. *I never should have doubted her.*

"She did it, Kristy," I whisper, emotion lodging in my throat. "She fucking did it."

Eden took the emperor down.

And now there's only one more thing left to do.

With a smirk, I hover over his body...and drop the candle.

I take one last drag of my cigarette, smiling from ear to ear as the flames engulf him.

"Rot in hell, Cain Carter."

I'll be joining you soon.

My grin grows as I make my way out of the house.

For every action...there is a consequence.

For every transgression...there is an outcome.

For every act of vengeance...a debt must be paid.

I close the front door behind me and drop the knife.

And I'll gladly pay the price for hers.

Chapter 47

*E*den doesn't drive. She also doesn't have any friends or any favorite local hangouts.

There aren't many places she'd run off to in her current state.

In fact, I can only think of one.

The graveyard located half a mile from Cain's burning house.

My boots crunch over the grass and little white flurries trickle out of the sky as I pass through rows of graves and monuments.

Black Hallows doesn't usually get snow in November, but given the events of the night, it's oddly fitting.

I blow a puff of breath into my hands, then dig them in my pockets for warmth. I'm about to call this a bust and turn back when I hear something a few rows over.

My chest tightens when I turn my head.

Eden's hugging Kristy's marble headstone, her small body wracking with sobs.

I should walk away, give her the time she deserves, but it's freezing outside and she's only wearing the suit jacket I gave her earlier.

Crouching down, I pry her off Kristy's grave.

"It's cold, baby," I say when she protests.

295

She claws at my chest as I scoop her into my arms. "I never got to meet her."

I know.

"I wanted a mom so bad," she rasps as I begin carrying her to the car.

I know you did.

"It hurts." A guttural scream rips from her throat. "It hurts so much."

I know it does. "I'm sorry."

It's the first time I've ever uttered those words.

It's the only thing I've ever been truly sorry for.

Eden's shivering so much her teeth chatter as I bring her into the house. I turned the heat on high during the drive, but given how cold she still is, it wasn't enough.

"Oh my God," Geoffrey utters when I pass him on the stairs. "I'll draw a bath."

"I'll do it."

He nods, looking her over. "While you do that, I'll call a doctor."

"No."

He blinks. "She's bleeding, sir."

"Get lost or find a new job," I growl, pushing past him.

Geoffrey is devoted, but there are some situations you can't trust anyone.

"Don't touch anything right now," I tell Eden as we enter the bathroom and I set her down. "Not until you get out of the bath."

The last thing I need is investigators finding a bloody fingerprint belonging to Eden.

She hasn't said a word since we left the graveyard. I'm not sure if it's because she's seriously sick or in shock.

Probably both.

I turn to her as the tub begins to fill. "We need to get these off." I place her hand on my shoulder for support. "Lean on me."

I take her shoes off first, placing them on a bath towel I laid down. The jacket she's wearing quickly follows.

My pulse speeds up when I see all the blood covering her body until I remind myself it's Cain's and not hers.

She winces when it's time to take off her panties and I soon realize why. They're damp and smell like piss.

Cain got off too easy.

Once again I swallow my rage as I help her into the bathtub.

I'm not a tender or kind person. Taking care of others isn't my thing. Never has been. But I do my best with Eden, being as gentle as I can while I wash all the blood off. When the water turns red and she cringes, I drain it and fill it back up. And when she starts to shiver again, I strip my clothes off and get in the tub with her.

"It's gonna be okay." I press the washcloth to her back. "He won't hurt you ever again."

"Sir, I'm sorry, but she needs to see a doctor—" Geoffrey starts to say as he barges in. His expression changes when he looks at the pile of bloody clothes and then at us.

Irritation skitters up my spine. "Geoff—"

"I'll take care of these." He picks up the clothes before I can stop him. "I already have a fire started in the library fireplace."

"You tell a soul and—"

"Your secrets are safe with me, sir." He looks at Eden and his face softens. "I'm sure it was deserved."

He has no idea.

"By the way," he says as he walks out. "The governor passed away."

Oh, *how the mighty have fallen.*

"Looks like everyone got what they deserved tonight."

"I didn't feel anything, Damien," Eden says, her voice barely above a whisper.

"Wha—"

"When I killed him. I thought I'd feel remorse…but I didn't. I

297

still don't." She draws her knees up to her chest. "How long do you think it will be before the police come looking for me?"

"Don't worry about that." I kiss her shoulder. "You should get some rest."

She tilts her head to look at me. "Cain said there was a bullet with your name on it."

I'd laugh if she didn't look so serious. Cain was nothing if not a manipulative liar. "Did he say that when he was still tied up?"

She nods and her expression turns grim. "It was my breaking point. I didn't want him to take another person…" She shakes her head. "I got tired of him taking everything good in my life."

He'll never take anything from her again. His death is her fresh start.

She stands up and reaches for the oversized towel on the sink. "Thanks for the bath. I'll see myself out in a few."

I'm right behind her when she leaves the bathroom. She's not going anywhere. Not until I know the police arrest the right person.

"Don't leave."

She fastens the towel around her. "I don't have a reason to stay."

I let that shot roll off my back. She's angry. She's entitled to it. But I'm still not letting her leave.

"Eden—"

"No." She spins around. "I already spent time with one dead guy tonight. I have no desire to do it with two."

Frustration burrows in my gut. I'm trying to do everything I can to help her. "What the fuck do you want from me?"

She shrugs helplessly. "Something I can never have."

She's not making any sense. All she has to do is say the word and I'd give it to her. "I don't know—"

"*You.* I want to erase the last eight hours of my life so I can have you again." She balls her fists. "It hurts. But it hurts a hell of a lot worse without you."

Our gazes lock as she takes a step closer.

"Look me in the eyes and tell me you don't love me."

Saying the words will only make things worse.

If we had a chance at a future. If I could change the past...I'd tell her. Hell, I'd scream it at the top of my lungs.

But we don't.

We never will.

～

The sun has already risen when I creep into her bedroom.

The news reported the fire at Cain's house a little over two hours ago. It won't be long before they get here.

Eden wakes with a start when I crawl into her bed. "What are you doing?"

I crush my mouth against hers. I can't say the words, but it doesn't mean I don't feel it.

"Being selfish."

Memorizing every single part of her body.

My mouth dips to her neck and I suck the soft skin as I pull off her shorts and panties. I want to go slow and take my time. But I don't know how much of it I have left.

"Damien." Her eyes are sad, desperate. "I'm gonna miss you so much."

My hand cups her cheek. *I'm gonna miss her more.*

She parts her thighs and I settle between them, sliding inside her inch by inch until I'm rooted to the hilt.

Eden sighs my name, combing her fingers through my hair as I thrust faster. Our breaths mingle in the dark as our hips rock.

"I love you," she whispers, wrapping her legs around me tighter. *Tell her.*

She moans, raising her hips as I pick up my pace. "More."

I grab the headboard, slamming into her harder. Giving it to her the way I know she wants it.

Her frantic gasps melt into my mouth as she clenches around my cock. I watch her face as she comes. Memorize every single perfect detail of it as she drains every drop of me. Not that I'd ever forget it.

Eden has my heart. All the blackened, fucked-up parts of it.

She drapes her body over mine and closes her eyes. It's only when I'm certain she's asleep that I whisper the words I shouldn't.

"I love you."

And I'll never stop.

Chapter 48

EDEN

*T*here's a smile on my face as I wake up…until all the events of last night come rushing back to me like a tidal wave.

Lies, heartbreak, *murder.*

A shudder runs through me as I look at my hands. These hands have taken a life.

And yet, I can't seem to find a lick of remorse. Not even so much as one tiny kernel of guilt. *Maybe I do belong in prison after all.*

I stretch my arms over my head and look toward the other side of the bed.

It's *empty*. My heart protests the injustice.

I was hoping to have a little more time with Damien before I turn myself in.

I know Damien will talk me out of it and will most definitely try to stop me, but I don't want to spend the rest of my life running.

I killed Cain Carter because he deserved to die.

That's my story and I'm sticking to it.

I'll take my chances with the legal system.

I grab a robe from the closet before I venture downstairs. I want to eat a hearty breakfast, take another shower, ask Damien if he knows any good lawyers, and head down to the precinct.

"Hey." I smile at Geoffrey as I pass him on the staircase.

He doesn't return it.

Probably because I'm freaking him out. Who the hell kills a man and then smiles the next morning like it's no big deal?

Maybe I should put 'contact therapist' on my list of to-do things. Bile surges up my throat. *Or not.*

"Is Damien in his office?"

Geoffrey shakes his head.

"Exercise room?"

Another head shake.

"Kitchen?"

"No."

And now we're three for three. Something is definitely wrong.

"Geoffrey?"

"Yes?"

"Where's Damien?"

He wrings his hands. "He was arrested about an hour ago."

I stare at him for a few seconds, wondering if I misheard him. "Why in the world would they ar—" My hands fly to my face. I figured with Cain dead, Damien would be in the clear. "It's polling day. Damien didn't kill Cain's family, Geoffrey. We have to do something."

Now Geoffrey's the one who looks confused. "I believe someone *already* did. Cain Carter's home was nearly burned to the ground last night…while he was still in it."

Blood rushes in my ears and I swallow hard. *This can't be happening.*

I clutch my stomach. Damien didn't have to cover it up.

The room sways and I grip the banister.

"Are you okay?"

I can't let him go down for something he didn't do. I won't. I'm not Cain.

"I need a ride to the precinct."

He frowns. "I'm afraid I can't do that. I'm under strict orders to bring you to the airport in twenty minutes."

Yeah, that's not happening. Damien told me I could either be the lamb or the slaughterer.

Last night I was definitely the slaughterer...and I guess today I'm going to need to be one again. *It seems to be the only way people take you seriously.*

I grab Geoffrey's collar. "Last night I killed a man in cold blood. Slit his throat and then plunged a knife straight into his heart. If you bring me to the fucking airport instead of the precinct so I can save Damien...I will *not* hesitate to do the same thing to you. Got it?"

He pales. "Yes, miss."

∾

"I need to see Chief Trejo," I tell the officer at the front desk.

He raises an eyebrow before his eyes wander downward.

That's right. *Soak it all up.*

I chose a black low cut, silk dress along with blood red heels, red lips, and red nails.

The glazed over look in the young officer's eyes tells me I chose right.

"He's..." He visibly swallows. "In a meeting."

I lean over just enough to give him a peek of my cleavage. "Can you tell him it's urgent?"

He nods so hard I think his head's going to fall off. "Sure can." He fumbles with the phone for a moment before he says, "What's your name, miss?"

"Eden King."

∾

Trejo's eyes light up like firecrackers when I walk into his office.

He better be in the mood to pull some strings, because I'm not leaving this precinct until I know Damien is free and clear.

If blackmailing him doesn't work. I'll seduce the bastard.

And if neither of those work, I'll turn myself in. Either way, Damien is being released by the time I leave.

I point to the door. "Mind if I close this?"

He leans back in his chair, lacing his fingers across his gut, and gives me a skeevy smile. "Not at all."

"Are there any video cameras in here?"

His eyebrows shoot up to his hairline. "Wh—"

I slap the manila folder on his desk. "Trust me, I'm asking for *your* benefit, Chief. Not mine."

That gets his attention.

He sits upright. "It's clear."

He starts to open the folder, but I place my finger on top of it. "We'll get to this in a minute. First, I'd like to know why you're holding Damien King."

I need to know exactly what evidence they have on him.

"That's official police business."

"You and I both know he didn't do it. More than half the town can account for his whereabouts last night considering he was hosting the masquerade ball."

"I only know what the evidence tells me," he grits through his teeth. "So if you came here to hassle me for information, you're wasting your time."

I pick up the folder. "I actually came here to help *you*." Shrugging, I open it and thumb through the photos. "On second thought, I think I should do the right thing and tell your wife instead."

He bristles. "Tell my wife what?"

"Were you and my stepfather close?"

The pensive expression on his face tells me he's not sure why I'm asking him that question.

"We were friends."

"Really?" I slap the first picture on his desk. It's the one of Cain blowing him. "It looks like you were a *little* bit more than that, Chief."

His eyes widen and he starts coughing.

"You okay?" I walk over to his side of the desk and pat his back. "Would you like some water? Because it's gonna get a whole lot worse." Opening the file, I spread the contents over his desk. "Anal, sixty-nine, golden——"

"What do you want?"

"I want to make a deal." I stride over to the chair on the other side of his desk and take a seat. "You open to hearing my terms?"

"Do I really have a choice?"

"We always have a choice, Chief." I cross my legs and smile. "Whether or not you make the right one is up to you."

"Just tell me what you want, and I'll see what I can do."

"I need you to let Damien King go. He didn't kill Cain."

"The knife with his fingerprints on it say otherwise."

Shit. I draw in a breath. I can't let him see me sweat. I try a different tactic.

"The house was nearly burned to the ground, correct?"

"Correct."

"Did you get the autopsy results back yet?"

"They're pending...but...uh." He rubs the back of his neck. "Let's just say if you wanted your stepfather to be cremated..." His voice trails off.

That's great news. "So, there's not a lot of evidence."

He shakes his head. "Apart from the bloody knife——no."

"Good. So the only thing you have to do is get rid of the knife."

He laughs. "I can't dispose of police evidence."

It's my turn to laugh. "Right. Because I'm sure no officer has ever taken money or drugs from a bust before?"

He blows out a breath. "Fine. Let's say I did get rid of the knife. What exactly am I supposed to tell people? They're going to want to know how Cain Carter died."

I pick my cuticles, recalling everything from last night. "He went home from the ball because he wasn't feeling well. You can confirm that with Margaret. He liked to drink whiskey and light candles when he was stressed. You're smart, Chief. I'm sure you can put all those pieces together and come up with something."

He rubs his chin, pondering. "It doesn't bode well for the department if we can't solve cases...but I'll figure something out." He pins me with a look. "As long as you can assure me you'll get rid of the pictures and stay away from my wife."

I place my hand over my heart. "You have my word."

But words don't mean shit. Which is why you should always keep backup files.

I flutter my eyelashes. "And Damien will be released when?"

"Give me a few hours to get rid of the knife and clean everything up."

I stand up and hold out my hand. "Thank you for your cooperation, Chief Trejo."

His expression is dour as he shakes it. "Don't mention it."

"Just out of curiosity, does the name Kristy Miller ring a bell?" I ask when I reach the door.

"Yeah, I remember that case like it was yesterday."

I swallow the lump in my throat. "If you're so worried about solving cases...you should know that she was innocent."

He sighs. "If she was innocent then who—"

"Cain Carter."

Chapter 49

EDEN

*N*erves bunch in my stomach as I wait for Damien to walk out of the precinct. It's been over four hours since I left Trejo's office.

Damien should have been out already.

I'm about to march back in there and raise hell...but that's when the doors open.

Butterflies swarm in my belly as he makes his way over to me, his confident strides eating up the concrete between us like a man on a mission.

It's a struggle to breathe as I look my fill, taking in everything from his gray suit that makes those piercing eyes of his pop even more to the dark stubble lining his strong line.

I watch as he pulls a cigarette out of his pocket and slowly brings it to his lips, his fingers curling around the filter as he lights it and inhales, causing the flames on his throat to flicker a little.

Only Damien King can make such a disgusting habit look so sexy.

As if sensing my reaction, the corner of his lip tugs up in a smug smirk.

I'm grateful I'm leaning against Geoffrey's car because my

mouth goes dry. My palms become sweaty. And my heart...well, the poor thing doesn't stand a chance. It never did.

Focus. Damien's not the only one on a mission.

If Damien wants me...he's going to have to prove it. I'm through accepting less than I deserve.

We have tons of shit to work out, but what we have underneath all that is worth the pain.

I just hope he finally realizes it.

I square my shoulders and straighten my spine. But if he doesn't...it's his loss.

Those icy blue orbs cut right through me like glass as he comes closer.

I don't wait. I can't. I have neither the time nor the patience. My life is out there waiting for me to live it.

"I came here to warn you that you're about to make the biggest mistake of your life," I tell him, raising my chin. "Because in the next hour, I'll be on a plane heading somewhere warm. And you will have lost the best damn thing that has ever happened to you." My heart races as I continue. "You have a choice to make, Damien and I suggest you make it quickly. You can either stop being a co—"

His jaw tightens. "Shut up."

Rage blurs my vision. He doesn't get to talk to me like that. Not unless he wants to lose a testicle. "Excuse me—"

"Shut up...so I can tell you I love you." He closes the distance between us, framing my face with his hands. "I don't need to hear the rest of your little speech, Eden. Because the only choice that will ever matter to me is the one that gives me you."

My heart beats so hard it pounds in my ears. "Oh—"

I don't get to finish that sentence either because Damien crushes his mouth against mine. Tingles zip up and down my spine, settling between my legs as he presses me against the car and explores every inch of my mouth.

"Damien—"

His teeth nip my bottom lip as his hand wraps around my

throat, lightly squeezing. My temperature skyrockets as he inclines his head, his stubble scraping my skin.

"If you break my heart." There's a dangerous edge to his voice. "I'll fucking kill you."

Damien knows damn well his heart is safe with me.

"Same goes for you." Smirking, I pull him closer. "Just think about what happened to the last man who broke mine."

Epilogue

*M*y heart pounds like a drum as I watch her out on the balcony of her house.

Sun-kissed skin. Long blonde hair. Little white string bikini covering her perfect curvy body. A pair of headphones in her ears.

She thought she could get away from me. *She should know better.*

I always get what I want. And what I want...will always be her.

A smile pulls at my lips. Eden doesn't know I'm behind her.

She has no idea just how long I've been *watching* her. Waiting for the perfect opportunity to strike.

My cock thickens. She's even more beautiful than she was the last time I saw her.

My blood stirs as I open the patio door. She stills for a moment as if she senses danger right behind her before she turns her volume back up.

She's going to regret that decision in a moment.

Quick as lightning, I pin her wrists against the railing. She screams, her phone plummeting over the balcony as I clamp my hand over her pretty little mouth.

"Miss me?"

Her chest heaves as I slide my hand down her toned torso. "It's

311

okay, baby. You don't have to answer." I lick the side of her face. Savor her sweet skin. "I'd prefer to find out for myself."

My dick is hard as steel as I remove the hand covering her mouth and dip my fingers inside her bikini bottoms. I grind against her pert ass as her wetness soaks my fingers. I need her to know what she does to me.

I need to touch her. Taste her. Have her at my mercy, fulfilling every urge and desire of mine.

She struggles against me as I circle her clit. *So sensitive.*

Five years didn't dilute my craving for her. It only made it fester. Because my need for Eden is far too strong to be ignored or contained.

"I suggest you remove your hand from my pussy."

I chuckle darkly. *She's so adorable.* "Or what?"

"Or my husband's gonna kick your ass."

I plunge another finger inside her. "Is that so?"

She moans. "He'll be home any minute."

I pull on her bikini strings. "Is your husband scary?"

She shivers. "Petrifying."

Groaning, I spread her open and tease her with the head of my cock. "Does he make you come?"

"Several times a day."

I nip her earlobe as I slowly glide my dick inside her. "How much do you love him?"

She smiles. "So much it hurts."

My chest tightens. The woman tears me wide open and steals my fucking heart and soul each and every time.

I slap her ass as I sink my teeth into her neck. "He sounds like a very lucky man, Mrs. King."

Want to be notified about my upcoming releases? https://goo.gl/n5Azwv

Cards of Love Collection

The Devil is just one of the many stories in the Cards of Love Collection. Which card will you choose next?
www.cardsofloveromance.com

Acknowledgments

There's honestly no way I can possibly thank each and every one of you. You're all amazing and I can't do any of this without you. I'm also praying I didn't leave anyone vital out, because man, that would suck.

I won't go into how Devil's Advocate was the hardest book for me to write, or how risky it was because I knew where this story was going back when I wrote The Devil and how I know if I had spilled early readers would have jumped ship. For those who *stayed* and didn't give up on my vision—thank you. For those who loved it despite it being what you thought it would be—you have a piece of my heart. For those who loved it AND shared with others how much you did—you have a piece of my soul.

Kristy: I can't thank you enough. Thank you for letting helping me out of my creative spiral and letting me talk and plot your ear off and untangling my brain when I was going crazy. I'm pretty sure I'd still be sitting at my desk having a panic attack over whether or not I could put my big girl panties on, pull the trigger, and write the damn story if it wasn't for you. And that was just with the Devil. With Advocate you went above and beyond. There will never be a way to thank you that would do it justice, so just accept my lifetime of gratitude. This book wouldn't have been finished without you, and I can't thank you enough for not only being my right hand cheerleader, but bringing a special voice to Kristy. I'm sorry about killing you though.

Ellie: I love your face. I'm keeping you. Thank you for everything. I know it's not easy working with my schedule and I know I probably drive you crazy. Even though you claim I don't. I don't know many editors who will do what you did for me. I love the crap out of you and I'm so thankful. Also, #PiranhaBlowJobsForTheWin

Brandi, Vickie, Jackie, Crystal, Rebecca, Mary, Dee (Chief Trejo), Jodie, and Kris.

You all have been *vital* to this process. Thank you so much for trusting me and giving me your input. Thank you for being there at all hours of the morning (or night) and putting everything aside to read my words. Thank you for your continued support and for being my cheerleaders. <3

Stacy Garcia: I love you. Thank you for not only reading Devil's Advocate as I was writing, but also making gorgeous teasers!! You're amazing, lady!!!

Candi: I think you deserve two awards. One for being so organized. And one for ***patience***. Holy cannoli. If I had a penny for every time something changed with this release…I could probably by myself a notebook to write down deadlines and stick to them. Thank you so much for sticking with me!!!

Stephanie: Bahaha. I don't know whether to apologize profusely or just keep saying thank you. I'm sure you didn't expect all this…um, *excitement* when you signed on to be my agent. Thank you for sticking with me and being so incredible at what you do.

Lori—Thank you (yet again) for such a gorgeous cover and for making my vision come to life! You are such a beautiful, talented woman.

A ***VERY*** special shout out to these ***amazing authors*** who not only took a chance on this duet, but were so gracious and shared it with their own readers!

Isabella Starling, Tabatha Vargo, Kate Stewart, Lexi Ryan, Melissa Andrea, Mira lyn Kelly, Hayley Faiman, Abby Gale, Kailee Samuels, CoraLee June, Parker S. Huntington, Jade West, Amara Kent, and Lucy Smoke.

I seriously can't thank you all enough.

And Readers,

Please—read them, Fall in love with them. And tell everyone you know about them. They are immensely talented, and they work their butts off. These authors don't just bring you words on a page. They bring you stories that will break your heart in one chapter only to mend it the next. Stories that drive you outside your boxes (and usually your comfort zone). Stories that challenge you. Heal you. Stories that make you laugh. Make you cry. Inspire you. Make you angry. Make you swoon.

Stories that never fail to always make you feel. And THEN they go out of their way to tell you about books and authors THEY love. How amazing is that?

So please—review our books, spread the word, and share your knowledge of them with others just like they have. <3

My reader group—I have the best *Angry Girls* on the planet. I love you all so much. Thank you for all of your support and giving me someplace where I can be me and connect with all of you. You guys rock.

And Jesus...let me mention this because I forgot him in the last one. Mike. I love you. You're my strength, my weakness, my everything. <3

Last but not least—to all my fellow ***underdogs*** in the world. We're just Eden's in the making, babes. Don't give up. <3

About the Author

Ashley Jade craves tackling different genres and tropes within romance. Her first loves are New Adult Romance and Romantic Suspense, but she also writes everything in between including: contemporary romance, erotica, and dark romance.

Her characters are flawed and complex, and chances are you will hate them before you fall head over heels in love with them.

She's a die-hard lover of oxford commas, em dashes, music, coffee, and anything thought provoking...except for math.

Books make her heart beat faster and writing makes her soul come alive. She's always read books growing up and scribbled stories in her journal, and after having a strange dream one night; she decided to just go for it and publish her first series.

It was the best decision she ever made.

If she's not paying off student loan debt, working, or writing a novel—you can usually find her listening to music, hanging out with her readers online, and pondering the meaning of life.

Check out her social media pages for future novels.

She recently became hip and joined Twitter, so you can find her there, too.

She loves connecting with her readers—they make her world go round'.

~Happy Reading~

～

Feel free to email her with any questions / comments: ashleyjadeauthor@gmail.com

For more news about what I'm working on next: Follow me on my Facebook page: https://www.facebook.com/pages/Ashley-Jade/788137781302982

Other Books Written By Ashley Jade

Blame It on the Pain - Standalone

Blame It on the Shame - Trilogy (Parts 1-3)

Complicated Hearts - Duet (Books 1 & 2)

Complicated Parts - Series (Books 1 & 2 Out Now)

Older Work

Twisted Fate - Series (Books 1-4)

The Best Deception [Standalone]

～

Thanks for Reading!
Please follow me online for more.
<3 Ashley Jade

Made in United States
Orlando, FL
12 June 2023